Other Titles Available by this Author

The Forgotten Earth Series

The Forgotten Earth

The Forgotten Flame

The Forgotten Sea (coming 2026)

Blurred
Between Good and Evil. Between Love and Betrayal

Brilynn O'Neal

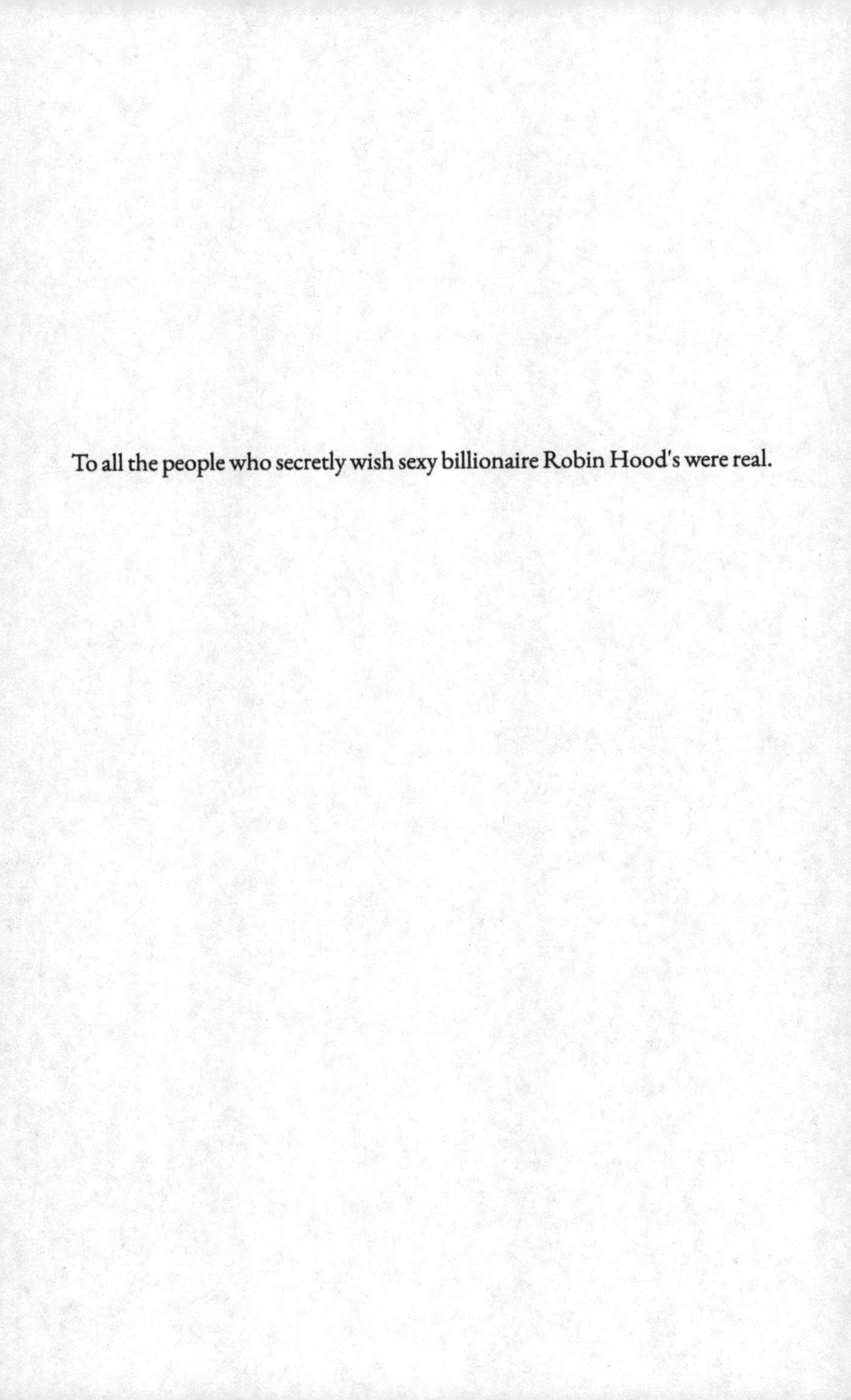

To all the people who secretly wish sexy billionaire Robin Hood's were real.

Author Note

Please note that the ideas and themes of this book are *fictional*. They do not reflect the express views or opinions of the author.

Not all themes may be suitable for all readers. Please observe the trigger warnings for this story.

Trigger warnings:
One open-door romance scene, talk of murder, violence, and grief. Themes of unwanted touch, inappropriate behaviors in a work setting, trafficking, gang violence, and descriptions of wounds.

Prologue

All I hear are screams. All I see is red.

How everything could have gone to shit so quickly and unexpectedly grates at me. I grind my teeth and take cover behind a market stall that sells jewelry. The vendor fled minutes ago.

Bullets fly everywhere, their target unknown to me.

This was clearly a setup.

But how? For whom?

I'd never screwed up an assignment as thoroughly as I've messed up this one. My civilian casualty count was five until today. That number has jumped by more than thirty, if I had to guess.

"Fuck!" I whisper to myself, trying to determine my next course of action.

If I want to get out of here alive, I need to make it to the rendezvous spot, but it lies between me and a dozen bullets.

I'm not much of a crier, but if I were, this whole situation would have me sobbing. Not only have I caused the death of innocents, but my target got away, and my intel was wrong. I'm back to square one with this case. A case I've been working on for almost five years.

Worse, this kind of fuck-up on my part will likely end my career.

I'll be lucky if I don't also end up in jail.

But I can't think about that right now. I need to focus on saving my own ass.

I peek around the wooden leg of the market stand and see a few more bodies fall to the ground. Rivulets of red stream from each one, staining the cobblestones. I squeeze my eyes shut, forcing down my rising emotion.

Now is not the time to panic. Nor is it the time to feel guilty. That can, and will, come later.

I press on the comm in my ear, trying to reach my team. "Anyone have anything? I'm a sitting duck here."

Silence answers, and my heart thuds harder in my chest.

"Gray? Come in, Gray," I say, my voice squeaking with my rising anxiety.

There's slight static through the comm, and Gray's worried voice comes through. "Nova?"

"Status? Escape route?" I ask, knowing I don't have time to chit-chat.

"Status?" he asks, his tone full of confusion. "I can't get a hold of the rest of the team. Their comms went dead a few minutes ago."

"Shit," I run a hand through my sweat-soaked hair, fearing the worst. "You're still safe?"

"Yes. Still at the rendezvous spot."

"Stay there. I'm coming."

"Without backup?" Gray sounds downright afraid.

"What choice do I have? I'm seconds from getting a bullet through my head."

The line is silent for a few moments.

"What can I do?" Gray asks.

"Secure the rendezvous spot and get us some damn backup. I don't care if you have to call the president himself."

"Copy." I can hear him typing away on his computer. If anyone can find us help in a pinch, it's him. He's the best tech guy we have at the CIA.

"I'll see you in a few minutes," I say and cut the line.

Numbing my fear like I've done a thousand times before, I hone my senses, watching and listening. People race away from the chaos, some moving north and some south. Several collide with one another. Others stop to help the injured. There's no pattern to the chaos, just as there's no pattern to the bullets.

The next stall is only thirty feet from me. Its vendor has also fled, but a few civilians crouch beneath the wooden table covered in Italian spices. Some of the bowls have been overturned, the spices speckling the table and cobblestones below. Their scent is preferable to the growing stench of iron-rich blood filling the air.

I can't stay here, frozen. I'm not sure how long the bullets will fly. For all I know, I'm their target. If I want to minimize the death count, I need to get out.

Or die.

Exposure to the bullets would only be a second if I make a beeline for the spice table. Maybe then I could also get some of the people out from under there safely.

Determining it's my only option, I balance on my toes, ready to sprint.

I blot out the noise around me, focusing on steadying my rapid breathing. I listen to the cadence of the gunshots, waiting for a split second of a lull.

When I hear it, I sprint as fast as my legs will carry me, almost tumbling into the two people trembling beneath the spices.

Their eyes widen at my sudden presence.

I nod, acknowledging them, but don't waste time assessing the situation. There's a large metal garbage bin behind the stall, and beyond that is an alleyway that appears to lead out of the market.

"It's not safe here," I say in broken Italian. "Go to the trash bin, and I will cover you. From there, get out."

They both nod, but I can tell the two teenage boys are in a state of shock. Not so badly that they can't get themselves out, but enough that they are desperate and would probably walk into the bullets if I told them to.

"On the count of three," I say, and they both get ready to run.

I can't really cover them, since I cannot see where the bullets are coming from or who is firing them, but I pull out my gun anyway, hopefully giving them a sense of safety and control.

"One. Two. Three. Run!" I shout, and they take off behind me. They both reach it safely, and my shoulders drop as their forms disappear down the alley.

Two. I was able to save at least two.

Not much of a consolation, but I'll take it.

I focus back on my own situation. I need to make it to the rendezvous spot where my partner should be waiting to get me out of here. Except I still have almost a quarter mile to go, and I've only moved thirty-five feet.

This is going to take a while.

Hopefully the bullets will stop and give me a better chance, but even when the people have mostly cleared out, or are hiding beneath or behind market stalls, the bullets continue to soar.

Somewhere in the distance, I hear sirens, but their sounds don't deter the gunmen. If I had to guess, and based on what I know, whoever is behind this has corrupted the police force.

I'm on my own.

So are all these people.

And it's all my fault.

I swear again under my breath, racing to the next stall. I arrive safely then repeat the process a few more times until I'm only two stalls away from the door that will lead me out.

I almost reach the door when a sharp, searing pain goes straight through my shoulder. The force of the bullet throws my momentum forward, and

I crash into the door. Grappling for the handle, warm blood soaks my shirt and drips down my arm. The blood makes the door handle slick, and my vision blurs.

Switching hands, I finally get the door open and close it behind me, also shutting out the sounds of screams and bullets. But now, it's dark inside, and I have nothing to light my way.

I stumble to the wall, running my hand along it to help me along. I don't expect the stairs, and a single step has me tumbling into the blackness.

I don't register the pain, only focusing on when I'll stop falling, but my head slams into something hard, and the world disappears.

Chapter 1

"You look like shit this morning."

That is not what you want to hear after you've been overseas for months on an undercover assignment that unintentionally led to multiple civilian deaths—which is now under international investigation.

"Thanks, Ella," I reply, throwing the strap of my bag across my desk chair and falling into it.

"Can I get you a coffee?" she asks a bit more hesitantly.

I nod, staring at the blank computer screen in front of me. "I'll need a gallon of it."

When I don't hear movement, I turn to face her. She's studying me.

"I'm sorry, Nova," she says cautiously, ignoring my attempt at keeping the situation light.

"Thanks," I repeat, returning my gaze to the blank computer screen before me, willing my fingers to turn it on.

I'm too much of a coward to do it.

"Can I get you anything else?" Ella asks.

"A dismissal of my trial?" I ask miserably.

She doesn't say anything right away, probably trying to gauge my mood and wondering if I'll break down in tears.

"It'll work out, Nova. It always does," she tries.

I huff. "Not this time. But thanks for the vote of confidence."

I switch on my computer, the brightness causing me to squint. I stare at the hundreds of new messages in my inbox. Scrolling through them, I land on the trial date set for six months from now—the trial that will determine my fate as a field agent for the CIA.

I find another message from my director, sent an hour ago. There's no subject line. I hesitate before clicking on the message, already tensing.

Meet me in my office immediately upon arrival this morning.

Shit.

Pushing back my chair, I stand, straightening my black blazer over a simple white blouse. My black pants are tight-fitting, and I paired them with simple red heels that click as I slowly make my way to the director's office. My heart beats almost as fast as it does when I'm in the field.

It's an odd thing to be as fearful of a job as facing the possibility of death. But this position is all I have and all I've known for the entirety of my adult life.

I knock lightly, hearing soft voices on the other side. The rustling of clothes and the soft pad of shoes make me step back from the handle. A short male I don't recognize opens the door. He has thinning hair, a sharp nose, and a sneer that would make most cower.

He stops and blatantly assesses me, running his gaze down my body from my head to my toes, lingering far too long on my chest.

"Apologies for the intrusion." I don't hide my disdain. My mouth turns down in a scowl.

He doesn't say anything as he returns his attention to my face, simply waving me off.

I almost punch the man but fear that won't help my trial. Instead, I grit my teeth and enter the office. The man leaves without another glance in my direction, not bothering to shut the door behind him.

"I know that look, Nova," my director says without even taking his eyes off his computer screen.

I tilt my head. "What look is that, Dec?"

"The one you give when you want to stick a knife through someone's throat." Declan finally tears his eyes away from the screen, offering a slight and all-too-familiar smirk.

"That obvious?"

He chuckles. "Sit." He motions to the chair in front of his large mahogany desk, which is meticulously organized.

Declan was hired as a CIA field agent around the same time as me, and we worked on a dozen assignments together. We became close friends during that time, but he was promoted to director six months ago, and I couldn't help but feel slightly abandoned. Now, I'd just completely botched my first assignment without him. And *under* his command. I not only doomed myself but may have also doomed him.

My stomach churns as I stare at his perfectly angular facial features. Features I'd memorized over the years.

"I know what you're going to say," I begin, trying to get ahead of what I know is inevitable. He is going to take me out of the field.

He raises a dark brow.

"I fucked up, Dec. I'm sorry. I miscalculated. I knew it was too public, but I didn't want to lose the lead."

Declan holds up a hand. "Stop, Nova."

I shut my mouth, staring at the wrinkle between his brow. The one he always gets when he's considering how to be logical and fair.

"The trial is six months from now. I don't want to hear your excuses. I need you to gather your evidence and prepare your defense with the lawyer. Do exactly as they say." Declan emphasizes the last part.

I nod.

He pauses and studies me for another minute. "In the meantime, I have an assignment for you."

My eyes widen.

Declan laughs. "You didn't think I'd let you mope around the office for six months, did you?"

"I thought..." I pause, stumbling over my words and my own thoughts. "I thought I'd be benched until the verdict."

"You aren't guilty until proven, so I will act like you're innocent until someone tells me you aren't. You're my best agent, and this assignment requires your particular skill set." He smirks at the last part.

I groan. That always means he needs my looks to help infiltrate the world of my target.

"This assignment is local, too, so you won't have to go off-grid in some random country. You can stay in touch the whole time."

"So you can babysit me?"

Declan chuckles. "Believe me, you don't need babysitting. The location was a coincidence."

"What's the assignment?"

"A billionaire CEO is suspected of acquiring other billion-dollar companies and then murdering the CEOs of those companies."

My mouth involuntarily falls open. "Excuse me?"

Declan smirks. "You heard me correctly."

"What method of murder?"

Declan runs a hand through his short, brown hair, and the furrow between his brow is evident.

"You don't know the method?" I ask, stunned.

"No, that's not it. The three victims have all been found with traces of poison in their systems. The oddity is that they are all different compounds and in quantities that suggest that the poison might not have been the primary cause of death, which makes it hard to convict anyone. However, all three victims are billionaire CEOs of companies recently acquired by Regenerative Industries, which is run by Owen Mills. The timing is what alerted the authorities. All three deaths occurred within a month of the acquisitions."

"Owen Mills? The cocky bastard who claims he's saving the world? The one that's always on The Morning Show?"

"That's the one."

I sigh. "Great."

"Owen's looking for a personal assistant to manage his various foundations and charities."

"And that's where I come in."

Standing, I pace around the room, my mind instantly questioning how to insert myself into his life. What might he be like, and how I can protect myself from someone like him, should I have to? Is he your typical, hot guy billionaire? Or is he something worse?

He's accused of murder, so probably worse.

"It won't be easy, Nova," Declan interrupts my thoughts. "I couldn't get you an interview for a position in his acquisitions department. You'll be hard-pressed to get evidence working with his charities, but at least it's a personal assistant position. You might still be able to find a way in."

I stop pacing and look at him. "You doubt me?"

Declan smiles genuinely. "I would never doubt you." He pauses again, as if debating whether or not to say the next part. "I know how you are with guys like him. You're going to have to pretend to actually like him."

"So no punching, kicking, or knives to the throat?" I ask, grinning innocently.

Declan rolls his eyes. "You can punish the bastard by putting him behind bars."

"Not nearly as fun," I mumble.

He laughs, loud and genuine this time. "Go do your research. Your interview is in two days."

Chapter 2

Two days fly by, and I don't feel prepared, even with all my research. I'm accustomed to targets who already have established records and primarily work within crime syndicates. Those bastards are easy to take out because no one cares if they are found dead or alive. They are also easy to manipulate with a racy outfit and shameless flirting. They are all the same—thinking pretty women have no brains and are only after a slice of their fortune.

Owen Mills is a different story. Although he has a reputation with the ladies, it's clear that he vets his employees with meticulous attention to detail. He requires extensive interviews, background checks, references, years of experience, the highest degrees an education can buy, and even a trial period.

All for a personal assistant position.

The strangest requirement is "a love of plants."

I fly through the initial interviews with a panel of his employees, playing a part I know well. No one suspects the lies that easily spill from my lips during the video calls.

They buy it all.

My extensive research into the company pays off, which is how I find myself staring into captivating green eyes on the other side of my computer screen a few days later. My sparsely-decorated office is the perfect place for the interview. It's quiet and unassuming, giving nothing away.

"Good morning, Miss Riley. My team seems quite taken with you." Owen's voice is deep and rich, and I almost roll my eyes at his insinuating tone.

"It's nice to meet you, Mr. Mills," I reply, adding a sweet smile to finish off my image.

He smirks back, appearing satisfied that I didn't take the bait. "You seem to check all the boxes, Miss Riley. I only have a few questions for you before we give this a trial run." I nod when he pauses. He continues, "What is your opinion on the food system here in America?"

An odd question to ask, but since his charities are mainly focused on changing agriculture, I'm prepared with an answer. "The food system is not only insufficient, creating more waste than necessary while still not supplying enough to everyone, it is also at risk of failure due to climate change and loss of topsoil." I pause, gauging his reaction, worried my response was too rehearsed. Too rigid.

His brow furrows as he watches me, the smirk gone. He sits up straighter when I begin to speak again.

"But if you're asking me my personal opinion," I add, taking a sip of my cappuccino, "Then I think the power needs to go back to local small farmers. They need the resources and money to switch to regenerative ways of tending the land. And not just farmers—everyone. Even if all they have is a small apartment balcony or a window box. The money shouldn't be going into the hands of large farm owners, regardless of their promises to switch to regenerative agriculture. Farming shouldn't be a monopoly run by billionaires. It should be a community effort. It should be something everyone buys into and controls."

Mr. Mills smiles, and this time it isn't a cordial one. It's an authentic one, lighting up his whole face and causing a single dimple to appear on the left side. It's nice, until he opens his mouth. "There is more to you than what's on the surface. I see why my employees like you."

Once again, I grit my teeth at the insinuation. He can't be more than thirty-five years old, and despite my hate for him, he's more than easy on the eyes. Yet he's a billionaire CEO and has the nerve to assume I'm all surface-level. He's captivating, with dark hair, light brown skin, and the brightest green eyes I've ever seen. His messy hair falls to his brow, and even through a computer screen, I have the urge to brush it aside.

I don't know how to respond to his little comment, so I say simply, "Thank you, Mr. Mills."

"Owen."

I raise my brows.

"If you're going to be my personal assistant, Miss Riley, you don't need to use the formalities."

"In that case, you may call me Nora." I don't flinch at the lie. After all, my real name has only a one-letter difference.

He smiles, but this one appears to be another forced one. "I'll see you tomorrow at nine, Nora."

"That's it? No other questions?" I blurt, my calm composure slipping a little. I expected more of an interrogation.

He almost laughs, his mouth twitching. "No. My employees were comprehensive with their interviews, and I read their extensive reports on you. I did a little research, myself."

"Oh?" He has me sweating as I stare at the almost conspiratorial look on his face. I take a sip of coffee to hide my surprise and rising panic.

"You never mentioned your modeling career in the interviews."

I almost spit out my drink. I've never had a modeling career, and I have a feeling I know where he got that information.

"It was very short-lived," I comment, trying to sound sincere, but it comes out through clenched teeth. Squeezing my fists beneath the surface of the desk, I try not to hang up and go straight to Ella, who is the one responsible for my fake identity with each assignment.

She failed to mention that little detail about my "past." Likely because she knew I'd hate it.

"Not your thing, Miss Riley?"

I thought I told him to call me Nora?

"No. Not enough action for my liking."

"Action?" The ghost of his dimple reappears.

I could punch the insinuation off his face, but I smile sweetly. "I need lots of different types of tasks that keep me on my toes, Mr. Mills."

He doesn't miss me calling him Mr. Mills instead of Owen.

His smile broadens. "I'll see you tomorrow, Miss Riley."

His image disappears, leaving me staring at the post-video blue and white screen.

"Ella!" I call from my desk.

From the slow way the door opens, I can tell she knows I'm unhappy with her.

"Yes?" she squeaks.

I swivel my chair around, finding her poking only her head through the doorway, her red curls falling in front of her face.

"A modeling career?" I drawl, but I can't help the quirk of my lips.

Ella laughs nervously. "Seemed appropriate for the literal hottest, richest bachelor on the planet."

"I appreciate the thought, Ella, but the man is not interested in looks when it comes to his employees. He only wants brains and a good work ethic. He made that very, very clear in our conversation."

"Really?" Ella sounds horrified that she made such a terrible miscalculation.

I sigh. "It didn't cost me the position, but he only asked me two questions, and one of them was about my 'modeling career.'"

Ella opens the door so her entire body is visible. "Perhaps he was just curious?"

I snort. "The man couldn't stop making assumptions based on my looks."

"Like every other man who ever meets you?"

I drop my head into my hands. "Is using plastic surgery to make you look uglier a thing?" I mumble through my fingers.

Ella laughs, plopping herself down on my desk. "No, Nova. It's not a thing."

"It should be."

She doesn't entertain my little comment. "Can I get you anything? Are you ready for your trial run with Mr. Mills?"

I peel my face from my hands and look at her. "No, I don't need anything, and I'm overprepared for it."

Little do I know, I'm not even remotely prepared for Owen Mills.

Chapter 3

"Everyone's excited to meet you, Miss Riley," a petite woman with dark hair and dark skin blurts out as she escorts me to Mr. Mills' primary office. It is on the top floor of a thirty-story skyscraper. It's a private room set on the far side, but the rest of the building is open and welcoming. The employees chat and work with an easy air, smiling and laughing. There's a quaint kitchen off to the side, hosting a variety of them, who are chatting by the coffee machine. Most people aren't at their desks yet, happily catching up on their weekend adventures.

It's an atmosphere I could get used to if I weren't a field agent constantly changing assignments, locations, and identities.

"Really?" I ask in response to the woman's statement, genuinely surprised.

"Oh, yes. Everyone was very impressed with your background and skill set. In fact, I think you're a bit overqualified."

When researching the company, it was challenging to determine how far to extend my training, education, and expertise. I admit I might have made myself look a little too good, especially on paper.

I laugh, trying to sound surprised by her comment even as my body tenses. "I realize I'm overqualified, but the position interests me."

"I bet it does," the woman chirps.

I almost roll my eyes, knowing what she's implying about our looks. "I'm extremely interested in his mission statement for his charities. I believe in what he's trying to do, Miss...?" I ask since we weren't properly introduced earlier.

She waves her hand at me. "Call me Laura." She stops in front of large, wooden, double doors. "Here we are. Good luck, Miss Riley."

Laura disappears back across the office floor before I can say anything or thank her. Though it's not part of my job description to become friends with the other employees, I'd still like not to alienate myself. So far, I'm not off to a great start.

Staring at the door before me, I can't understand my nervousness. I've pretended to be other people for ten years now. Why does this time feel so different?

Knocking softly, I take a step back.

I expected Mr. Mills, but I did *not* expect a sweaty, half-dressed Mr. Mills to open the door.

Stumbling in my red heels, I catch myself right before crashing into him. Mr. Mills smirks, and I quickly compose myself.

"Apologies. I didn't realize I was intruding," I say, my voice a little shaky.

"You didn't. Come in." He steps aside, that stupid hint of a dimple appearing.

He's definitely used to flustered women.

Straightening, I walk past him, ignoring his muscled chest damp with sweat.

A moment later, I realize why: Half of his office is a gym. Dumbbells and a barbell are on the floor, along with kettlebells and medicine balls. There are even ropes and a pull-up bar, as well as other various types of gym equipment.

"Do you work out, Miss Riley?" he asks, seemingly aware of my attention.

I face him, finally composing myself. "Yes, sir. I do."

He raises a brow but doesn't ask anything else. Instead, he walks to a bench and grabs a clean, white T-shirt. He pulls it over his head and runs his hand through his hair, pushing it back from his eyes.

"Am I early?" I ask, confused as to why I'm staring at a man who clearly isn't ready for work.

"No, you're right on time."

"Then, you're late?"

He laughs. The sound is alarmingly and annoyingly alluring. "No. I'm also right on time. Have a seat, Miss Riley."

Okay. So he's a casual boss. Clearly. His desk is unorganized, and papers litter every unoccupied space. An empty coffee mug sits next to his keyboard, while a steaming cup sits on the other side. He has a pile of dirty laundry pushed into a corner of his office, and reusable water bottles are scattered around the room.

"I think you need a cleaner, not an assistant," I comment before I can stop myself.

He laughs again. "Perhaps you can find a good one for me, Miss Riley? But I bet you don't know any. Let me guess, you're annoyingly organized and neat?" His eyes sweep over my body. I'm wearing a clean, pressed black suit with a modest, white shirt underneath. His gaze drifts to my red heels and holds before traveling back up.

I eye him, wanting to give him a piece of my mind. Instead, I reply sweetly, "I like order, Mr. Mills. I'd be happy to find someone to clean your office if that's what you want, but if not, I'm glad to do it."

His smile grows wider. For unknown reasons, he seems to be finding this whole situation amusing, while it's only making me feel more uncomfortable. I've never felt so far off my game before. I try to convince myself it's because of my impending trial and not the man in front of me.

"No need to find me a cleaner, Miss Riley, and it's not in your job description."

I almost roll my eyes as he walks around his desk and falls into his chair, motioning for me to do the same.

"This trial run will only be a week, Miss Riley, but I doubt it will take me that long to decide." He pauses and keeps his stare on me, but I keep my face neutral. He continues, "I have a few charity galas coming up that are poorly planned since my last assistant retired. I want you to start by vetting the current venues and event planners and ensuring they are up to the standard of our previous galas."

I nod.

"The list is on the desk over there." He points to a small desk opposite his gym. It's next to a small bar that looks like it's been used far too many times. Dirty glasses litter the small counter, and the alcohol bottles that decorate the shelves are almost empty.

I return my gaze to find him watching me far too intently.

"I'll get started," I say, wanting to put some distance between us but not understanding why. I've dealt with men far worse than him. Why am I feeling so flustered?

I hear him pushing papers around his desk and then the clicking of keys as he gets to work.

Looking down, I focus on my task, wondering how I'm going to find the evidence I need to convict him if all I'm doing is planning fancy parties for rich people. I try to remind myself what I'm best at: getting close to notoriously difficult people.

I glance at Mr. Mills as he answers a phone call, surprised by the easy way he speaks. He's all charm, and I wonder if it's genuine or part of an act to keep people from thinking he's a murderer.

"Do you need something from me, Miss Riley?"

My eyes widen when I realize I've been staring. "No, Mr. Mills, I was just thinking."

An amused grin lifts his lips. "About?"

Luckily, I'm much more intelligent than the last ten minutes would suggest. "Instead of multiple galas, which I'm sure you're tired of, why not make it a combined event in a larger venue? Fewer logistics, less time, and combining patrons and your different charities might be a good thing. Might lead to more connections and bigger money." Not to mention, it'd make this task easier for me.

Mr. Mills cocks his head to the side. "If you can pull it off, Miss Riley, by all means."

I smile. "Nora. Please call me Nora."

He smirks back. "Only if you call me Owen."

I sigh, giving in. "Fine, Owen, I'll put together the logistics and run it by you."

He winks. "Deal."

We spend the next couple of hours both lost in our respective tasks. Combining events proves to be less complicated than I expected. His charities are all nonprofit organizations, focusing on either regenerative agriculture education, urban agriculture education, or organizations involved in converting monocropped farms into regenerative ones. They all have a common theme. He has a few small charities, though, that don't have a clear mission or name and only deal in small amounts of money. Those catch my eye, and I search for more specifics.

The more I research the charities, the more frustrated I become. There appears to be no red flags or suspicious activity. There are no connections between the acquired companies and the murdered CEOs and any of the charities. Perhaps money is involved, but that's not obvious. Just because funds are transferred to these charities, it doesn't mean there's any wrongdoing.

I start to wonder if I'm in way over my head with this assignment. Perhaps Declan should have put my partner, Gray, on this assignment. He's the tech genius.

Coming out of my thoughts, I find Owen watching me as I frown at the computer.

"Something wrong, Miss Riley?"

"Nothing's wrong. In fact, everything's perfect!" I chirp.

God, I sound like an idiot.

His lips quirk, turning up into a half-smile. "Did you eat?"

His question throws me a bit, and I look at the clock on my computer. It reads 3:30 pm.

My eyes widen, and I shake my head.

"Here," Owen says, standing and walking the short distance to my desk.

He deposits a small, brown, paper bag on the tabletop and waits, arms crossed, for me to open it.

"You didn't need to give me your lunch," I say, reaching for the bag.

"It's not mine. It's yours."

I scrunch my nose, peering into the bag. There's a perfectly wrapped sandwich inside next to a receipt. Angling my head, I read it. Owen did, in fact, order two different sandwiches.

"How'd you know what I like?" I ask, pulling out the sandwich and unwrapping it.

Owen's half-smile turns into a full one, with that annoying, charming dimple and, what I imagine is, his usual mischief. "I don't. I got you my favorite."

I stare at the Italian sandwich made on a French baguette, burrata cheese spilling down the sides, and my mouth waters. He may not know my favorite sandwich, but damn does this one look good.

Owen chuckles at my reaction and moves back to his desk, grabbing his coat. "I'm off to a few meetings for the rest of the day. Feel free to leave whenever you need to."

With that, he's out the door, and I'm no closer to finding evidence or even a lead. What's worse: my traitorous brain is actually starting to think this man is a decent human being.

But that can't be right.

"How'd the first day on the job go?" Declan's familiar voice comes through the cell phone I have pressed between my ear and shoulder.

In an apartment that agents use as a safe house in San Francisco, I make myself a quick bowl of pasta with sausage. The place looks out over the Bay Bridge and is furnished but sparsely decorated. If you didn't look closely, you'd think no one lived here.

It's no home.

"Can't say it was easy," I reply, "though I'm grateful to not have to fear a gun to my head every five seconds."

Declan chuckles. "No, you'll just have to check your coffee every morning."

It was meant as a joke, but I'm not sure what to make of that.

He continues, "How can I make it easier?"

Thinking, I pour through what I've learned about him and the company over the last eight hours before replying. "He's pretty secretive and observant as hell. He won't be easy to deceive. I'm likely going to need hackers. I don't think he'll willingly give me access to his phone records and emails."

"You can be pretty convincing, you know." I hear the amusement in Declan's voice.

"Not with Owen. I don't think he likes the fact that his employees picked someone who looks like me. As I told Ella, I think we made a huge miscalculation in what he likes."

"You're saying he doesn't like pretty women?"

"I'm saying he doesn't want a pretty woman working in his office. I'm sure he loves them in his bed."

Declan laughs, and the sound is oddly comforting. "Interesting. I wonder why that is?"

"Distraction? How should I know?" I'm getting more frustrated as the conversation goes on, and I'm no closer to figuring out how to get closer to Owen. And if I can't, I won't find what I need.

"I'll work on getting you a hacker, but you're going to have to tell them where to look. You'll have to have an idea at least."

I sigh, switching the phone to between my other shoulder and ear while stirring the boiling pasta. "I'm far better suited for assassinations, I think."

"The last assignment nearly destroyed you, Nova. And I'm not talking about the trial."

I hate how spot on he is. I can barely stand to think about it without panic surging through my chest and rendering me breathless.

"I know, Dec. But I don't know how to get close to this guy. I'm not charming like he is. I'm a ticking time bomb."

"Truer words have never been spoken."

Ignoring his barb, I continue, "I can't promise this guy won't end up with a knife through him. A punch to the face would be me holding back."

Declan laughs again. "Maybe he's into that kind of thing?"

"Not helpful," I grumble, straining the pasta and throwing it in a pristine, white bowl that's probably never been used.

"I have faith in you, but Nova?"

"Mmm?"

"Don't forget to prepare your testimony for the trial. *That* is a priority, not Owen Mills."

"I know. I'm sitting down to work on it now." It's the truth, even if I'd rather pretend Italy didn't happen.

"Good. Any new memories or leads coming through?" Declan suddenly sounds oddly fearful, which is very unlike him. He's usually the steady and stable one in our duo.

"No. The memories of that day are still fuzzy. I lost a lot of blood. I'm working on a timeline and identifying faces of the people involved."

Declan is quiet for a few moments. "Be careful who you indulge all of this with. I don't want anything to go wrong with your trial."

I find it odd that Declan wants me to be so secretive, but I know he's worried about me.

"Oh, and don't forget to take care of yourself," he adds.

"I will, Dec. Thanks."

"Talk tomorrow."

When he hangs up, I'm left alone in a dark, cold apartment that is eerily silent. I chew my food, a lump in my throat every time I swallow, knowing I'm in way over my head with two completely separate problems.

Chapter 4

My second day on the job starts without a hitch. I jump back into the gala prep and research the charities that will be featured at the event. Though I look for anything out of the ordinary, I come up empty-handed. The charity side of the company seems squeaky clean.

My frustration grows, but I'm almost relieved that there's nothing nefarious going on with the charities. I'm starting to think there's something to Owen's claim of saving the world on all the morning shows.

It's something I'd never admit to him or anyone else, though.

Owen is gone most of the morning in meetings. He finally allowed me to access his calendar so I can help him with scheduling. Scanning it, I discover nothing but the usual business meetings. Nothing suspicious.

I'm wondering if there even is any evidence to be found when Owen's voice interrupts my thoughts. "Time for lunch, Miss Riley. I won't let my employees starve while on the clock." He's leaning casually against the office door, watching me.

"You're oddly worried about my food intake, Mr. Mills."

He smirks but doesn't respond, so I do as he asks, grabbing my proposal for the combined charity event. Maybe I can ask him over lunch what the smaller charities are for since I can't find anything about them in the company's system.

"What do you like to eat?" he asks, holding the door open for me.

"I'm not picky."

"No?" He raises a brow.

"Just because I like to be organized doesn't mean I'm picky. Or high maintenance," I add since that's what most people think when they look at me. "I'm rather easy to please."

"Is that so?" The amusement hasn't left his voice.

I roll my eyes, which he catches out of the side of his eye, but doesn't comment on.

We both wait in silence as the elevator takes us to the first floor. I feel his gaze on me a few times before we step out into the lobby. He lets me lead, following behind, even though I have no idea where we're going.

"Good afternoon, Mr. Mills. Your car is ready." An employee occupying the front desk beams at him.

I eye Owen. Why does he want me to call him by his first name when no one else here does?

"Thank you, Miss Auburn," he says, holding the door open for me, a knowing look in his eyes.

I walk out, my heels clicking loudly on the concrete, and stop in front of an obscenely expensive, red SF90 Stradale Ferrari. I expected he owned expensive cars; he's a billionaire after all. What I didn't anticipate was riding in one. I figured he had people who drove him everywhere.

"Do you have something against sports cars, Miss Riley?"

Realizing that I am staring at the car while he holds the passenger door open for me, I quickly compose myself. "Nothing against them. In fact, I quite enjoy driving them."

He halts me as I attempt to duck into the passenger seat. "Why don't you drive us to lunch, Miss Riley? That way you can have some fun, and I can learn what you like to eat."

Is this some sort of test? Seeing whether I'm telling the truth? If it is, two can play this game.

Not hesitating, I walk over to the driver's side, pulling off my heels and throwing them into his lap as he settles himself next to me. He lets out an amused chuckle, clutching my shoes and staring at my bare feet.

I adjust the seat and mirrors. He's much larger than I am, and everything is programmed to his height. When I'm satisfied, I turn and find him watching me with a look I can't read.

When his gaze finds mine, he asks, "Where to?"

I smirk, turning my attention back to the road. "You'll see."

Driving the short distance to the coast, we make our way north on the winding roads that line the cliffs leading to the ocean. It's my favorite drive, and the car easily glides around the tight turns. Before I know it, my whole body relaxes into the easy feel of the wheel beneath my hands and the road beneath the tires.

"Where'd you learn to drive cars like this?" Owen asks out of the blue.

"My father. He was into fast cars."

"Was?"

I nod, not wanting to explain. Not wanting to relive what happened. Not needing his pity.

Owen seems to understand and changes the subject. "Where are we going? I'm starting to think you're kidnapping me."

I smile deceptively. "Perhaps I am, but if I were, I'm not sure you'd be mad about it."

Owen raises a brow, a half-smirk on his lips. I can't read his face, though, and I'm worried I've already crossed a boundary on only my second day of work.

I slow the car, turning left into a small, gravel parking lot, suddenly aware he might not want me parking his expensive car in the dirt.

He doesn't say anything about it, however. Instead, he looks around, his gaze flicking from the restaurant to the scenery around it.

"This is my favorite restaurant in the whole Bay Area," I explain.

It's a small place that looks more like a shack than a restaurant, but it overlooks the water, and the seafood is to die for.

"I've never even heard of it." He sounds surprised as he passes me my shoes.

"It's a locals' spot. Secret for a reason."

"And you trust me with this knowledge, Miss Riley? You do know the influence and connections I have."

I roll my eyes, unable to help myself. "You're kind of an arrogant ass, aren't you?"

Clapping a hand over my traitorous mouth, I moan at my true colors beginning to show without my permission. Usually, I don't have a problem playing the role I'm supposed to and abandoning who I really am. This time, though, it slips easily.

"And you're not as zipped up as you appear," he shoots back at me, but the glint in his eye gives away his playfulness.

I put on my heels and step out of the car without answering. Before I know it, he's at my side, scanning the small wooden building in front of us. The blue and white paint is slowly peeling, revealing the graying wood beneath. There's no sign hinting at the name of the restaurant, and I don't offer it as we step through the creaky, wooden door.

I smile as we approach the old, wooden bar inside, its body worn and faded from almost a hundred years of use.

"Jax!" I shout.

He turns, a towel and a bar glass in his hand, and his eyes widen in surprise, as if he'd seen a ghost. A second later, he's around the other side of the bar, wrapping me in a rough hug that I return in earnest. I missed him while I was overseas, and my heart squeezes at the sight of him.

"Still in one piece, I see," he comments, stepping back to assess me.

I cringe. Jax knows what I do, even if I can't ever tell him the details.

Seeing Owen's eyebrows raise, I immediately explain. "I travel a lot."

Realization dawns on Jax's face, and without giving Owen a chance to say anything, I answer Jax. "I'm home, safe and sound. This is my new boss, or possibly my new boss, Owen Mills."

Jax's brow furrows. The name must sound familiar to him, but I am relieved when he clearly can't place it. "Nice to meet you, mate," he says in his Australian accent, extending a hand to Owen, who assesses him far too intently.

Jax is your quintessential Australian surfer. He has tanned skin, long blond hair pulled back in a man bun while he works, and he's wearing a Hawaiian button-up shirt, paired with khaki shorts and flip flops. Like me, his looks suggest he has little in the way of brains, but also like me, he's secretly very intelligent.

"Jax is doing research for the marine mammal center along with running this place," I explain to Owen, who grabs Jax's hand and squeezes firmly.

"Nice to meet you," Owen says, and Jax smiles at him before returning his attention to me.

"The usual, Nova?" Jax asks, and suddenly I'm panicking at his use of my real name. A second later, Jax's eyes widen.

Fortunately, Owen doesn't seem to notice. With Jax's accent, it sounds similar enough.

I remind myself to bring up this little complication to Declan and Jax tonight when I get back to my apartment.

I nod. "The usual, except double it."

Jax eyes Owen for confirmation, and he nods in return.

Leading Owen to my usual table by the window, he slips into the chair across from me. The sky is foggy and gray, and the ocean is calm today. The atmosphere in the dimly-lit restaurant is cozy, and the exhaustion from the last few months hits me without warning.

Owen observes my wide yawn without comment, instead asking the question I knew was coming. "How do you know Jax?" The question is casual, but there's a hint of something else under his words.

I decide to be truthful since it's likely that Owen would find out if I'm lying. "I've known Jax a long time, actually. He came to the States when he was fourteen, and we went to high school together."

"High school sweethearts?" he asks, once again far too relaxed.

"No. Despite how badly I wanted him, he just never wanted me back."

That clearly gets his attention, his eyes widening, and I laugh at his reaction. "Jax is into men, Owen. I'm definitely not his type. But we've been best friends ever since I pretended to be his girlfriend to keep the bullies away."

"What did this pretending entail?"

"You're shameless, you know? Do you act this way with all your employees?" This gets him to shut his mouth. His brows furrow as if he is thinking seriously about my question.

"No. I suppose you're right. I'll behave." He sounds serious, but I can't tell if he's joking.

Jax comes over and sets two clean plates in front of us. We both thank him, and he rushes back to the kitchen. Owen watches Jax's exit. The look that crosses Owen's face is different this time, but what unnerves me is how observant he is. Like he sees through the lies and knows what's real.

"So, I was finishing my proposal to combine the events and came across a few unlabeled charities. I was wondering what those were so I could place them correctly," I say, shaking the thoughts from my head.

Owen waves a hand at me. "Don't worry about those. I hold different charity events for the smaller ones. I'll send you a list of patrons to invite. They don't need to be featured in the auction."

That doesn't help my suspicion or my questions, but I jot down a note on the proposal about acquiring a list of patrons and hand it to Owen.

He scans it, brow furrowed, then looks up at me with a charming smile that I try to ignore. "This looks great, Miss Riley. I give you my permission to go ahead with the plan."

"That's it? No other questions?"

"You're very detailed, Miss Riley. No other questions necessary."

Jax shows up with our food, placing a bowl in front of me first and then Owen. Owen studies his with amused interest.

"So, Barbie, how've you been? And don't just give me the 'I'm fine' speech," Jax says, which has Owen looking at *me* with apparent amused interest now.

"Barbie was my nickname in high school," I explain.

"For obvious reasons." Jax chuckles.

I huff. "I'm *fine*, Jax. Got back from Sicily a week ago, and I'm missing the seafood."

"You mean you're missing my charming company."

I smile. "Always."

Jax hesitates, eyeing the two of us as if worried he's interrupting. "I'll leave you to your lunch meeting."

Without another word, he disappears into the kitchen.

I turn to find Owen staring at me, looking at me as though he can't quite figure me out.

Doing an undercover job this close to home is going to be far harder than I thought. I'm supposed to be playing a role, but this doesn't feel like one.

"What?" I ask at his bemused expression.

"I'm beginning to think you have more than one side to you."

Shrugging, I stuff a large bite of cioppino in my mouth. "Don't we all?"

With that, he spoons a mouthful, and his eyes widen. He chews slowly, and when he swallows, he looks stunned.

"This is really good," he says through another bite.

A grin is my only response, and we consume the rest of our meals in silence. The quiet should make me uneasy, but it doesn't.

After we're finished, Owen pays, and I ask him to wait for me in the car so I can say goodbye to Jax. He doesn't argue, shouting a quick "nice to meet you" at Jax before ducking out the door.

"That boss of yours is pretty cute. You sure there isn't something more going on there? He did take you out to lunch." Jax wiggles his eyebrows.

"I don't even officially have the job yet. I can assure you there's nothing going on." Not to mention, he's a murder suspect who I'm supposed to be gathering evidence to convict.

"Be careful there, Nova. He looks dangerous," he says mischievously.

I know he means a man that attractive can be dangerous, but he has no idea. Attractive and murderous is a bad combination.

"It's good to see you, Jax. I promise I'll be around more now that I'm home."

Jax studies me for a moment. "You better. Also, I know something's going on with you. You aren't yourself. I plan on squeezing that info out of you soon. Just a warning." He comes back around the bar and wraps me in a hug.

I press my cheek against his warm chest, finally allowing my shoulders to slump as my weight presses into him.

"You don't have to do everything alone, you know," he whispers into my hair.

I pull back enough to look up into his blue eyes. "I know. I know. We'll catch up soon. I promise."

Jax lets me go, and I make it to the door before he shouts, "I'm holding you to that!"

I smile and walk to the passenger side of Owen's car and ease myself into the dark red, leather seats.

Owen is watching me with another one of his amused expressions.

"Do I have something on my face?" I ask, harsher than I intended.

He smirks. "No."

With that, he peels out of the parking lot, and we head back to the office. The thought of what I'll have to do has me feeling a little queasy, and I'm still unsure why.

Chapter 5

I’ve been stalking the target for weeks, finally tracking him down in the middle of Palermo—the largest and most populated city in Sicily. He’s walking through the market with his two main bodyguards. Others trail him, not bothering to conceal their guns as they keep their eyes alert to any threat. I can’t see them, but I expect more guards are stationed ahead. There are likely ten of them.

Ten against one.

“Nova.” The communication comes through my headphones from my new partner.

I slink behind a rack of beautifully colored summer dresses. “What do you have for me, Gray?”

“It’s too crowded. You can’t take him out here. Too many witnesses.”

“I’ve been tracking this guy for years, Gray, and now that I have eyes on him, I’m not going to let him go.” I can’t help the frustration in my voice.

I hear Gray let out a long breath as I stick my head out to make sure I haven’t lost my target.

“Wait until he’s past the market, but don’t miss the escape location we agreed on,” he says at last.

“Copy.”

I slink out from behind the dresses, and that’s when everything goes to shit.

I wake, shaking and soaked in sweat. Throwing the soft, satin sheets off my body, I stand. I pace around the room for a few minutes, my bare feet pounding against the cool, wooden floors. It takes me that long to stop hyperventilating.

Looking at the clock, which reads 4:45 am, I realize there is no way I'm going back to sleep, so instead, I dress in workout gear and pack my work clothes in a garment bag, slinging it over my shoulder. My stomach is in knots, making me feel queasy, so I don't bother with breakfast or coffee.

I decide to take up Owen on his offer to use the equipment in his office before he gets there. The CIA gym is too far away from the apartment and the office anyway. Plus, I plan to do some snooping while I clean the disgustingly dirty space.

The streets are mostly silent as I make my way to the thirty-story office building that serves as the headquarters for Regenerative Industries. I pull out my newly-made keycard and enter the silent building, slowly making my way up to the top floor, and slip into his office.

It's dark and quiet inside. Switching on the lights, I notice everything is as it was when I left the evening before. After depositing my garment bag across the back of my desk chair, I start by cleaning up the empty cups and glasses on the bar. I move to the laundry in the corner next, depositing it in a clothes basket and placing it by the door. I gather up the papers, quickly scanning each one and organizing them into piles based on what's on them. None have any of the information I'm looking for, not that I expected them to.

I suspect Owen is smarter than he looks. In that, we have something in common.

Moving to Owen's desk, I start with the empty coffee cups, bringing them to the sink to wash before organizing the papers on his desk like I did with the others. Sweeping the last of them off, my gaze catches on a small Post-it note beside his keyboard. On it is only one name: Peyton Radd. No other information. I quickly snap a photo of the Post-it, and then I look around at my clean-up job.

When I'm satisfied, I make my way to the gym equipment.

Instinct instantly takes over, and the movement is calming. I move through the familiar motions, lifting weights until my muscles feel like Jello. I finish with the punching bag in the corner. It's covered with white leather and looks as though it's hardly been used.

This is where I truly lose myself, working out every inch of pure rage that lives in my body, always at risk of exploding.

I don't know how long I pommel the bag, but I feel the rawness of my knuckles when a familiar voice breaks the silence. "Remind me not to get on your bad side, Miss Riley."

Instantly dropping my arms, I swing around to face him. Stray strands of blonde hair cling to my face, and I brush them away, finally noticing the blood.

Shit. I tore my knuckles.

Owen looks past me at the bag, and I follow his gaze to find blood spattered on the white leather. I groan. Who buys a white punching bag anyway?

"I'll wash it," I say and turn to meet his gaze.

He's watching me as though he's trying to piece together some puzzle. "You need to get that looked at?" His eyes drop to my bloody knuckles.

I cover them as best I can. "No. I'll wrap them."

"I take it this isn't the first time you've beaten a bag until your knuckles bled?"

I shake my head.

Owen's eyes drift from my face to the rest of me, and suddenly I'm all too aware that I'm standing in front of him in only a sports bra and a pair of tight-fitting leggings, and I'm dripping with sweat. I hadn't expected to still be like this when he walked through the door, but I lost track of time.

"I'm sorry I'm late," I say hastily, trying to cover the scar on my shoulder and hoping he hasn't already noticed.

He turns and scans the rest of the room, the corner of his mouth kicking up. "I see you've been busy."

"Couldn't sleep."

He regards me with curiosity. "Let me know if you ever need a real sparring partner. I used to box."

I raise a brow. "Your bag looks brand new."

"It is. I killed the last one," he says as he strolls to his desk and drops a gym bag next to his chair, also placing a coffee cup near to his keyboard. His eyes drop to the sticky note, widening almost imperceptibly before his features return to neutrality, and he looks back at me.

Interesting.

"I haven't had a true opponent in a while Miss Riley. I'd be honored to train with you."

I don't know what to say to that. Getting close to him is part of the job, and I do want to punch the smirk off his face, but it isn't exactly professional. I haven't even officially gotten the position.

My curiosity overpowers my common sense. "Love to, Mr. Mills. Name the date and time."

He smiles, that damn dimple appearing. "As it seems we both cannot sleep, how about I meet you here at 5:30 tomorrow morning."

I nod, not thinking too hard about it. I'm supposed to earn his trust. What better way than beating the shit out of him?

"Let me get out of your way. I'll shower and be back to work in a few minutes," I say, heading for his personal bathroom next to the bar.

He observes my retreat with a look I cannot read. The sound of weights being moved and dropped pierces the silence as I slip through the door and close it firmly.

Well, I have a name on a Post-it: Peyton Radd. It's not much to go on in terms of evidence, but it's a start. What I don't have is my sanity, and I will my heart to stop beating so fast.

Coming out of the bathroom, I find Owen still working out—shirtless now. I brush my hands through my wet hair, unsuccessful in locating a hairdryer. Not that I expected one.

Owen stops for a moment, his expression veiled but his eyes on me, before he resumes his workout without a word.

Switching on my computer, I get straight to work, going over the names and compiling a list of the patrons who should get invitations for the gala.

"You have a venue yet?" Owen calls from across the room.

"Yes," I reply, not looking up from my work.

"And?"

"And it's a surprise, Mr. Mills."

"Once again, Miss Riley, you are making me feel a bit afraid for my life."

My gaze shoots to his, but instead of seriousness, his eyes sparkle with mirth.

"Once again, Mr. Mills, I didn't kidnap you yesterday. You can trust me."

I inwardly cringe at the lie. Everything about this situation is a lie. Everything I do is bringing him one step closer to a lifetime in prison. I'm the last person he should trust.

I'm so lost in my thoughts that I don't notice he crossed the room until he's sitting on my desk, trying to steal a peek at my computer screen.

I swat at his head, and he ducks, chuckling. "So violent, Miss Riley."

"What do you not understand about the word surprise?" I ask, trying to sound stern.

"I don't like surprises."

Cocking my head to the side, I study him. "You'll like this one."

He snorts. "I don't doubt it, Miss Riley."

We stare at each other for a moment before I return my attention to the screen, wanting to get the gala details out of the way so I can continue with my real purpose.

Owen doesn't move from my desk, but he doesn't try to look at my computer screen.

"Is there something else you need from me?" I ask, not pulling my eyes from the work in front of me.

He shifts his weight as though he's going to stand but thinks better of it. "Did you eat, Miss Riley?"

The question has me snapping my attention to him. He notices my wrapped knuckles hovering above the keyboard.

"No," I say.

That's when his eyes find mine.

"Come." He stands, grabbing a shirt and throwing it on before heading out of the office not bothering to see if I'm following.

We make our way to the cafe in the lobby, once again in companionable silence. Owen orders two coffees and two chocolate croissants and places one of each in front of me at a small, two-person cafe table by the front office windows that look out onto the busy sidewalk.

I thank him, and he nods in response.

Chewing the croissant, I think of all I know about the man in front of me. My research came up with only basic information, which isn't surprising given that big names usually have a good PR team to keep them mostly anonymous.

He's an only child. His mother doesn't appear to be in the picture, though I couldn't figure out what happened to her. His father used to own the company but signed it over to Owen a few years ago, giving him complete control of the company and the finances. He's been labeled the richest man under forty by Forbes magazine, as well as the hottest billionaire under forty. And he won hottest man alive by People magazine last year. I almost roll my eyes but remember my company and smile instead.

"Do you have any siblings, Mr. Mills?" I ask as people pass and stare at us with curiosity. Owen greets most of them with a cheery smile.

"One," he replies, taking a sip of his second coffee of the day. "Half-brother, technically."

I wasn't expecting that. My research didn't mention any siblings.

"He runs one of the charities. You'll meet him before the gala."

"So, I'm hired?" I ask, the corner of my mouth turning up.

He halts, slowly dropping the cup from his mouth, and his lips quirk. "Yes, Miss Riley. You have the job."

Resisting the girlish desire to squeal, I bite my lower lip. He watches my mouth as I do.

"Thank you, Owen, really."

His eyes travel to my eyes and hold. "You called me Owen."

"Isn't that what you told me to call you?"

He opens his mouth to say something but is cut off by a sultry voice. "Owen Mills. I've been looking for you."

I don't miss the slight flinch and widening of his eyes. He eyes the woman approaching from behind me. I don't turn, waiting until she comes into my line of sight to assess her.

"I thought I'd find you here," she says cheerily.

"Noell, what can I do for you?" Owen's tone is oddly low, with a hint of anger. Or maybe annoyance? Something else? I don't miss his use of her first name, though.

She finally pretends to notice me. "Oh, and who's this?" she asks, staring at me as though I'm an inconvenience.

Owen goes to introduce me, but I meet her challenge and interrupt. "I'm Nora Riley, Mr. Mills' new personal assistant." I extend my hand, smiling. At least I think I'm smiling. I could be scowling.

Noell gives me a fake smile, weakly clutching my hand for a split second before dropping it and returning her attention to Owen. The reality is: I'm used to people dismissing me the second they look at me. All I've ever been good for is my looks.

"Finally caved and hired a new assistant? Interesting choice, I must say," Noell drawls.

I scoff, but she acts like I'm not even there.

"The work was getting overwhelming. What can I do for you, Noell?" Owen glances at me, offering an apologetic look as Noell goes off on a tangent.

"The integration of the new companies is starting to become a problem, Owen. We have to do a restructure. The company can't be profitable if we keep every employee."

I raise a brow, suddenly much more interested in what this woman has to say.

"Restructure isn't necessary," he replies curtly.

"But—"

Owen cuts her off. "Are you not paid enough, Noell? Are you out of a job? This company pays all employees *more* than they are worth, according to the market."

"But this company can't keep affording to do so."

"Perhaps not. But for now, we have no problem." Owen acts as if that's the end of the conversation, returning his attention to his coffee and taking another large sip in a clear dismissal.

Noell huffs in frustration. "Your father was right. You're going to run this company into the ground."

With that, she storms off, and I'm left staring at her retreating form, wondering what their relationship is. She's clearly close to the family, but she also works for them. There's a familiarity that doesn't exist with the rest of Owen's employees. And what she said...

Owen pulls me out of my thoughts when he sighs. "Sorry you had to witness that," he mumbles, rubbing a hand through his black hair, the muscle in his arm tensing.

I pretend not to notice and shrug. "Accounting isn't my thing."

He finally turns his gaze on me. "No. I suspect your skill set is much less black and white."

I'm not sure what he means by that, but before I can ask, he stands, taking my empty plate and depositing it on the cafe counter. He thanks the baristas, who smile at him, before leading me back to the office.

I ask only one question before finishing up the gala invitations. "What's your brother's name?"

"Parker Mills."

My eyebrows shoot up. "The famous Calvin Klein underwear model?"

Owen smirks from across the room. "That's the one."

Chapter 6

"**I** have a name, Dec. Peyton Radd," I say over the phone later that night, already curled up in the large, four-poster bed. Which is far too large for one person. "It was on a sticky note I found next to Owen's keyboard."

"Have you looked it up?" he asks, though I'm sure he knows I have.

"Google came up with nothing."

"Send it to Ella. Have her search the CIA database."

"Already did. She said she'd get back to me in the morning."

There's a long pause on the other end of the phone. I can't tell if he's distracted or debating what to say to me.

"Dec?" I ask.

"Are you doing ok? I've been worried sick about you. I've been going over the mission reports from your last assignment. It was... I just want to know you're ok. That you're taking care of yourself." His concern is genuine. His friendship is sincere, and suddenly I'm on the verge of tears.

I take a moment to compose myself.

"Nova, tell me you're talking to someone about it. Tell me you aren't alone in this."

I sniffle, hoping he doesn't hear it through the phone. "I haven't had time to find anyone to talk to."

"We have counselors on site, Nova."

I cut him off before he can continue. "I know. I know. I'll make an appointment. I think I'm still in shock. I've been trying to write the report for the trial, but my memory has holes. I'm completely unsure of the order of events. I thought time would help me piece it back together."

"We're only missing the information from when everything went to shit until you met Gray at the rendezvous spot."

That's the problem, though. My memory of those few minutes are hazy and filled with screams, death, and my own pain and blood.

I realize I haven't said anything when Declan whispers, "I will do absolutely anything to clear your name, Nova. Anything at all. You need to tell me how I can help."

The thing is: I believe him. Declan has always been that partner who would do anything for me—even take a bullet. The thought that he might lose his job by helping me keep mine has my throat tightening.

"I'll send over my report when I'm done with it. Maybe there is something in it you can help with."

Declan takes a deep breath. "Deal. But in the meantime, promise me you'll talk to someone."

"I promise."

Another long pause has me fiddling with the end of the sheets, weaving them between my fingers.

"Goodnight, Nova. Please don't take out all that anger on your target. We don't need more investigations," Declan says, trying, as always, to lighten the mood.

"I plan to beat the shit out of him tomorrow. Don't worry," I jest, except I can't really say it's a joke since it was Owen's idea to become early morning sparring partners.

Declan chuckles. "Night."

"Night, Dec."

After switching off the light to try to get some sleep, the phone rings again. I blindly reach for it on the bedside table, expecting to find Declan's name on the screen. Besides Ella, he's the only one who calls me after work hours.

I'm surprised when I see my new partner's name pop up on the screen.

"Gray?" I ask, unable to hide the slight clip of concern in my tone.

There's an almost inaudible sniffle on the other end before he clears his throat. "Nova, this is all so fucked up."

I don't have to guess what he means, but I sit up taller in the bed, my body tensing.

"I know. Listen, I'm fully aware I might be the reason you lose your new position. I never intended to pull you into this mess. I've talked to my lawyer, and we are doing everything we can to make sure you don't lose your job or serve any jail time."

I can almost hear Gray shaking his head on the other end. "It's not that." He sniffles again. "I'm worried about you."

I flinch. I wasn't expecting concern.

Gray has been working at the CIA for ten years. His previous position was designing new tech for field agents. He'd only recently been promoted right before our mission. He'd always been quiet but confident and committed to his job.

And I'd fucked him on his first field assignment.

"I've been reviewing all the recorded comms and reports," he continues. "Besides when you decided to go off the books and follow your lead, there's nothing. No wrongdoing whatsoever."

"When there are that many civilian deaths, there's always wrongdoing, and it doesn't matter who's at fault. Justice needs to be served, and sometimes it's easier to serve it to the person most directly involved."

"What about the investigation?" There's a hint of hope in his voice that I'm very much about to squash.

"If we couldn't get to the bottom of it after years of tracking these guys, you think investigators, who've never been involved, can figure it out?" It's a rhetorical question, and when Gray doesn't respond, I can tell he knows it.

Another shaky inhale is all I hear on the other end for what seems like minutes.

"What can I do to help you?" he asks in almost a whisper, and my heart breaks a little bit.

This man, who's worked with me only one time, cares enough to call in the middle of the night and ask how he can help me, instead of worrying about himself.

At that moment, I know what I have to do, even if it means the end of my career and possible jail time. I need to damn myself and clear his name.

"Nothing, Gray. I've been through these things before." A blatant lie. "Take care of your report and tell the whole truth. I've got myself covered."

This time, his breathing sounds steadier, like a weight has been lifted from his shoulders.

"Ok," he says more confidently. "But let me know if you need any of the comms from the mission for your report. I know you lost a lot of blood and hit your head, so your memory might be a little patchy."

If only he knew the extent of it.

"Thanks, Gray. And thanks for checking in. I really appreciate the support."

"Anytime, Nova. You're the best of the best, and I wouldn't want to lose you. I've been crossing all fingers and toes that I'd be partnered with you. Because, with you, I feel safe."

My heart squeezes, and I suddenly feel like I can't breathe.

"Thank you. You won't lose me." Another blatant lie. "Night, Gray."

"Night, Nova." This time, he sounds almost cheery, even if my heart is bleeding.

Chapter 7

It was a setup. It has to be.

Bullets fly everywhere around the market. Screaming and the color red are all I register. How did this happen? I hadn't even shown myself out in the open. I hadn't drawn my gun. They couldn't have known I was on their tail, and yet...

A girl who can't be more than ten falls at my feet, a bullet through her eye. I turn away, wanting to retch. Gray's words echo in my head. "Don't miss the exit point we agreed upon."

It's the only thing I can do now. Make it to the rendezvous.

I finally move, crouching low and ducking behind overturned market stalls. It's chaos as people try to run. Only a few cower behind wooden crates or tables.

Five hundred feet. I only have to make it five hundred feet. I take in a shaky breath and move again, keeping my attention on the directions the bullets are coming from.

I almost make it to the next stall that was selling fresh fish from the Mediterranean when I feel the sharp pain of a bullet and the hot trail of blood running down my shoulder.

Bolting upright, I'm once again drenched in sweat. I let my head fall into my trembling hands, wanting to cry. Nothing comes. Only the hot embers of rage boiling deep within me.

Too familiar a feeling.

Taking a few deep breaths, I finally move from the lonely bed and make my way to the shower. I drown the anger and shaking hands with scalding water. When I'm finished, I dress in my workout gear. I know it's early—not yet 5 am—but I make my way to the office anyway. I plan to warm up and hopefully get the memories to leave my head before Owen shows up.

The moment the key card clicks open the door, I know I shouldn't have come early. A flash of long, brown hair whips around, belonging to a half-naked woman. Strong arms wrap around her, and green eyes meet mine across the room. Stumbling backward, I immediately close the door.

My heart races, and the sight of Owen with that woman does nothing to help the rage that's already there.

I make to leave when I hear the door open behind me.

His voice is a low, rough rumble with a hint of laughter. "Leaving so soon, Miss Riley?"

Of course, he finds this situation amusing.

I freeze and take a deep breath, plastering a sweet smile on my face before turning around. "I didn't mean to interrupt..." I wave my hands awkwardly. "Whatever that is."

What is wrong with me?

Owen smiles and, of course, it's large enough to see that dimple. He cocks his head to the side. "She was just leaving."

I take a step closer to him. "That didn't look like leaving to me."

Owen doesn't stop smiling as he takes a step toward me. "And what did it look like, Miss Riley?"

Narrowing my gaze, I try to decide if this is another test. Of course, I know his reputation. Everyone does. And I'm too tired and angry from my dream to give a shit.

I decide to be myself. "It looked like you were making out with a half-naked, beautiful woman, and I interrupted."

Owen's eyes widen slightly, the only indication of his surprise, but he's all charm as he responds, "It was a goodbye kiss. As I said, she was just leaving."

"Don't have her leave on my account. I can grab a coffee and some breakfast. Maybe take a long, looong walk. Or perhaps you only need me to take a *short* walk?" I can't help the sarcasm or the anger that wants release.

Owen shocks me by laughing, without noticing he's moved only inches from me. "A kind offer, but she's going."

As if on cue, the beautiful woman walks out of the office, dressed in a barely-there, black, sparkly dress, hiding the lacy lingerie I spotted only minutes ago.

She stops and kisses Owen on the cheek. He doesn't turn to face her, holding my stare the whole time.

"See you later, Owen," she says. "Thanks for the ride last night."

I choke on a laugh as she continues down the hallway, not even acknowledging my presence.

Owen smiles. "Something funny, Miss Riley?"

Shaking my head, I side-step him and make my way into the office. "Was it a long ride? A good one?" I can't help myself, though I know the words are highly inappropriate for an employee.

He laughs. The kind of laugh that makes you want to hear it over and over again. One that energizes the whole room.

I turn. He's leaned against the door frame, arms crossed. Shirtless, of course.

"You didn't list sense of humor on your resume, Miss Riley."

Shrugging, I drop my bag on my office chair and scan the room again. At least they were neat, except for the bar, which is littered with more dirty glasses and empty alcohol bottles.

"You don't look ready for a fight, Mr. Mills," I comment, returning my attention to him.

He pushes off the door, stopping at the space in the middle of all the gym equipment. He sweeps his hands around. "Never been more ready, Miss Riley."

Reaching into my bag, I pull out a cloth to wrap my raw knuckles, hopefully preventing them from ripping open again.

Owen watches me. "No need to fear. Only a light sparring session to get the blood flowing this morning."

"You didn't just do that?" I ask, trying to sound genuine, but my smile gives me away.

"I didn't know I'd have to dodge your bad jokes when I hired you," he says, but the grin gives him away, too.

I step in front of him. Whether I want to admit it or not, fighting is my happy place. It's the only thing that keeps me sane. "We warm up first. Take turns with practice jabs and hooks, then we can play."

He grins back at me and nods. "Ladies first."

Ignoring the tone of his voice and the insinuation, I start moving, bouncing on the balls of my feet. I raise my arms. He does the same, splaying his hands so I can aim for them.

I hit his palms over and over again, and everything else falls away. Even my rage lowers to a light simmer as sweat begins to pour down my chest.

Owen doesn't speak when it's his turn, clearly lost in the same trance. His hits are practiced. Perfect. Beautiful even.

Of course, I'd never admit that to him.

Owen suddenly stops and pulls back. He's breathing hard and staring at me.

I drop my arms.

"You ready, Miss Riley?" he asks, recovering his breath shockingly fast.

"As I'll ever be. What are the rules?"

"The only rule is we can't knock each other out, and no swollen faces. I have meetings I need to look pretty for." He smirks.

"Meetings? Or beautiful women?"

"Both?"

Rolling my eyes, I raise my arms again, anxious to finish this. "Let's go. I won't damage your pretty face, don't worry."

"You think I'm pretty?" The words are barely out of his mouth when I swing my fist toward his so-called pretty face. He ducks at the last second, backing up.

The bastard has the nerve to smile.

I don't give him time to recover, swinging with my left arm. He blocks it, and I come up with my right, making contact with his jaw.

It is hard enough for him to feel, but it shouldn't leave a mark.

He recovers quickly, his smile gone now. He manages to get in a few hits, but the majority go to me.

"Protect your left side," I bark at him.

He laughs. "So bossy."

"I'm desperately trying not to damage that beautiful face of yours, but you're making it too goddamn easy."

He puffs out air. "Cocky, are we, Miss Riley? And did you now promote me to beaut—"

He doesn't finish the sentence as a series of punches steals the air from his lungs. He taps out.

I step back, allowing him to crumple at the waist, gasping for breath.

When he recovers enough to speak, he says, "Once again, don't ever let me get on your bad side, Miss Riley. If that was only a fraction of what you can do, I have no desire to know what one hundred percent looks like."

I laugh, which has Owen straightening and meeting my blue eyes with his green ones.

"I must admit, Mr. Mills, that was quite fun. You also don't give yourself much credit. You're the strongest partner I've had in a long time."

It's the truth. We used to have boxing competitions with the field agents. I won almost every one of them. The only person who could ever beat me was Declan, and now that he's the director, he doesn't compete. As a result, I don't either. I don't find them quite the same as they used to be.

This match with Owen was a surprise. A good surprise. One that has the rage melting away as he stares at me.

"That was definitely not on your resume, Miss Riley."

I laugh again. "Didn't know that was a necessary skill to list for a personal assistant position."

He studies me with such intensity that I want to cower, but I hold my ground.

"It sure is an interesting one. Who taught you to fight like that?" he asks.

I run a hand across my sweaty brow, suddenly needing to look anywhere but at him. "After my father died, a friend of mine taught me. He said it'd help with the grief. And the anger." None of it is a lie, and I wonder why the hell I am telling him so many truths. This isn't the role I'm supposed to be playing. I'm supposed to be someone else.

"And does it?"

I look up at his calculating eyes. "Yes."

My stomach twists as his dimple appears. "Well then, I'll see you here again tomorrow. Same time."

Nodding, though I can't fathom why I'm agreeing, I move toward the bathroom. "As long as I don't have to walk in on any naked or half-naked women, you have a deal."

Owen chuckles. "No naked women. I promise."

I open the door to the bathroom, grabbing my bag on the way.

"Oh, and Miss Riley?"

I turn my head, gripping the handle of the door.

"I knew you thought I was beautiful."

Chapter 8

Traversing the wide-open office space, where people both socialize and work, Owen leads me to the conference room on the opposite side. He's walking next to me, closer than necessary, and the hair on my arms stands on end, but not out of fear.

It's aggravating how much his nearness affects me.

"I need you to take notes," Owen explains as people eye us with curiosity. "I won't always be able to attend these meetings, and I want you to be able to facilitate them. This one is with a few of my smaller charities."

"The unlisted ones?" Suddenly, I'm far more interested in this meeting, and I try to ignore the stares and hushed whispers.

"Yes. You'll see why they're unlisted in a moment. Oh, and—"

Owen suddenly halts and grabs my arm, turning me to face him. I tilt my head to meet his eyes.

"My brother runs this division," he continues. "You'll have to work with him."

"Why do you seem so worried about that, Mr. Mills?" I ask, cocking my head to the side.

He laughs awkwardly, dropping his hand from my arm and looking away. "My brother can be shameless?"

"Is that a question? Or is he shameless?"

Owen grins. "He's shameless."

"So it runs in the family?"

"You are—" he starts, but we're interrupted by a deep, sultry voice.

"Now, who's this beautiful thing? Who have you been hiding from me, brother?"

I look over to find a stunning man standing only a few feet away. The similarities in stature and bone structure are obvious, but Parker's hair is blond, long, and wavy, and his skin is a few shades lighter. His eyes are hazel, not green, and locked on me.

He runs his gaze from my head to my toes. I hate when men do that, but for some reason, I'm not all that upset when Parker Mills does it.

"This is my new charity management assistant, Nora Riley. She'll be helping with the gala and the charities," Owen says through gritted teeth, apparently noticing his brother's wandering eyes.

"So we'll be working closely?" He sounds so thrilled that I almost laugh.

Owen catches my half-snort but quickly switches his attention back to Parker. "Yes. She'll be owning your ass, little brother."

He raises a brow, intrigued. "Is that so?"

I scoff, walking past the two men and into the conference room, unsure how they both make me more flustered than I've ever felt. I've assassinated notorious killers for fucks' sake.

I'm aware of the eyes tracking me while I stride to an open seat. They aren't the stares I'm expecting, though. These aren't high-strung execs; these are everyday people. People from all walks of life. Even children.

The next thing I know, a small boy, no more than four years old, squeals with excitement and races to the door, leaping into Owen's arms. Owen smiles broadly and catches the boy, tugging him close and whispering something in his ear. The boy laughs and plants a wet kiss on Owen's cheek before Owen places him back on the ground. A woman, who appears to be the boy's mother, approaches Owen. She says something I don't catch, and Owen leans over and embraces her.

Parker observes me with a bemused expression. "Not what you expected, Miss Riley?"

I peel my eyes from the scene to meet a matching dimple on Parker's cheek.

Damn it.

"No," I say truthfully. "I was expecting tight-ass execs or more arrogant asses like you and your brother." Without waiting for his reaction, I find my seat, but not before I hear Parker bark out a laugh behind me.

Owen takes the seat to my left. Not a second later, Parker claps his brother on the shoulder, angling his head toward me. "I like her. Mostly because you have no chance."

I have no idea what that means, but I could guess. I decide not to give it much thought.

Parker winks at me before taking a seat on the opposite side of Owen. Owen glances over, and I pretend to be busy organizing my notes on each charity, not wanting to think about either of the Mills men.

"I know I don't," Owen replies so quietly that I'm the only one who hears it.

For unknown reasons, my heart picks up speed.

"Owen!" The young boy races over, providing a needed distraction. "I forgot! I made this for you!"

The boy jumps into Owen's lap and hands him a homemade card. He proceeds to open it and explain every detail. Owen listens intently, nodding along and asking nonsensical questions that light up the boy's eyes.

"Charlie, it's time to come sit," his mother calls from down the table when it's clear everyone's found their seats.

Charlie lets out a *humph* and refuses to move.

"It's ok, Charlotte. He can stay," Owen says then shifts his attention to Charlie. "Though you'll be super bored. Your mother brought markers. I have no such treasure."

"And snacks," his mother chimes in.

That gets him, and Charlie jumps from Owen's lap and sprints into his mother's open arms.

With that, Owen begins the meeting. I take notes. I had no idea what these charities were, but after listening, I understand why my answer to his interview question helped me get the job. He's putting the power and money in the hands of small farmers, setting up education and resources to help them transform the land into regenerative arcs that serve as ecological strongholds while also feeding underfunded communities—communities that were previously and notoriously food deserts.

The more I listen, the crazier it gets. The charities don't have names, so they can't be traced back to Owen and Regenerative Industries because he doesn't want the credit. He only desires to provide the funding and help the communities create the arcs on their own. He wants the power completely in their hands.

I'm so lost in thought, questioning everything I know about this man and what I'm supposed to be doing here, that I don't hear his question.

I shake my head. "I'm sorry, what did you say?"

Owen smiles. "I asked, since you'll be taking over the company's admin work for these charities, if you wanted to visit them?"

Everyone looks at me with unblinking stares, and the answer slips easily from my lips. "I'd love that."

Charlie claps his hands as if it's the best news he's ever heard, and the room fills with laughter.

Leaning to speak Owen, so only he can hear me, I ask, "How come you didn't tell me about all of this before the meeting?"

The mischievous look on his face, as he half-turns toward me, has my stomach doing flips without my consent. "Because they're not my charities, Miss Riley."

I understand his meaning, but I still don't know why he didn't tell me about them if I was going to work with them.

He must notice the question in my eyes because he leans even closer, his breath skating along my ear. "Their voices are the important ones. What they need from you must come from them, not me. This is their community and their project. I am a participant in their community, but I am not their leader. I own none of this, and I control none of it, too."

Suddenly, my heart is speeding too fast. All the alarm bells are going off in my head, but not the ones I expected. This siren is one of confusion. One that is telling me that nothing is what it seems, and there is more to this story. One that is screaming that Owen isn't who and what he's accused of—he's so much more. But more of what? The bad guy? The hero?

And worst of all: does any of this even matter if he murdered three people?

Before I know it, the room is clearing out, and I'm gathering my things, trying to ignore my thoughts and warring instincts, when Parker sits down on top of the table, next to me. "You're a bit of a conundrum, Miss Riley."

I stop and stare at him. "And how's that, Mr. Mills?"

"My brother never hires attractive women to be his assistants. Don't get me wrong; you're perfect for the position."

I hold up a hand to stop him. "If you're so curious, why don't you ask him? All I know is that I'm qualified, and he offered it."

Rising from my seat, I clutch the information on the charities close to my chest.

Parker also stands, and I find myself too close to him, so I step back, the chair rolling away from my legs.

He smirks. "My brother won't give up his secrets."

Intending to drop the subject, I make to leave, but my stupid curiosity gets the better of me. I eye Parker, and he looks as if he's already expecting the question. I internally curse myself before it slips from my lips. "Why won't he hire attractive assistants?"

Parker shrugs. "Thought that'd be obvious. He got burned by one."

"Oh." I don't know what to say to that. I'm about to burn him, too, just not in the same way.

The thought makes me a little sick, for reasons I cannot explain, as the rest of the room clears out. Charlotte and Charlie leave last. The boy hugs Owen again while waving his tiny hand in my direction.

The biggest smile lights up the boy's face, and Owen is practically glowing from that blaze.

There's no amount of logic to explain what I'm witnessing. The whole situation isn't one I'm used to. Murder suspects don't act this way, and they certainly don't try to give money and power away. I should know. I've put away hundreds of murderers.

So, what the hell is going on here?

Chapter 9

Ella calls me after the meeting, and I lock myself in the bathroom, speaking in a hushed voice.

"Peyton Radd is one of the alias names used by a hired, private assassin," she explains. "He's been arrested a few times, but there wasn't enough evidence to convict him. It says he's still on the loose."

"Shit," I mumble.

The information isn't surprising, but it only creates more questions than it answers.

"You think Mr. Mills hired him to kill those other billionaires?" she asks.

"I don't know. Does it say his supposed method of assassination?"

There is silence on the other end of the phone as Ella searches the file. "He's suspected to be one hell of a sniper. Trained by the Marines."

"No mentions of poison?"

"No."

"Shit," I repeat, even though poisons aren't usually on any assassin forms because they are extremely hard to track.

I sigh, switching the phone to my other ear. "Thanks, Ella."

"I'll keep looking. He goes by other names. There might be a file I missed."

"Thanks. How's that new hacker boyfriend of yours?" I ask, changing the subject. I need to get my mind off the situation I find myself in.

"Shhh," she whispers harshly.

Ella works for the CIA, and yet she's dating an illegal hacker. The irony is not lost on anyone. He's a good one, though, and the CIA would be lucky to have him, but Ella can't ask him to join the CIA without admitting she works for the CIA to begin with.

"I'm sorry." I laugh. "I mean, how's your *hot* boyfriend doing?"

She lets out a long breath. "He's perfect, Nova. I can't believe I have to live this lie around him. I want to talk shop and show that I know exactly what he's talking about instead of pretending I'm clueless. It's exhausting, but he's worth it."

I smile even though she can't see it. "I'm happy for you, Ella. Can't wait to meet up with you two for a drink."

"You should!" She squeals. "And you should bring that underwear model."

I snort. "I'm not bringing my boss's brother."

"You mean your target's brother?" The question was definitely intentional.

"Yes. Same thing."

"Is it?"

I huff. "Bye, Ella. Talk later."

She chuckles. "Bye, Nova. Enjoy two sexy men while you can."

She ends the call before I can mutter a retort, and I find myself smirking for no good reason.

A knock on the door makes me jump.

"You fall in, Miss Riley?"

I roll my eyes, though I know Owen can't see me. When I open the door, he's standing there, arms crossed, and I try my best to ignore the enticing look on his face.

I shrug. "I did what everyone does when they use the bathroom. I texted my friends."

He raises a brow, and I push past him.

"Gala invitations go out tomorrow. Do you want to check them before I send them?" I ask, avoiding all other subjects aside from the work I was sent here to do.

"No need. I trust you."

There's that damn word again: trust. My gut twists. I've always played the fraud, but this time it doesn't feel right. Like an itch I can't scratch—persistent and getting worse with each moment I spend with him.

The worst part is: I'm starting to want him to trust me, and I'm finding myself beginning to trust him. It's beyond logic and reason, and I can't snap myself out of it.

"It's too close to home, Dec. I can't separate the role I'm supposed to be playing from who I really am."

Silence takes up the space on the other side of the phone while I pace back and forth on the cold tile floor of my soulless apartment.

"I can put someone else on it," he finally offers, but he doesn't sound happy about it.

"I'm already in. It'd be too much work to pull me out and replace me." It's the truth, and I've already put Declan through too much to ask that of him. He deserves for this case to go smoothly. Hell, I deserve for this case to go smoothly, too.

There's more silence on the other end.

"Have you made an appointment with a counselor yet?" he finally asks.

Shit.

"Yes," I lie. It's not that I don't want to make an appointment. It's more that I don't have the time to do so.

He takes an audible breath. "Did you finish your trial report?"

Now it's my turn to be silent for a moment.

"No," I say at last.

"I want you to take the weekend to do something for yourself. No work." I go to complain, but he cuts me off. "No, Nova. Give Ella everything you have on Mr. Mills so far, and she can continue the research. I want you to take two measly days off and do something for yourself."

An awkward silence ensues again.

"Nova?" he finally asks, his voice betraying his worry.

"What the hell am I going to do, Dec? The CIA is my whole life."

Declan sighs heavily. "Call Jax. That's an order. Or go out with someone from your new job."

Declan knows Jax, and Jax knows Declan. Though my career is supposed to be a secret, certain people are contractual exceptions. Jax knows what I do for a living, even if he doesn't know the details, and he's under contract to keep it a secret from everyone else.

"And further the lie I'm living? To be ripped out of their lives after I put their boss in jail and cause them all to lose their jobs? No thanks," I say miserably.

"You haven't had a problem before."

"That's because everyone I put behind bars was a murdering rapist asshole!" I shout before lowering my voice to almost a whisper. "Not a hot Robin Hood who murders rich bastards then steals from them and gives to the poor."

Declan lets out an awkward laugh. "You seem to be ignoring the murdering part."

"We've had this conversation already. I'm also a murdering asshole. I just do it legally."

Declan has no retort, and when the silence grows too long, I finally let him go. "I'll text Jax. I'll take a day off. One, not two."

He doesn't argue.

Chapter 10

"Are you kidding me?" I shout the next morning when I open the office door at exactly 5:30 am to find a completely nude woman exiting the bathroom. My anger ignites, and warmth rushes to my cheeks.

Luckily, Owen is dressed. Kind of. He's wearing his normal sweats with no shirt.

His head snaps in my direction, and I glare at him, holding the door handle so tightly that my scabbed knuckles crack and new blood rises to the surface.

He glances at the naked woman who's completely unfazed by the situation as she grabs her clothes from his desk.

When his gaze finds mine again, he looks oddly apologetic instead of arrogant.

"You promised," I hiss.

Owen flinches. "I know. I'm sorry."

Again, I'm shocked at the woman who seems completely unaware. Uncaring. Where does he find these women?

She slowly dresses, clearly in no hurry.

Finally releasing the poor door handle, I stalk to my desk, dumping my bag in the chair. I rustle through it, trying to find my first aid kit, when I sense him hovering.

Looking up, I find him only inches from me, holding out gauze and tape. "I'm sorry," he repeats.

Inhaling, I reach for the first aid supplies. "Thank you."

He nods and takes a step back, giving me space, but not daring to move too far. I look around to find the woman already gone, and my gaze shifts to the bar. More dirty glasses and empty bottles are haphazardly spread across the counter.

"How do you even function consuming that much alcohol every day?" I ask before I realize how inappropriate that question is, but I don't care because I walked in on my boss with a naked woman, which is far more inappropriate.

"I'm sure I'd be better off without it." He shrugs. "Habit."

Narrowing my gaze, I know full well there's more to it than that, but I drop it. Though I'm supposed to be earning his trust and getting to know him, there is only so far I will go. Traumatic pasts is where I draw the line.

And perhaps that's because I keep my own locked up tight.

"How about I make it up to you by allowing you to damage my beautiful face?" He smirks, the dimple appearing. "If you can."

I scoff while I finish wrapping my hand. "You have no idea how I'd like to mess up that pretty face of yours, especially after you broke our promise. But you're still my boss, and you still need that face to help you save the world."

I hear a sharp intake of breath. "You surprise me, Miss Riley."

My gaze snaps to his. "How so?"

"I can't quite tell if you hate me or love me."

"I can't either," I deadpan.

His warm, deep laugh has my stomach doing flips.

"Let's go before I change my mind and decide to mess up that face," I say, standing and crossing the room. The scent of the rubber mats and gym equipment hits me like a long-lost friend, and I almost sigh.

"Beautiful face," he corrects.

Instead of quipping back, I shake my head dramatically, and then we're both lost in our movements.

Later, Owen drives me east to the suburbs, toward the regenerative projects in the low-income areas. I take in the landscape as we pass hundreds of monocropped farms. Large swaths of uncovered dirt kicks up in the wind, carrying away the fertile topsoil. Owen clenches his teeth and squeezes the wheel tighter.

Even after miles of these types of farms, he doesn't relax.

"If you love plants so much, why don't you have any in your office?" I ask, wanting to ease his tension but not knowing how.

He cocks his head slightly, never taking his eyes off the road. "I guess I've always considered the office my father's, not mine."

"I take it you don't get along with him?" I remember the comment from Noell about Owen's father being disappointed with him.

He smiles, but it's not a happy one. "Not exactly."

"Too much like you that you butt heads? Or too different that you cannot see eye-to-eye?"

Owen is quiet for a few moments, his jaw tight. "In a way, it's both." He sighs. "My father has a different view of money. He always wants more of it, even though he has enough to feed a small country. I, on the other hand, have plenty and want to give it to people who need it much more than I do. He thinks I'm destroying everything he's built by giving his money away."

"But then why did he sign the company over to you?"

"He doesn't trust anyone outside of his own blood, and he thought he'd be able to manipulate me. Parker is too reckless, even if my father trusts him. I was the obvious choice, groomed from birth to take over the company. I knew the competition and had good business relationships with the other companies we eventually acquired."

I take note of that in my head. A previous relationship could lead to motive and evidence.

"Why'd you acquire those companies?" I try to act like I don't know anything.

"It was good business."

It wasn't the answer I was hoping for, but I drop it, sensing Owen doesn't want to talk about it, and I don't want to seem overly interested. He's too observant. He'd pick up on it and shut down.

"What about you?" he asks. "Why so many different jobs? Someone with your intelligence and experience could have any position. Why a personal assistant?"

I shrug. "I wanted to be home for once. Maybe even put down roots. Get some plants of my own." I huff out an awkward laugh. "Your position opened up, and I thought it'd be a good fit."

Part of me wants all that to be true. Part of it *is* true. Sometimes, I imagine quitting the CIA and settling down with a less dangerous job that doesn't require me to be away for so long. But then I remember I have no reason to settle. I have no one to settle for, and I fear I'd be bored. Or, worse, lonely.

"And your family?" he asks.

I decide not to lie. "I don't have any family." An awkward silence ensues, which makes me want to fill it up. "I have no siblings. My mother died of cancer when I was young, and my father was murdered when I was eighteen. He was an engineer and mechanic who worked on Formula 1 cars. That's how I know how to drive fast cars. I know how to fix them, too." I add the last part to soften the news that always renders people speechless.

The look on Owen's face makes me want to take it all back and tell him a complete lie.

"It was a long time ago, Owen."

"I'm not sure any of that can be fixed by time, Nora. That shit becomes a part of you."

He has no idea how right he is. My father's murder led to me joining the CIA so I could put other killers behind bars or in the grave. I don't miss Owen's use of my first name, though.

I inhale and exhale slowly. "I'm buying you plants for your office."

It was a deliberate change of subject, and I suspect Owen knows that since he smiles. Genuinely.

"Our office," he corrects.

My heart almost stops in my chest.

Chapter 11

"You're funding schools, too?" I ask incredulously as Charlie gives us a tour, bouncing from room to room, exclaiming each one is his favorite. They serve low-income elementary students here and educate approximately one hundred children.

The building and classrooms are nothing special, even though they *feel* special. There are small rooms with a variety of desks, chairs, and school supplies. Each schoolroom is decorated according to the teacher's personality and features various art projects created by the students.

Owen smiles but doesn't respond as Charlie tugs on my hand and pulls me through large double doors that lead outside, behind the school.

I almost gasp, taking in the scene before me. The kids are spread out among rows and rows of food crops, berry bushes, fruit trees, and beautiful, flowering plants. Some of them sow seeds while others water, though most of them chase each other between the vegetation or steal ripe berries from bushes.

I'm not surprised this is how he spends his money—funding schools makes sense based on what Owen's trying to do with his charity.

I can't wrap my head around this man. On paper, he's a murderer. In reality, it's much more complicated.

"Something wrong, Miss Riley?" I'm pulled from my stupor by Owen's deep voice far too close to my ear.

I step to the side, Charlie still clinging to my hand and trying to yank me forward. I laugh at his impatience and shrug at Owen as Charlie once again sweeps me away.

We're almost running through the strawberry patch when Charlie's mother, Charlotte, steps in front of him and holds up a hand. Charlie halts, dropping mine.

She looks stern, but her face soon melts into a smile. "Charlie, shouldn't you be helping?"

Charlie groans and reluctantly obeys. He walks toward the group of young students planting far too many seeds in the small areas of dirt, plops down next to a little blond-haired girl, and starts stealing from her supply.

Charlotte sighs, watching, before returning her attention to me. She scans my body, a frown forming on her lips. "You can't help in those clothes, Miss Riley."

"I was not informed I'd be getting my hands dirty, or I would have come better prepared." I pointedly glare at Own.

Charlotte's gaze lands on him beside me. "You didn't tell her?"

Owen's laugh is low, menacing. "I didn't know if Miss Riley would want to get her hands dirty."

"And why wouldn't I want to help?" I cross my arms.

Owen holds up his hands in surrender. "My fault. I apologize, Miss Riley. I'm sure Charlotte can find you something suitable to wear."

She frowns. "Of course I can, but may I advise that you bring your staff prepared for work next time? I'm not a clothing store, Mr. Mills." She turns and starts walking back to the building.

I finally meet Owen's eyes. They are full of amusement as he stares at me. I huff and stomp past him, racing to catch up with Charlotte. We walk in silence until we reach the doors.

She holds it open for me. "He must like you, Miss Riley."

"Nora. Please call me Nora."

Charlotte nods and follows me inside. "He doesn't usually bring anyone from the office."

"Not even his old assistant?" I ask, my intrigue growing.

She shakes her head.

His words of trust drift into my thoughts, and I can't help the shiver that snakes down my spine. It should be a win—getting a target to trust me means the assignment is all but in the bag. So then why do I feel like shit?

Charlotte opens a storage closet and pulls out faded, denim overalls that look about the right size. She also grabs a worn pair of men's work boots and holds them up in front of her face. Her brow furrows, and her gaze shoots to my red heels.

"I can go barefoot," I offer.

She cocks her head to the side. "Are you sure? I'm sure these would do for a short while."

"I'm sure."

"There's a bathroom down the hall. You can hang your clothes in here when you're done."

I thank her. She nods, heading back in the direction of the garden.

I take a deep breath, my palms clammy. This was not what I was expecting when Declan pitched the job to me, and now I'm not so sure how I feel about all of it. I've never been so conflicted in my entire life.

I quickly change and sweep my blond hair into a high ponytail before rolling up the sleeves of my white blouse. When I'm finished, I walk back to the garden, letting my bare feet sink into the soft earth.

Owen and Charlotte are desperately trying to keep the four-year-olds under control as they toss seeds everywhere. I can't hide my smile at the chaos before me. It's pandemonium, but it's also joy.

"So much for an organized garden," Charlotte huffs, frustrated.

"Perhaps the young ones would be better off on watering duty?" I offer, and both their heads swing in my direction.

Owen sweeps his gaze over my attire, the corner of his mouth kicking up. When his stare catches my feet, he arches a brow.

I ignore his silent question as Charlotte stands and takes my advice. "Time to water the flowers!" she yells, followed by enthusiastic squealing.

Owen gets up, dusting the dirt from his hands and knees. "Ready, Miss Riley?"

After I nod, he leads me to the flower garden, assigning me to pull weeds. The monotonous task has me lost in a meditative state. I revel in the dirt beneath my fingers. I'm so used to death and blood that planting life feels better than it probably should.

It doesn't take long for the weeding to take an interesting turn when the light patter of water falls into my hair. The children hold hoses straight up, dousing everything like rain.

I smile at their laughter and soaked hair and clothes. Charlotte stands with her hands on her hips, but she's smiling and chuckling along with the children.

Too focused on the kids, I don't notice Owen behind me until a strong stream of water pelts me in the back. As I swing around, I'm blasted in the chest with another.

Yelping, I dodge the stream, trying not to trample the plants in the process. My feet slide on the dirt that has suddenly become mud. Rushing forward, I grab a free hose as another stream of water hits my head, soaking my hair. My fingers curl around a free hose, and I turn on him. In an instant, his shirt is drenched.

Owen appears shocked, pausing his pursuit of me. But a devious grin soon replaces his surprise, and he runs toward me.

I squeal, laughing, and dart out of the way, shooting the water behind me, hoping to catch him as he speeds after me. We chase each other until every inch of us is dripping, but we still don't stop, both of us wanting to best the other.

It takes Charlotte turning off the main valve to get the children to stop, including us. The water slows to a trickle from the head of the hose.

"Time for lunch!" she yells at the children, who run for the outdoor tables next to the school, leaving the hoses and sprawled seed packets where they are.

Dropping my hose, I put both hands on my knees, trying to catch my breath. There is mud everywhere now. It covers every inch of the ground and travels up my borrowed overalls. Big, brown spots dot my white blouse and bare forearms. I reach up to find more mud caked in my hair, and I laugh.

Owen watches me with a smile large enough that his dimple is on full display. He's covered in the same amount of mud, and his blue T-shirt clings to his body, revealing every detail of his muscular torso.

"You ruined my fun, you know," I say, trudging toward him and in the direction of the building.

He raises a brow.

"I was quite enjoying my weeding duties," I clarify.

He chuckles, stepping to my side. "Your smile would indicate our hose war was just as fun."

I catch myself. He's right. I'm smiling like a child. I quickly firm my lips into a straight line.

Owen catches me and laughs harder. "You seem like all business, Miss Riley, but you surprise me."

I realize we've both stopped walking and are far too close to each other, but I find myself not wanting to move away.

"I know how to have fun, Mr. Mills."

"Is that so?" he baits me, but I step back, and he lets me.

"Why a school?" I need to change the subject.

"These kids didn't have a great start in life, and they can't learn in high-stress situations. I wanted to give them a more relaxed place, with lots of time outside. They needed a safe place."

"But you don't run it?"

"The idea was mine, but Charlotte took it and made it her own. I let her. She certainly knows what these kids need better than I do. She grew up here with no family and very little money or opportunity."

Owen begins to walk, and I follow him, my head reeling. Can this man really be a murderer?

"This is what your father believes you're throwing away the company's money on?" I ask, though I already know the answer.

He stops and holds the door open for me. As our eyes meet, he nods. "I don't see it that way."

"I don't, either." I'm not sure why my voice is so quiet or why my heartbeat has picked up.

Owen suddenly scrunches his nose in the most adorable way. "I think maybe I should get you a towel before you come in. You'll leave muddy footprints all over the school."

Glancing at my feet, I wiggle my toes.

The sound of Owen's chuckle has my attention going to his mouth and lingering far too long.

He snaps me out of it. "Wait here." Kicking off his muddy shoes, he disappears behind the door.

Sighing, I lean against the building, letting the sun warm my cold, wet body.

I'm definitely fucked.

Chapter 12

"**G**ray hacked into the security cameras. He found footage of meetings with the victims. No sound, of course, but he discovered something really interesting."

I wait for Ella to continue and pace my apartment. Yet again, my palms are sweaty for reasons I can't quite understand.

"Peyton Radd is present in all the meetings leading up to the third victim's death," she continues. "He seems to be acting like an intern."

"For whom?"

"Unclear. No one speaks to him."

"That's strange."

"Yeah." Ella sighs and sounds exhausted.

"Can you have Gray try to hack emails sent between Mr. Mills and the third victim? The three months leading up to his death?"

"Sure." I hear Ella typing furiously, likely taking extensive notes.

"Oh, and Ella?"

"Mmm?" she says, though I can tell her mind is already far away.

"Go home and get some sleep. Give that boyfriend of yours a kiss. This can wait."

In reality, I don't want to wait. Something feels wrong with this entire case, and it's not just that Owen isn't acting like the murderers I've put behind bars in the past.

She chuckles. "You have no idea how nice that sounds, but I have to finish up here. Sometimes I wish I could have Eagan help. We'd probably already have the evidence to convict this guy."

That gives me an idea. A terrible one. "He might be able to help."

Ella almost sounds like she's choking. "What?"

"All of Mr. Mill's charities and foundations are nonprofits. They are open to the public. That means Eagan can look at any information about them without suspicion being raised, even if he got caught."

"You want him to hack into the charity emails?"

"Exactly. See if he can find any mention of lethal plants or poisons. After all, most of the charities are plant-related."

She enthusiastically replies, "I'll ask him tonight!"

"Good. It'll be nice to have more eyes out there."

"Thanks, Nova."

"Don't mention it, Ella. Talk tomorrow."

I hang up the phone and instantly regret my decision to involve Eagan. Though nothing we're doing is against any rules, he could easily find out that Ella works for the CIA, and that could get both of us into more trouble than we already are.

There are bodies everywhere. Enough to make me believe this was all a set-up. But how? And why? This specific crime syndicate isn't this brutal. There must be at least twenty shooters. I lost sight of the target, but that's not surprising.

This is a cover-up for something larger. I know it is, but I can't figure out for what. Or why they would go to these lengths. No mission I've ever been on has had this much public display of violence and loss of civilian life. There has to be a reason for it.

I stumble toward the rendezvous point, fighting the pain and blood loss, my vision blurring. I know I won't be able to figure this out right now, so I try to bury it in my subconscious.

I have to get to Gray. I have to get out of here. Then I can figure out what happened.

A few steps into the dark, I find myself falling. The blood loss has me too dizzy to catch myself, and I trip, my head colliding with the edge of something hard.

Everything goes black.

Snapping my eyes open, I'm not surprised to find my shirt soaked with sweat. I sit up and grab my phone, my hands shaking as I jot down notes from my dream, trying to piece together what happened. Trying to make sense of it. Trying to have a coherent report for the lawyer's defense.

I groan while reading through what I've already written. None of it makes sense.

Looking at the clock next to the bed, it reads 4:15 am. It's too early to go into the office, but I can't stay here. I'm too anxious. Getting up, I turn on the shower and wash the sweat away.

When I step out, there's a message notification on my phone.

Owen: *You awake?*

My heart doubles in speed.

Me: *Yes.*

The typing bubble appears, and I don't understand my anxiety.

Owen: *Couldn't sleep again?*

Me: *No.*

Owen: *Do you ever text more than one-word answers?*

Me: *No.*

A laughing emoji appears.

Owen: *Why does that not surprise me?*

I send a shrugging emoji.

Owen: *I can't sleep either. Meet me at the office?*

Me: *As long as there are no naked women and you're sober.*

The typing bubble appears, but disappears.

I wait.

After what feels like forever, he finally sends his reply.

Owen: *No naked women. Not drunk, but is hungover OK?*

I roll my eyes, even if he can't see it.

Me: *You'll still reek of alcohol.*

Owen: *I will sweat it out.*

Me: *Gross.*

Another laughing emoji. He replies a second later. *Please?*

Putting down the phone and toweling off my wet hair, I consider his offer.

I pick the phone back up.

Me: *Fine. I'll be there in fifteen minutes.*

What am I doing?

Owen slouches in the large, plush chair in front of his desk. He's shirtless, of course. His hair is tousled like he just woke up.

"Did you sleep here?" I ask, throwing my bag on the ground and crossing my arms.

"What of it?" he asks, chewing gum.

I almost laugh, knowing he's trying to mask the scent of alcohol. He's not hungover.

I narrow my gaze. "You're still drunk."

"So observant, Miss Riley."

Suddenly, I'm annoyed. "You lied."

He swings his legs over the side of the chair and stands. Once he has his balance, he stumbles toward me.

"You wouldn't have come," he says, stopping a foot from me.

"Lied and manipulated. You make a habit of those things? Is that how you get all those women into your bed?"

I don't mean to let all that slip, but I can't help it. I'm so flustered and angry and confused, and I don't know which way is up. He's a murder suspect, and yet he's only been kind. He's done nothing but help people, including me, which has me not wanting to look too far into why.

He takes another wobbly step toward me, and now I have to crane my neck to look at him. "What if it is?" he growls. His eyes are narrow slits, the green in them darkening almost to black in the dim light.

"So honorable," I mumble sarcastically.

"You know nothing about me, Miss Riley." His voice is a deep growl. A flash of anger passes across his eyes.

In any other situation, I'd be on high alert. Ready for a fight. Ready for the abuse that often follows when a person's emotion finally snaps. But with Owen, I don't feel afraid.

"Then tell me!" I yell at him. "Tell me why you drink every night? Why you have a different girl in your bed every night? Why you sleep in your office almost every night?"

He raises a brow. Does he think me so daft I wouldn't notice he doesn't go home at night?

His fury deflates. "Because...because..." He trails off and looks at the ceiling, sucking in a deep breath. His chest is so close. "Because money doesn't buy you happiness, Miss Riley. It buys you loneliness."

Now it's my turn to suck in a breath. I didn't expect him to say that. "What about your brother?"

Owen meets my gaze again, and this time his eyes are softer. Sad. "We didn't grow up together. He grew up with his mother, while I lived with my father, spending most of my time here, sleeping under my father's desk most nights."

This company was his whole life, whether he wanted it to be or not. Even as a child, he had no choice. My chest constricts at the thought of the little boy under the desk, living and breathing his father's career. Did that little boy ever have a childhood? It sounds like Parker did. I'm doubting Owen did.

He continues, "We only recently became close now that he's helping with the charities."

I go to place a hand on his chest and stop myself, dropping it to my side.

Owen's gaze tracks the movement.

I step back. "You can't fight me in this condition. I'll surely give that pretty face of yours a black eye. You're no match for me drunk."

He laughs, the sound causing a flutter low in my gut.

"I'm no match for you sober, Miss Riley. What do you propose?"

"Coffee, food, a shower, new clothes, a toothbrush, and lots of water. I think I have some electrolyte powder." I bend down and pick up my bag, shuffling around the contents until my hands land on a small plastic bag full of electrolyte packs.

I hold them out to him and find his stare is on me. The look pierces me, and goosebumps travel up my arms.

He takes the packets, his hand lingering too long on mine. I snatch it away and turn, trying to compose myself.

"Thank you, Miss Riley." His voice follows me to my desk.

Nodding, I move to the coffee machine, adding a filter and ground coffee beans. Then I flip on the spigot and hold the pitcher under the stream.

"I'm not lonely. Not with you here." His confession is almost a breathless whisper.

I halt, water spilling from the top of the coffee pot, but I'm unable to move.

Owen steps behind me and reaches over to shut off the spigot. His front presses against my back, trapping me against the sink.

I don't move. Neither does he.

My heartbeat speeds up. I pretend not to notice my body's response or the fact that Owen hasn't moved away. With shaking hands, I dump some of the water out of the overfull coffee pot.

He steps back suddenly, as if just realizing how close he was.

"Go take a shower. I'll find us something to eat," I say to him, my voice more raspy than I intended.

He obeys without a word, and as I'm switching on the coffee machine, I hear the bathroom door shut.

Relaxing my shoulders, I let my head fall into my hands.

What the hell happened? And why do I seem to care so much?

He's a fucking murder suspect.

Chapter 13

I make it through the day unscathed, avoiding Owen as much as I can. Instead, I focus on various admin tasks for his charities and managing last minute gala items. I do some research on the companies he has recently acquired.

The further I dig, the more interesting it becomes. All three companies were tied to big oil, and all three had inquiries into human trafficking, along with a surprising number of sexual harassment lawsuits.

"Ella," I whisper into the phone in the bathroom while Owen takes a business call on the other side of the door, "Can you have Eagan look into something else for me?"

"Does this have to do with your hot boss?" she teases.

I ignore her little comment. "I need some off-record digging."

"What are you up to, Nova?"

"It's probably nothing, but I found an interesting link between the three companies Owen acquired. It doesn't help with evidence against him, but it might lead to an interesting motive."

"We're on a first-name basis now?" she teases a second time.

Once again, I ignore her comment. "Can you have Eagan look into the personal lawsuits against each of the three victims leading up to their deaths? And lawsuits against the companies themselves? Most are not public record and were handled behind the scenes, but I want to know specifics.

What they were about and how they were settled. You think he can do that?"

"He'll have no problem, but Nova, this sounds like you might get into some trouble if Dec finds out."

I take a deep breath. "I know. I'm willing to risk it."

I don't want to leave Declan out, but I'm going a bit against protocol with my digging, and I don't want this to reflect poorly on his career if I'm caught.

Ella doesn't say anything for a few seconds. "I'll have Eagan start today."

"Thanks, Ella. I owe you both big time."

She laughs. "We'll be expecting a very fancy dinner."

"Deal."

"Oh, and Eagan hasn't found anything suspicious with those charities, but I'll have him keep digging."

"Thanks."

"Tell Jax hi for me!" she chirps.

"I will," I reply before hanging up.

I stand and flush the toilet to make it sound like I was in the bathroom for a reason, before changing out of my regular black suit jacket and black pants and into a pair of jeans and a tight-fitting, red top. I pair the outfit with black Converse. Finished, I step out of the bathroom.

Owen's stare is instantly on me. "Date tonight, Miss Riley?" he asks with a hint of a smirk.

"I'm meeting Jax and his boyfriend, which is really none of your business," I snap back at him.

His smile only grows. "Need a ride?"

"Not from you." I gather my phone and stuff a few papers into my bag before meeting his gaze across the room.

"Ouch. I just thought it'd be a nice way to say thank you for not killing me this morning and helping me out."

I narrow my eyes.

Owen laughs. "I'm not going to kidnap you, Miss Riley."

I roll my eyes at his attempt at a joke, throwing his own words in my face. "We're meeting at his restaurant. You sure you want to drive all the way out there?"

I'm secretly hoping he says no. Or am I hoping he says yes? I can't quite seem to figure out how I feel about this man.

He gets up, grabbing a jacket from the back of his desk chair. "I don't mind."

"You sure you don't have someone you need to meet?" I ask, perhaps hoping he does. Or maybe I'm curious.

He looks at me, and I can't read him. "Not tonight."

I step out from behind my desk and throw the strap of my bag over my shoulder. "It's Friday."

He comes to stand next to me. "I'm not as busy as you think I am, Miss Riley."

"Really?" I ask sarcastically. "I'd say those two naked women this week would be evidence of the contrary, Mr. Mills."

I don't wait for his reaction and head for the door. He beats me to it, grabbing the handle before I can.

I finally look at him. His green eyes are full of an emotion I can't quite read. It appears as though he wants to say something, but he pulls the door open instead.

"After you, Miss Riley."

Turning, I walk out of the office. He follows in silence.

"Nova!" Evan shouts as he comes around the wooden bar at the restaurant and wraps me in his strong arms, lifting me off the floor.

I laugh, clutching him like he's the only person keeping me tied to this earth.

"Oh, how I've missed you! You always smell so damn good," Evan comments, burying his head in the crook of my neck.

Laughing harder, I playfully slap his shoulder. "I don't even wear perfume."

"That's why you always smell so good. You smell like you."

"Let her down already, Evan. No hogging," Jax says, coming around and peeling me from Evan's arms.

I hug Jax, and he also buries his head in my neck. "He's right, though," he says when he lifts his head. "You always smell so good. Like home."

I smile, that comment affecting me more than it should.

I'm so happy to see them that I forget entirely about Owen standing behind us until Evan drawls, "Who's this delicious man?" He extends his hand toward Owen.

Whirling around, I discover Owen's amused expression and observe as Evan takes Owen's hand and kisses him on the knuckles.

Owen chuckles. "I'm her new boss." He pulls his hand away slowly.

"Boss?" he asks me with a wink and a waggle of his eyebrows. "Or *boss*, boss?"

I laugh, and Owen surprises me by laughing too.

"Boss, boss," I respond.

"Oh, shit. Sorry boss-man. I didn't realize real bosses drove their employees out on a Friday night."

Owen cocks his head to the side, as if considering those words. Leave it to Evan to always make everything awkward.

"He owed me a favor because I'm such an amazing employee and do far more than what's in my job description," I explain, realizing a moment later, when Evan's eyebrows shoot up, that I gave him more ammunition.

"More, huh?" he insinuates.

I huff. "You're impossible. Get me a drink already, will you?"

Evan winks at both of us before hurrying off to grab me what I asked for. Bottles clink, and the low hum of conversation fills my ears.

Jax leans casually against the bar, watching me. His eyes dart to Owen for a brief moment before settling on me again. The question he isn't voicing sparkles in his eyes.

I turn to Owen. "Do you want to stay for a drink? No pressure."

"Oh, do stay! I'd love to stare at you a little longer," Evan chirps as he sets down my drink. It's a simple vodka soda with a splash of lemon. I rarely drink, and I probably shouldn't do so now. Not when my target seems as though he might take me up on my offer to hang around.

Part of me doesn't care. I'm in no danger with him, and my body knows it, even if my mind won't catch up.

Owen eyes the drink before his eyes meet mine. There's another unspoken question in the furrow of his brow.

"Despite Evan's very inappropriate statement, you are welcome to stay if you want," I say "I can promise you won't be bored with these two, but I can't promise you won't be hit on and almost convinced to go home with them by the end of the night."

"Hey, I'll be good!" Evan sounds almost offended, but his teasing tone gives him away.

Owen's smile grows until the dimple is visible, and he's only looking at me. My stomach instantly drops.

"How do you know they can be convincing?"

It's definitely not the question I was expecting.

Evan beats me to a response. "Because we almost convinced her to come home with us one night. Funny story, actually—"

I cut him off. "You did not almost convince me, and you are men's men, through and through. You never would have actually taken me home. Plus, this is a highly unprofessional conversation we're having in front of my boss."

Evan and Jax both laugh, but it's Evan who responds. "First, you could do with being a little less professional, Barbie. And two, have you seen yourself? I may not be into women, but I'd make an exception for you any day."

I almost choke on the sip I'd just taken and glance at Jax, who appears to be finding all of this far too entertaining.

"Are you gonna help me out?" I ask Jax.

He takes a sip of his own drink. "No. There's a reason I love him."

Chucking, I take another long drink from my cup. "You two are insufferable."

"But that's why you love us," Evan says.

I sigh. "Perhaps." I almost jump when I remember Owen is standing next to me. "Are you sure you don't have somewhere more important to be? This will only get worse as they drink more."

Owen smiles, and it's only for me. "I don't have anywhere to be, Miss Riley." His voice is so deep; it seems to vibrate through my entire body.

I turn back to Evan, who winks at me, and I down the rest of my drink.

Wrapping my arms around myself to keep warm, I pace outside the bar, wanting to be back inside laughing with three beautiful men. But I'm eager to figure out if Eagan's found anything about Owen.

"He's still looking," Ella says, and my heart sinks. I should have known it might take a while, but I can't shake the feeling that something's wrong.

I must be silent for too long because she asks, "How's the trial stuff going?" Her voice is careful, like she's talking to a small child that might throw a tantrum if provoked.

She wouldn't be wrong about that.

I sigh. "There are so many holes in my memory. Between the chaos and blood loss, I can't seem to piece together anything substantial. I'm afraid my testimony won't help me."

"What about Gray? Have you spoken to him?"

"We talked about it one time. We compared notes, and he filled in some of the holes, but it still doesn't make sense. He agrees we missed critical intel."

"Is he worried about the trial?"

"I can't tell. It's mostly on me. I was the lead. He was tech and communications. None of what happened was his fault. He even tried to warn me off before everything went to shit. In fact, most of my statement will be in defense of him. He did nothing wrong."

"You did nothing wrong either, Nova. I hope you know that. I've read all the reports. No one saw it coming."

"We're the CIA for fucks' sake. How did we not see that coming? Another thing that bothers me is that they knew I was in that market. They *knew*."

"A trap just for you? Seems excessive to have twenty gunmen in a public market to only take you out."

"I'm missing some critical information. I know I am." I can't help the frustration.

Ella changes the subject. "Got a text from Jax a few minutes ago."

"What did the fucker say? I know he blew it way out of proportion. He always does."

Ella may be my personal assistant, but she's also my friend, and she's no stranger to Jax and Evan's antics.

"He said your boss is there." She says the statement cautiously but with a hint of mischief.

"He gave me a ride, and being the polite person I am, I asked him to stay for a drink. He agreed."

"There was also something about taking him home with them and karaoke and the fact that Jax thinks he's the hottest man alive." She says it all like it's a question, and I know she's trying to pry my thoughts from my head.

I grumble. "Says everyone."

Ella laughs. "You don't agree?"

I find myself pouting into the phone. "I never said I didn't agree. I just don't know why everyone always has to bring it up."

Ella laughs harder. "Careful, Nova. Hot, murderous men are super dangerous."

"Thanks for the reminder," I groan.

She's right. He *is* dangerous, and I keep forgetting that.

Her voice changes again, turning quiet and serious—almost scared. "Nova, if Eagan does find out that the companies Owen acquired were evil in some way, the deaths of those CEOs don't get rid of the illegal activity—or the people that were involved in the illegal activity."

"What are you saying?" Though I already know the answer.

"I'm saying you need to be more careful. Mr. Mills may be in danger, and you might be too."

Something catches my eye, and I hang up the phone. A shadow moves silently through the trees outside the restaurant.

I freeze, straining my ears to listen for any movement. A chill races down my spine. The telltale sign I'm being watched.

My instincts kick in, having been in this exact scenario more times than I can count. I reach into my bag, pretending to search for something, acting oblivious to my surroundings.

Though I appear calm and clueless, my palms start to sweat, and I'm internally berating myself for not being more alert. I have no idea how much of the conversation the person in the shadows caught.

Finally wrapping my fingers around a red lipstick tube and a hand mirror, I pull them out and face the restaurant.

Usually, I would never turn my back on a potential threat, but if they wanted to harm me, they would have already done it. They are here for information.

But I'm here for the same thing, so I find myself in a bit of a standoff with the person in the shadows. Who will make the first move?

I take my time, applying the lipstick slowly, as if trying to make sure I get it exactly right. While I'm doing that, I peer at the mirror, watching for the shadows to shift.

As expected, they do not wait for me to go back inside. Meaning, they either got the information they needed, or they think I'm clueless and useless. Likely the latter, or they wouldn't have moved.

The shadow is large, probably a man. He retreats further into the trees, moving slowly in a straight path.

I inch backward, keeping my steps silent even though I know he's already turned and cannot see me.

When his shadow disappears out of sight, I spin and stash my lipstick and mirror roughly into my purse and follow him on silent feet.

I rely on men thinking women are clueless in this business, and they rarely surprise me. If I'd been a man, this guy wouldn't have so carelessly let me follow him.

He keeps a straight path through the trees, still quiet and out of direct light from nearby buildings, but he doesn't look back once. Stopping before the tree line, he surveys an empty parking lot lit up with street lamps. It appears to be a warehouse parking lot, but the cracks in the pavement and the plants growing through them suggest this warehouse isn't currently in use.

The man finally steps into the light, though his all black clothing and black beanie cover most of his features, and I can't see his face. Which means, following him may have led to a dead end unless he turns his face or I can figure out where he's going.

The man proceeds across the parking lot, his black boots silent against the pavement. The crickets and frogs drown out all sound.

I wait until he moves out of sight on the other side of the building before quickly skirting the parking lot, staying within the trees. Moving at a faster pace so I don't lose him, I round the building to the other side. The man gets into a black, unmarked car and drives away.

Cursing, I pull out my phone and snap a few blurry photos of the back of the car on the off chance there's some distinguishable markings that Gray can track down for me.

I sigh, finally slumping my tense shoulders, and walk over to the warehouse door. There's a padlock over the handles, and no windows in sight.

Another dead end.

Giving up, I pull my phone out, dialing Gray, and make my way back through the trees, wondering if I've been away too long that Owen might become suspicious. Or worse, worried, and come try to find me.

"Nova?" Gray asks, picking up after two rings.

"Could you do me a favor for my new assignment? Dec mentioned if I needed tech help, I could ask you."

"Sure," he answers almost cheerily, and my chest constricts at the sound, knowing I'm the reason he likely hasn't been assigned anything interesting since our last mission went to hell.

"I'm sending you some photos of an unmarked car. Can you enhance the photos and see if there's any way to ID it?"

"Absolutely!" he chirps.

"And there's a warehouse north of Ed's, the seafood restaurant. It appears abandoned, but could you check it out and find out who owns it, and see if we can get a look inside?"

Gray doesn't ask questions, and I can hear him already clicking away at his computer.

"I'll have the info to you by the end of the night," he murmurs, finally remembering I'm still on the line, too lost in what he does best.

I chuckle. "Thanks, Gray. I owe you."

I sense him waving off my statement. "No problem."

Hanging up the phone, I hurry the rest of the way back to the restaurant.

Owen, Jax, and Evan haven't texted or called, and there's no one outside shouting my name, so I take a deep breath and step back into the restaurant, pretending I didn't follow a man who was clearly sent to get information from either me or someone inside.

Or both.

As I lock eyes with Owen, the man whom I was sent to lock up, a shiver runs down my spine.

Something isn't right with this case.

The three men are singing loudly, arms wrapped around each other's shoulders. Owen is in the middle. I want to laugh and smile and join them, but my heart is beating a million miles an hour.

Owen stops singing all of a sudden, and his face drops. "What's wrong?" he asks, peeling himself away from Jax and Evan, who keep singing. Oblivious, likely due to the empty glasses sitting next to them.

Shaking my head, I try to plaster a smile on my face even though my stomach feels sour. "Nothing. Had too much to drink."

"You want me to take you home?" He searches my face, standing way too close.

I nod because I don't want to pretend.

He spins and grabs his coat. No questions. No complaints. When he turns back, he hands me my jacket.

Jax and Evan notice and stop their singing.

"You aren't leaving so soon?" Evan asks, sounding disappointed.

I walk over and wrap him in a hug. "I'm sorry. I promise I'll be back tomorrow."

Evan glances over my shoulder. "As long as you bring boss-man."

Chuckling, I pull away. "As long as you stop calling him boss-man."

Evan winks, and Jax wraps his arms around me. "I know there is something up with you," he whispers into my hair. "And I'm going to get it out of you soon. I haven't forgotten."

Tears well in my eyes without warning.

I step back, and I know Jax can see all of it. He always could.

Jax leans in and whispers in my ear. "He's a good one, you know. Not all pretty men will break your heart."

This one most certainly will, and I suddenly want to know what Jax would say if he knew the whole story.

He pulls away from my ear, and I stare at him pointedly.

"He's my boss," I mouth, trying to get him to understand that he's not just my boss at Regenerative Industries—he's my assignment.

Jax shrugs, pretending to not understand. Or perhaps he does know but somehow doesn't believe it. Either way, he gives me a sympathetic smile and a pat on the shoulder.

"Nice to meet you, Owen," Evan shouts after us.

Owen turns and waves. "Nice to meet you, too."

When we're in the parking lot, Owen opens the car door for me.

"Are you ok to drive?" I ask, not remembering how many drinks he had.

"I'm perfectly sober, Miss Riley. I only drank sparkling water with lemon." I must look shocked because he laughs. "Get in the car, Miss Riley. I promise I won't kidnap you, and you'll arrive at your apartment in one piece."

I do as he asks, not saying a word. Far too many things are going on for my brain to process at the moment, and it leads to my mind aching to turn off and my body that's desperate to sleep despite not being able to.

We don't speak for most of the thirty-minute drive back to the city. I want to learn everything Owen knows about the companies he acquired. What information am I missing? Did he really kill those men? But, of course, I can't ask him any of that.

"What I wouldn't pay to know what's going on in that brain of yours right now, Miss Riley," Owen says out of the blue, and when I glance at him, I realize he's probably been studying me for most of the thirty minutes, and I've been oblivious.

"How about a thought for a thought, Mr. Mills?"

He smiles—a devious sort of smile.

I don't choose the question that might lead me to answers. Instead, I ask the one that's been simmering ever since visiting the school Owen's charity built. "You have the money and power to do whatever you want. Why give it away?"

Owen doesn't say anything for a minute, and the smile disappears as he loses himself in thought. "I figured that was obvious, Miss Riley. I want to help. To use my money and power for something good."

"Those are dangerous things, Mr. Mills. Everyone is after them. You must have enemies."

I regret the statement the second it leaves my lips. Gone is the teasing man who was laughing with my best friends, replaced by something much darker.

"As I said earlier, money and power do not buy you friends, but you're correct. They can buy you enemies."

I don't know what to say to that. His confession all but confirms my suspicions about the person I followed, but I don't know how to ask the questions I need or how to get him to keep speaking.

For the first time in my career, I have no idea what I'm doing.

"A deal is a deal, Miss Riley." He finally cuts through my swirling thoughts.

Of course, I don't tell him what I'm really thinking. Instead, I selfishly try to bring back his easy smile. "I was thinking what a lovely threesome you'd make with Jax and Evan."

He side-eyes me, the corner of his mouth kicking up. "A fantasy of yours, Miss Riley? Three doting men?"

I laugh, and his smile grows until that damn dimple appears again. "It wasn't until now."

Owen turns his head, his eyes widening. I laugh harder, squealing at him to keep his eyes on the road. He snaps his head forward again, but he laughs with me.

We both fall into companionable silence, and before I know it, the car is stopped in front of my building. Grabbing my bag, I unhook my seatbelt. When I look at Owen, he's watching me.

"Thanks for the ride." I get out of the vehicle.

"Thanks for taking care of me this morning."

I bend down and place my hand on the outside of the car door. "It was no problem." I go to shut it but blurt, "Oh, and Mr. Mills... a girl can dream."

I slam the door and turn, Owen's laughter chasing me to my building.

Chapter 14

I get home to messages from Gray asking me to call immediately. He must have found some information about the warehouse, and I don't hesitate to dial his number.

Gray doesn't even bother with a hello, launching into what he needs to say. "The warehouse has been abandoned for years. The state bought the land from a logging company in the eighties, and it's been unused since."

"Great," I mumble.

Another dead end.

"As for the car," he continues, "I couldn't find anything but the make and model of it. It's unregistered."

That's not surprising, but my heart still sinks. I'd had some hope that something would turn up—any sort of lead.

"Thanks," I say, trying not to sound disappointed.

Gray is silent for a few seconds, and I realize that I'm starting to understand him a little better. I know he's not the best at expressing sympathy, but he tries.

"We'll figure it out. At least you know what to look out for now." He tries to sound optimistic but ends up sounding overly so.

I smile into the phone. "I know we will."

And somehow, I believe it. I'm not alone in this. I have Ella, Dec, and now Gray. And in some roundabout way, I also know I have Jax and Evan on my side.

But when I think about Owen, I can't shake the odd sense of doom. I can't tell if the feeling is aimed at Owen or me. Probably both.

"Any leads on the evidence?" Gray asks, and I know it's because we need a win when everything else is turning into a dead end. He hasn't asked me about the trial again. He has to be nervous.

I desperately wish I could ease his fears with the trial and Owen's case. But the reality is, I'm drowning in uncertainty.

"A few," I lie because I can't stand to disappoint him.

There's a short pause, and I hear him shuffling around on the other end of the line. I wonder where he is and if he's alone.

It never occurred to me to ask about his personal life.

"Hey, Gray?"

"Mmm?" he mumbles as though he's pressed the phone between his ear and shoulder.

"You have a girl? Or guy? A family? I feel horrible having never asked you."

Another pause has me second-guessing my question. Perhaps it was too personal.

"Not currently." He doesn't give me any more information, and I don't want to push, but when I'm about to say goodbye, he whispers, "She died of cancer a year ago."

Oh, fuck.

I'm such an ass. I should've known.

Everyone at the CIA knows about what happened to my dad and why I joined the CIA in the first place. No one asks about it, but they're at least aware. Here I am, not even realizing my new partner lost someone, too.

"That shit sticks with you. I'm so sorry, Gray." It's all I can offer, though I know it will never be sufficient. The hole they leave in your chest never quite goes away, no matter how much time has elapsed.

"Thanks, Nova," he replies softly. There's another long pause before he adds, "It's been an honor to work with you. Your strength in the face of adversity is admirable—inspirational."

My chest constricts. I'm no role model. I have anger issues, and I'm pretty sure I joined the CIA for revenge, chasing some unattainable justice.

"Get some sleep, Gray," I say instead of telling him about all the insecurities that have lived with me since the day my dad died.

"Only if you do." He chuckles, a bit of lightness returning to his voice.

"I'll try," I reply, though I'm sure he knows it's not true.

Not five minutes after I hang up the phone with Gray, Ella calls.

"Eagan found an interesting lead," she begins, her tone far too casual, which has me sitting up straighter.

I wait for her to continue, but she's intent on drawing out the drama.

"Ella," I grind out.

"The third company—and third victim—has been involved in some major cover-ups. Hushed lawsuits, employees disappearing. That kind of thing."

"What were they trying to hide?"

There's a long silence on the other end. "They covered their tracks well, but Eagan discovered some encrypted sites with discussion on the company. Human trafficking, drugs, and sexual assault were all mentioned."

Somehow, her revelation doesn't surprise me, but I let her finish.

"Eagan also found the name of a whistleblower that apparently the company tried to get rid of, but the person disappeared."

My body tenses, and my question comes out so hopeful that it's barely a whisper. "Do you have a location?"

I can almost hear Ella beaming on the other line. "Yes."

I jump out of bed, even though it's ten at night and I can't be sure the person is still in the area. They're likely halfway across the world if what Ella is saying is true.

"Want to hear the good news first? Or the bad?" she asks.

I frown but pull on black leggings and a fitted, long-sleeve, black shirt, sweeping my hair up in a ponytail. "Bad."

"They have one hell of a security system, and the house is out of comm range."

I swear under my breath. "And the good?"

"It's within driving distance."

Pausing by the large window in my bedroom that overlooks the Bay Bridge, I consider my options.

"You're planning on going tonight." It isn't a question, and I can hear the resignation in Ella's voice.

"What? No lecture?" I try to lighten the mood.

"As if you've ever listened to my lectures." I can almost hear her eye roll.

Owing her an explanation, or perhaps an excuse, I say, "I can't wait. I'm almost positive Owen isn't safe, and if this person has any information, I need it as soon as possible."

There's a long pause on the other end of the line before Ella puffs out an exasperated breath. "So we're saving your target now?"

It's such a loaded question. I don't know how to answer her, and my silence is telling.

Ella sighs. "Listen, Nova, I'm not just your assistant. I'm your friend, and from what Eagan has dug up, I know these companies are scum and we're better off without them." She pauses. "But...he *killed* them."

"We don't know that," I respond quickly. Too quickly. Ella immediately catches on.

"No, you're right," she says, her tone chastising. "But he's suspected of it, and you're supposed to be getting the evidence to prove it. Not off chasing bad guys that don't have anything to do with your actual assignment."

I let out a frustrated growl, and Ella chuckles. "I know that sound, and I'm damn glad I'm on the phone and not with you right now, otherwise I'd have to explain a black eye to Dec tomorrow."

"I'd never punch you."

"No, only use another unsuspecting hard object."

That gets me to smile, and I relent. "I understand your concern." When she snorts, I choose to ignore it and continue, "And I'm still trying to find the evidence, but I can't just let this go. And no, it's not about Owen. It's about my safety, too. It's about getting *all* the bad guys."

"Oh, we're using first names now?" Ella quips.

I refrain from commenting, and say instead, "I won't try if it's too dangerous. I promise."

Ella sighs again. "I'm giving you one hour once you're there, and then I'm calling Dec and sending a team in."

I grin, because that's more than I deserve. "Thanks, Ella. I owe you one."

"You owe me a trillion, but who's counting?"

I laugh. "See you on the other side."

A grunt is all I get in response, and by the time I hang up the phone, I'm already heading inland to the coordinates Ella gave me, to what I hope will provide me answers. The problem is: I don't know what I need.

I push down the questions and the thoughts that follow. I've done this many times before in my life and career. It's easier to get the job done when you leave the emotion behind.

But for the first time since joining the CIA, I'm having a difficult time doing that.

Ella wasn't lying. The whistleblower's house is so far from civilization that I find myself driving for over an hour on an overgrown dirt path. I lost cell service thirty minutes ago, and there isn't a light to be seen for miles.

Knowing this person also has an intense security system and I'm quickly approaching the house, I slow the car, keeping my eyes peeled for the telltale signs of cameras, bugs, and other tech traps. I don't want an unsuspecting bullet through my head.

I brace for anything.

For a time, I feel like Ella was wrong about the security, but soon there's a disturbance in the dirt beside the road. I've been trained to spot any sign that a place has had human interference, and though it's subtle, I notice the slight imprint of a boot.

I stop the car and get out, straining to hear any sign that I'm not alone. The forest around me is alive with the chorus of crickets and frogs, but there are no sounds of human activity.

Bending down, I study the print. It looks new. Made within the last day or two. I follow the direction it points to and find bent bushes. A few branches look to have broken off. The cut seems new.

The path stops at a large tree, and, sure enough, there's a camera posted ten feet off the ground. I pull out a tool I've used often. It mimics the way a tree rat might chew through a camera wire. Cutting it, the faint red light flickers out of existence. Heading back the way I came, I make sure not to disturb the area further.

I abandon the car, needing my full senses to find other security traps. As I anticipated, there are a few more cameras, but instead of cutting the wires and raising an alarm, I skirt around them through the forest, careful not to make any noise or leave behind any evidence.

A few more minutes of maneuvering around the extensive system, and the house finally comes into view. There's a light outside, illuminating the front porch, but otherwise, the house looks almost abandoned. It's small and brown, blending in with the surrounding trees. There is no garden or any potted plants. The only sign that the place isn't completely abandoned is the footpath that leads from the house to the detached garage. Tire tracks indicate the person has left recently, but the grooves aren't deep.

This person doesn't go out often.

I'm so busy scouting the area that I fail to notice my attacker until they move out of the bushes to my right and tackle me to the ground.

The person is covered from head to toe in black and has one hell of a right hook. My stomach takes the brunt of the force, and I almost retch, but my training kicks in. I ignore the pain and hook one leg around their middle, rolling on top of them. Using my forearm, I crush their trachea while my other hand twists the wrist holding a knife. The person yelps and drops it.

Both of our breaths are heavy, though the exchange was over in a blink. Our chests move in sync, but since my arm is on their throat, their breathing is shallow.

"Can't breathe," they rasp. The voice sounds feminine.

I ease up, releasing her throat but keeping her subdued.

"Who sent you?" she asks, and this time I hear the fear—and paranoia.

"I came of my own volition." It's not a lie. "I'm looking for information about the company you used to work for."

Something flashes across her face, but I can't quite tell what it is. "I don't know what you're talking about."

I sigh, easing up even more. I've learned two things from this brief meeting: One, she's terrified, and two, she doesn't know how to protect herself and relies on her tech to keep her safe. This means she's not really a threat to me, and the only thing I can do is try to earn her trust so she will give me what I need.

I can also provide her something she wants.

Safety.

I decide to be truthful. "I work for the CIA, and I'm looking for information on your former boss. I have reason to believe he was involved in illegal activity."

She scoffs. "A *lot* of illegal activity."

I raise my brows.

She lets out a slow breath. "I have no reason to trust you, but you got past my security with ease, and there's no chance in hell I'm taking you out physically. So, I'm inclined to believe you."

With that declaration, I choose to trust her, too. Climbing off her, I stand, offering my hand. She eyes it warily but takes it, and I pull her to stand. She's shorter than me, but not by much, and her brown hair tumbles from the black beanie she's wearing. Her irises are a stunning shade of blue, and the lines on her face would indicate she's around my age, maybe a few years older.

She eyes me as if she's assessing me the way I am scrutinizing her.

"Come," she finally says, waving a hand and turning her back to me.

The ultimate test of trust in my line of work.

I follow. She takes me up the old wooden steps, skipping the third one, and I find out a moment later why: The step creaks so loudly, echoing through the trees, that the crickets silence their chirps for a moment.

"That step has saved me more times than my security system."

I chuckle. "I don't doubt it."

She opens the screen door, then the inner wooden one, and ushers me into the small space. The living room to the right is full of computers and tech equipment, all beeping away. To the left, the kitchen is covered in dirty dishes. It looks like weeks' worth.

She doesn't stop in either room and instead leads me down a small hallway that ends with two identical doors. She opens the one on the left, and I find myself in a small library. There's a couch under the window, and this room appears to be the cleanest.

She motions to the sofa, and I sit down, watching her. The slump of her shoulders gives away her exhaustion.

"Don't sleep much?" I ask as she sits in a small chair opposite me.

She shakes her head. "Not since they tried to kill me."

I arch a brow.

"That's what they did to anyone who knew too much," she continues. "I was his assistant. Though I acted dumb, I heard his conversations, and I kept track of the people who disappeared."

"What happened to them?"

She looks at me as though I'm not too bright. "They killed them."

"How'd they cover their tracks?"

She shrugs. "Most cases were declared suicides, but some were linked to serial killers. They'd use the same strategies to kill their victims."

I clench my jaw, and it doesn't go unnoticed.

"You're CIA. This must not be surprising."

I shake my head. "No, not surprising. I'm trying to put together many different puzzle pieces at the moment. You heard the CEO is dead, right?"

She nods. "But they still know I know."

I sit forward, placing my arms on my knees, softening my voice. "Who knows?"

It's like trying to calm a wounded animal. She's about to shut down or bolt. It's in the gleam of her eyes.

She shakes her head, dropping it into her hands. "I don't know. Whoever he was working with. Whoever controlled the drugs and human trafficking."

"What was his role in all of it?"

She raises her head, blue bloodshot eyes meeting mine. "He traded and sold people and drugs. They profit-shared. He kept the authorities away using money and influence, which allowed their operation to rake in billions."

None of this is surprising, but somehow, I didn't expect the scope of it.

"And you're afraid whoever he worked with is still after you?"

She nods. This time, moisture fills her eyes.

I reach out a hand and place it over her clammy one. "We're going to find them, and in the meantime, I'm going to put you up in a safehouse with the CIA."

Her eyes widen. "Really?" She almost chokes on her words, the relief evident.

"How long have you been here?"

"A year."

She's been living in seclusion and fear for a year? *Fuck.* How many others got out and are living the same life? I'm terrified to ask.

I pat her hand. "You ok to come with me now? Or would you like me to send someone tomorrow so you can get your affairs in order?"

She looks around the room, and as she does, I notice how skinny she is.

I change my mind.

"I think you should come with me." I'm firm, but my voice remains quiet.

Her eyes find mine again, and there's a bone-deep relief that takes over. She nods as I lead her out of the prison she's been living in.

She squeezes my hand until we reach my car, and I open the passenger door and let her slide in before shutting it. Walking to the driver's side, I shoot off a text to Ella.

Nova: *I need a safehouse for a witness.*

Ella: *Witness for Owen?*

Nova: *Witness for the crimes of the CEO of the third company.*

Text bubbles pop up then disappear. Because I don't want to scare the woman, I get in the car and put my phone away.

"Ready?" I ask.

The woman nods but doesn't look at me. Instead, she stares out the window into the dark forest. How much *does* she know, and how badly has it ruined her life?

I can't help the deep-seated rage that I often feel when I learn of the crimes of my targets, how they can get away with so many things and destroy so many lives and get away unscathed. Even worse, walk away with more power. More money.

It's nothing like the way I feel with Owen, and that has me both terrified and conflicted.

Chapter 15

When I regain consciousness, I'm somewhere dark. I'm shaking, but I'm not sure it's from the cold or the blood loss. My mouth feels like sandpaper, and my voice croaks.

"Where am I?"

It's Gray's voice that breaks the silence and darkness, though I can't see him. "A safehouse outside the city."

"How'd I get here?"

"When you didn't show up at the rendezvous spot, I went looking for you. Found you passed out and bleeding."

"You didn't call backup? Why'd you break protocol?"

"I knew you were close."

"You shouldn't have done that."

"I was supposed to let you die?"

Suddenly, I realize how much of an ass I am. "Shit. Sorry, Gray. I should be thanking you, not grilling you."

He chuckles. "I'm used to it by now, though I don't know how Dec lived with it for so long." His voice is teasing.

"I'd punch you if I could see anything, and if my shoulder didn't feel like it has a knife in it."

"Rest, Nova. I'm going out to get some supplies. Our transport will be here in a few hours."

"Why is it taking so long? We should be on a plane by now."

He doesn't say anything right away. "It was a bloodbath, Nova. A lot of civilian deaths. The CIA is trying to prevent a bigger political problem."

I wake with a start. After the late-night situation with the whistleblower, I didn't get home until 6 am Saturday and spent the rest of the day in and out of sleep. Eventually, I passed out for the night, but my sleep wasn't good. The dream proved that.

There's something about the timeframe from when I hit my head to when I woke up in a safe house with Gray. He went against protocol to get me out. He didn't call for backup. But didn't he say they were too busy handling the fallout?

I push the sweat-soaked hair out of my eyes and roll over to find that it's still only 4 am on a Sunday. I reach for my phone and find a handful of drunk texts from Jax and Evan. Seems they continued partying after I left them last night. Evan also sent some shirtless photos of Owen from magazine shoots he found online.

I roll my eyes and click out of the group text, only to find a few messages from Owen.

I open the chat and suddenly my heart rate kicks up.

"Ridiculous," I mumble to my beating chest.

Owen: *You awake?*

That text was sent at 2 am.

Owen: *I don't mean to keep bugging you, but when you wake, will you text?*

That was sent at 3 am.

Owen, thirty minutes later: *I'm not drunk or with a naked woman, I promise.*

When I attempt to reply, a text bubble pops up, and I halt. The bubble stops, too. I don't know what to make of all this.

Me: *I'm awake.*

Owen: *Sorry to bother you. I didn't know who else would be up at this hour.*

Me: *Did you sleep at all?*

Owen: *No.*

Me: *Why?*

Owen: *That's a complicated question, Miss Riley.*

What does that mean? Usually, his late nights are filled with drinking and women, so why not now? And why can't he sleep?

I don't know how to respond to that, so I wait for him to say something else. I don't have to wait long.

Owen: *You ever feel like the clock is ticking far faster than you expected?*

Oh shit.

Does he suspect me? Or does he think he's in danger? My brain goes into overdrive.

Me: *Life is short.*

It's the only response I can think of, and I find I have the urge to go to him. Every instinct in me believes he's in danger, and I can't shake it.

Owen: *That it is, Miss Riley.*

A pause before the text bubble pops back up.

Owen: *Want to go for a hike? Watch the sun rise? I know a good place.*

I should say no, but I can't shake my fear. I also find I *want* to say yes.

Me: *Sure. I'll be ready in ten minutes.*

Owen: *I'll be waiting.*

I throw my phone on the bed and let my head sink into my hands. I need answers and fast, because Owen is correct: time is running out.

"Brought you a coffee," Owen says as he opens the passenger door of his red sports car, parked on the empty street and in front of my apartment building, holding out the steaming cup.

It's still dark outside; only a few stars blink overhead. But the lights from the city block out most of them. The usually-foggy air is clear this morning, and I suck in a deep, cleansing breath and take the warm coffee from his hand, nodding my thanks.

"Do you ever drive a different car?" I ask when he comes around the other side and settles against the heated leather seats.

He puts his blinker on and pulls away from the curb. "This is my only car, Miss Riley. So, no."

"Why?" I've never met anyone with his kind of money who wasn't drowning in fancy cars.

"Why would I need more than one car?" he says as though it's obvious.

He's right, of course, but that information still surprises me.

"Why don't you sleep, Miss Riley?" he asks, surprising me with that particular question, even though I'd asked him the same one not thirty minutes ago.

"It's complicated, Mr. Mills."

He laughs at me, throwing his own words back in his face.

"I've had nightmares since I witnessed my father's murder." I don't know why I say it. I don't typically offer that information to anyone, let alone an assignment of mine. But for some reason, that information feels safe in his hands. Which is what scares me the most.

Owen's laughter instantly dies, and he narrows his gaze on the road. "I'm sorry. I didn't know you saw it."

"I couldn't save him," I whisper back, the tears I rarely allow to the surface threatening to spill.

He reaches over and grabs my hand, squeezing it. He doesn't let go, and I don't pull away. His rough calluses scrape along the softer skin of my palm, and I squeeze my eyes shut.

After a few moments, he breaks the silence. "I don't sleep because I'm afraid. I fill most nights with women and drinking because it makes me feel less alone. Less scared."

"What are you afraid of?" I ask sincerely.

"Losing everything I've built. Losing the few people that matter to me."

"You aren't afraid for yourself?" I dare to ask because I want to know if he suspects he'll be caught eventually for what he's suspected of. A small part of me, though, *needs* to know for reasons I haven't yet determined.

He doesn't hesitate. "No. Whatever happens to me doesn't matter as long as everything else is protected."

Shit.

This man. This selfless, stupid man.

I squeeze his hand back. "Why would you lose everything?" I feign innocence, though I already know the answer.

He doesn't answer my question for a long time as he swerves around tight curves, hugging the coast. The motion almost lulls me to sleep, and I finally register the months of little rest and what it's doing to me. I'm good at ignoring it, though, and right now I want to know his answer, so I force myself to stay awake.

"Because power and money are fleeting, Miss Riley. Neither of those lasts forever."

It isn't the answer I am expecting, but somehow it doesn't surprise me. How easily we forget that those things are fleeting. How little the money and power mean when they can easily be taken away. But I don't think he means just that. I think he knows eventually he'll be caught, and he doesn't want every good deed he's done to go down with him.

My heart constricts.

He pulls into an empty parking lot, everything still pitch-black outside. In the headlights, I can make out a small swath of redwoods surrounding the area. A small building along the edge of the trees looks to be a bathroom, and possibly a welcome center, but both are pitch-black. No lights are visible.

When he stops the car, he releases my hand, his hand flexing as he pulls it away. "Ready?"

What a loaded question. I'm not sure I'm ready for any of this. Especially not him.

I nod, and he pushes the door open, walking to the trunk of the car and pulling out a backpack and two flashlights. He turns on both and hands one to me.

"We can watch the sun rise from the sea cliffs then make our way through the old growth forest on the way back," he explains, shutting the trunk, the noise echoing through the desolate parking lot. The distant crashing of the waves is the only other sound.

I smile. "Lead the way."

He doesn't turn right away and instead searches my face in the indirect glow from the flashlights. "I'm glad I hired you, Miss Riley."

He doesn't wait for a response, seeming afraid that I will say the opposite. Instead, he heads through the dark parking lot, aiming for a small opening between the trees marking the beginning of the trail.

I swallow thickly, and it hits me what I'm doing to him and myself. I've gotten too close to my mark. I'm in too deep. But I don't know how to stop. I don't even think I want to. My instincts should be telling me to run. They should be warning me to put space between us. But they are oddly silent. Content almost.

I race to catch up, and we both slip through the forest in the pitch-black. The typical San Francisco fog remains offshore, but moisture clings to the branches of the trees, raining a light mist on our heads. The damp air, combined with the trees, creates an intoxicating smell, and I find myself taking deep breaths. The first ones I've had in a long while. The whole time,

Owen doesn't say a word but copies my breathing, and a slight grin paints his lips.

We walk in companionable silence until we reach the cliffs. Water pounds against the rock below us, much louder now. The sky is already beginning to lighten, turning it from black to a dark blue. The city twinkles in the distance, its light blotting out many of the stars above.

We sit on the tall grass and silently watch as the sky brightens further. The colors shift from blue to every pastel shade one could imagine. Time continues, neither of us speaking. As the colors fade, I finally turn my attention to Owen.

He's staring at me.

"Do I have something on my face, Mr. Mills?" I joke.

He smirks. "No. I was just thinking how, in this light, you look far less intimidating."

I don't know why, but a laugh escapes my lips. "Don't let it fool you." I stand and brush the dirt off my pants.

He's on his feet a moment later. "Oh, I know better than to do that."

A shifting of the light has me scanning the tree line behind Owen. I swear I sense movement.

Owen follows my gaze. "Probably an animal," he comments, but there's a quiver in his voice that makes me believe he might not trust his own words.

Perhaps I'm overthinking, but I can't shake the feeling that something isn't right. And those inklings are usually correct. They've saved my ass more than a few times in my line of work.

"Let's go, so I can buy you breakfast," Owen says, turning to lead the way down the trail that meanders along the cliffs and into the forest.

"Always so concerned with my eating habits," I mumble behind him, ignoring the movement and noise for now but keeping myself on high alert.

He chuckles. "Can't have you losing any of that muscle, or I'll soon be able to beat you in a fight."

I snort. "Unlikely."

A twig snaps behind us, and I'm instantly turning. Owen halts and does the same.

I scan the area again. My adrenaline releases in my veins, making me more alert.

"Like I said. It's probably an animal," Owen whispers.

Animals don't follow people. They're afraid of them. And animals don't step on twigs and break them. They don't weigh enough and are certainly not stupid enough to give themselves away to potential prey or predators.

Only humans do that.

Fuck.

I turn to Owen and surprise him by stepping into him, pressing my body against his. Rising on my toes, I put my mouth against his ear. The movement appears intimate to any onlookers—innocent and unaware.

"That's not an animal or other hikers. Don't move, and don't act surprised. We're being followed," I whisper, and despite the danger we find ourselves in, I can't help but notice the warmth of his hands as they press into my hips, or the movement of his chest as it moves up and down against mine. Both find a similar cadence, perfectly in sync.

His body stiffens, the only indication he understands. He doesn't contradict me either, which makes me believe he knew being followed was a possibility.

I suddenly don't care if he finds out what I am. All I want is to get him out of here. Make sure he's safe.

"I'm going to take your hand and pretend we're having an intimate moment. Then we're going to head back to the parking lot. Slowly. We need to stay out in the open and not let them suspect we know they're there."

The last person who followed Owen was only looking for information, not trying to harm him, so I'm secretly hoping this time is the same, even though every alarm bell is going off in my mind.

He dips his head until his lips brush against my ear. "Lead the way, Miss Riley." His voice is low and deep and shows no sign of fear. Suddenly, I'm feeling things I shouldn't be, considering the situation we find ourselves in.

I grab his hand. It dwarfs mine. His heat sinks into me, and my cold fingers suddenly turn warm.

I try to ignore the ever-increasing adrenaline running through my veins, causing my heart to pick up its pace, knowing it's not only due to the current threat we face. Instead, I turn us back up the trail, toward the parking lot. My senses are on high alert, listening and watching for any movement.

He's so close that I can feel the heat of him. I can hear his ragged breath, and the sound makes me think of other ways he might sound like that.

I shake my head, willing the inconvenient and inappropriate thoughts to vanish.

We walk quickly but not fast enough that anyone would suspect we know we're being followed. Turning, we follow the trail away from the coast, and I almost allow myself to believe that I was only being paranoid when a gunshot sounds behind us.

I want to freeze in terror, feeling the phantom pain of the gunshot in my shoulder, but my brain instantly shifts its attention to Owen. All I care about is getting him somewhere safe. I twist both of us and push him to the ground. When a second gunshot sounds, I fall on top of him.

I'm instantly up again, pulling him along with me. "Get to the trees," I growl, shoving him ahead of me.

"I thought you said—" he begins, and I can hear the panic in his voice.

"That was before I knew they had guns," I shout as we both sprint for the trees to the left of us.

Thank god Owen is fit and quick on his feet. He keeps pace with me as we crash into the underbrush and barrel through the forest, our steps loud over the dry leaves and fallen branches. Discretion is no longer needed—only survival.

Another gunshot sounds behind us and ricochets off a tree ahead. Owen halts, and I crash into his back. He stares at the bullet hole in the tree, almost as if he's about to go into a state of shock.

"Look at me," I demand, knowing we only have a few seconds at most.

He does. I ignore the terror on his face and the fact that my instructions and my calmness in this situation might get me found out. At the very least, they might cause some suspicion. I decide it's worth it. I decide *he's* worth it.

"I will distract them, pull them in the opposite direction. You need to run for the car. I'll be right behind you. Wait two minutes for me. No more. If I'm not there, go."

"I can't," he stammers.

"You can and you will." I push him away from me.

His face looks devastated, and I try my best to ignore it while turning away from him and sprinting in the opposite direction. I make as much noise as I can, drawing the gunman away from Owen. The plants grab at my clothes, tearing my skin under my leggings.

I may not have a gun, but I did strap a dagger to my thigh. I grab for it, not slowing. Counting the seconds, knowing I only have a minute before I need to head back toward the car, I use the numbers to steady myself.

The sound of another shot echoes behind me. It's close. Whoever's after Owen took the bait and followed me instead. I could sigh with relief if I didn't have to run for my life.

Sweat pours down my chest. When I reach sixty seconds, I switch directions. I catch the movement of my pursuer as I do, and I clutch the dagger harder until steel cuts grooves into my skin.

Come on.

I urge them to make a mistake. To come out into the open for a split second so that I can bury a dagger in them.

A moment later, I spot their silhouette step out from behind a tree, and I whip my arm toward them, turning my body to get the most momentum and releasing the dagger.

I hear the gunshot at the exact moment the dagger leaves my hand. Falling to the ground, searing pain rips through the skin on my arm, but my dagger hits its target, and the person goes down with a grunt of pain.

I hit his leg.

Not waiting for him to pull the trigger again, I push up, my arm screaming in pain, and sprint as fast as my legs will carry me.

The branches grab at my hair and pull it from its ponytail. I ignore my arm. I ignore everything, focused only on my one objective: the seconds I have left to get back to the car in time.

When I break through the tree line and stumble on the pavement of the parking lot, I let out a strangled noise. The shadow of his form waits in the driver's seat.

He didn't leave me.

When I get to the car, I yank open the door with my good arm and fall into the seat.

"Go!" I shout and slam the door shut. Owen doesn't wait as he peels out of the parking lot, his foot already poised over the gas.

We both don't say anything for a few moments, and I struggle to get my seatbelt fastened. He notices my arm and almost swerves off the road.

"Eyes on the road," I growl, sitting up straighter so I can get a better look at my wound. The bullet only grazed the skin of my upper arm.

I reach down and grab the end of my T-shirt, tearing it. I wrap it around my arm and cinch it tight, wincing at the pain.

At least I won't bleed all over his car.

Owen doesn't slow, and I brace myself around every corner, careful not to aggravate my injury.

Damn, he knows how to drive this thing.

"You have somewhere safe to go?" I ask, not quite sure why he hasn't spoken but also not sure what to say to him, either.

"Yes." His voice is deep and laced with a roughness that tells me he's been expecting something like this to happen.

I don't have it in me to say anything more, and he doesn't elaborate on his answer. Instead, he races along the coast, eventually turning inland. He drives for another ten minutes, turning off the main road and onto a dirt one. Another few minutes, and he slows the car to a crawl.

"You should probably call the cops," I rasp through the pain, even though I don't want him to get them involved. But I don't want to make an already-precarious situation worse. After this morning, if he doesn't suspect that there's more to me than meets the eye, then he's a fool.

I know he's not, though. I've seen my fair share of them, and he definitely isn't. Which means I need to be prepared for the questions I know he's going to ask, for the possibility that he will figure it out. That he will fire me and leave me with nothing.

He glances down at the blood-soaked T-shirt.

"We need to get you to a hospital." It doesn't surprise me that he ignores my plea to call the cops.

"I'm fine. I'll be fine. It's not deep." When we both fall into silence again, I ask him with a little more force, "Owen, who's trying to kill you? And why aren't you calling the police?"

I still need to try to act like the innocent assistant, even if I did throw a blade into the leg of our pursuer and am not panicking as much as I should be if I were just your average civilian.

Owen takes a deep breath as we come to the end of the dirt road, and he shuts off the car. "I'm not sure who would be trying to kill me, but I have an idea. I'm not calling the cops because"—he runs a hand through his dark hair— "because I can't have them poking around my company. I can't lose the money. I can't lose my charities." His voice is so desperate that I want to reassure him, but I can't.

"I understand," I say instead.

"You do?" he asks, surprised.

I sigh. "I don't want you to lose them either. Can we go inside so I can get cleaned up, and you can tell me everything? From the beginning. You owe me that much."

It's his turn to sigh as he nods and gets out. He comes around to open my door, helping me stand.

When I get to my feet, I sway a little and threaten to topple. Owen grabs me around the waist and steadies me.

"Low blood sugar and drop in adrenaline aren't a good combo," I mumble, allowing him to hold me up and walk me to the house.

I finally notice my surroundings. We're in the middle of the woods. It's dark under the canopy as the sun is still low in the sky. There's a bark path that leads from the dirt road up to a tiny wood cabin. A large porch encircles the whole house, and a stone chimney is visible above the roofline.

"It's my father's house. He doesn't come here anymore. Not since my mom died," Owen offers while he watches me take in my surroundings. He's still holding tight to my hips, and I can't help but sink further into him.

Instead of helping me walk, he sweeps me up in his arms like I weigh nothing. I let out a rush of air and tense.

"Felt like you might topple over. Figured this might be an easier way to get you inside," he says as a way of explanation, but I'm not complaining. I'm too tired and overwhelmed.

He carries me into the house and sets me on a large brown leather couch by an old wooden fireplace covered in rustic stone.

Grabbing a blanket from a basket next to the couch, he covers me and pulls out some kindling and a lighter from another basket beside the fireplace. Before I know it, he has a fire roaring.

When he finally faces me, I can do nothing but blink up at him. We stare at each other for a moment, neither of us apparently knowing what to say. I can't read his face, but his eyes feel sad. But there's something else there, too—something I don't want to think about.

His stare suddenly makes me too hot, and I throw off the blanket, making to stand and go clean myself up when he stops me with a hand on my shoulder.

"I know you're tough, Miss Riley, and I also know you've been on your own for a long time. You can take care of yourself, but for once, please let me help you. I need to." There is desperation in his voice, and my throat tightens while I swallow.

"The best part of this house is the tub," he continues. "I'll run a bath for you so you can clean yourself up. I have some clothes here. I'm the only one who uses this place."

I suddenly want to know why he's the only one. Why *does* he come here at all? I want to know everything about him, and not because we almost died, and not because I'm supposed to find evidence that will lock him up for life.

I want to know. To know *him*. And I have no idea what to do with that.

Sitting there like an idiot, I just stare at him. He continues, "I'll make you something to eat while you bathe, and once you're fed, I'll explain everything. I promise."

I nod because I don't know how else to respond.

He reaches for my hand, and I take his. Instead of pulling me to my feet though, he scoops his arms under mine and lifts me again. This time, I don't tense—I melt. I let my head fall into the crook of his neck and breathe deeply. The subtle scent of sweat and pine hit my nose, and I practically moan into his skin.

His breath halts at the sound, his muscles stiffening almost imperceptibly, but he continues to the bathroom as if nothing happened.

Setting me on a plush carpet in the center of a huge bathroom, he walks to the porcelain, free-standing tub under a large window that faces the redwood forest. The tub is big enough for two people—that doesn't go unnoticed.

He turns on the spout and tests the temperature with his hand. I watch him with curiosity and something else I can't, or won't, name. I chalk the intense feelings up to being shot. Again.

As the tub fills, he walks back to me and crouches down. He studies my tired, and likely scratched, face. "Do you need me to help you get undressed?"

I can't read his tone, but it almost seems like he's uncomfortable. That can't be. He's the cockiest bastard I've ever met.

I shake my head. "I can do it," I say, my voice a bit scratchy.

He stands. I reach for the bottom of my torn shirt and wince trying to raise it over my head.

Owen frowns down at me.

Switching strategies, I drop my arms, first trying to free my injured arm.

I know I can manage it, but Owen doesn't wait to find out. He bends over, taking the bottom of my shirt and slips it off my good arm then over my head, and finally he gently tugs it down my injured arm.

"Thanks," I mumble, fumbling with the bloody bandage.

He crouches, helping me untie it. He's careful and gentle. The fabric sticks a little to the drying blood, and I flinch as he peels it away from the laceration.

"Sorry," he whispers. His fingers trace the outline of the injury, assessing it. I close my eyes, not because it's painful but because the touch feels good. His fingers trail up my arm to my shoulder and halt.

My eyes fly open and find him staring in horror at my scarred shoulder. *Shit. Shit. Shit.*

How could I have forgotten about my bullet wound? I quickly search for some explanation and land on, "I also got shot when my father was murdered."

His eyes dart to mine, and inwardly I know that the scar looks too new, but it's the only thing I can think of as an excuse for its presence.

He glances at the mark and runs his fingers along the raised edges of it. I expect pain, real or phantom, but it doesn't come. I only feel his featherlight touch. Soothing. Comforting.

When he stops, I realize my eyes are closed again. This time, I open them slowly.

Owen's gaze pierces right through me, and I hold my breath. I expected pity. That's most people's reaction to my past—my visible and invisible scars. It's not what I find when Owen looks at me, though. It's more like grief and awe. But that can't be correct.

"Do you want to take a bath with your bra on?" he asks, and I'm brought back to the reality that I'm half-naked.

I look down at my sports bra and groan when I realize there's no way I'm getting the thing off without help.

"I can cut it off if you want," he offers with a chuckle.

"Get the scissors."

He raises a brow.

"It's gross, and I want it off," I explain, suddenly not caring that my fake boss is about to tear off my clothes with scissors.

I want to rid myself of all the swirling feelings, even though I know cutting off a bra won't do that.

He's back in less than a minute and helps me stand. I turn so my back is to him. He holds my good arm to steady me and brings the scissors to my back.

He halts. "You sure about this?"

I nod, and he starts cutting. It takes him a little while to cut through the thick fabric, but once he's done, I let it fall from my chest. It lands on the floor in front of my feet.

Owen takes a step back. "I'm assuming you don't need me to cut off your pants, too?" There's that familiar undertone of amusement in his voice, and I find myself smiling.

"I think I can manage from here, thanks," I say, looking over my shoulder at him.

He doesn't move right away; his gaze is caught on me. I try not to shiver as his eyes roam across every inch of exposed skin.

"Ok, then"—he coughs—"don't drown." With that, he turns and practically races out of the bathroom.

I laugh to myself. Owen doesn't easily get flustered, and a few inches of exposed skin had him hightailing it out of the bathroom.

After pulling down my pants with one hand, I step into the warm water. It stings my arm and all the minor scrapes from the branches, but eventually I relax into the warmth and close my eyes.

I try not to think of the mess I'm in. Instead, my mind drifts back to Owen, to thoughts I most definitely shouldn't be having. But the alternative is worse, so I indulge myself.

I think of the things I've learned about him. His kindness, his smugness, his humor, his ability to weasel his way into my thoughts, and his eyes. The way he looks at me...

The click of the door has me coming out of my thoughts, and I snap my head toward the sound, my breathing far too rapid for a peaceful bath.

"Sorry," Owen says as he reaches inside and places a towel and clean clothes on the floor. When he closes the door, I lean back, sinking my head beneath the warm water.

Fuck.

Chapter 16

The clothes are Owen's, and they are about four inches too long and hang off me like a child trying to wear adult clothes, but they smell like him.

I roll up the sweatpants and tighten the string around the waist, doing the same to the long sleeves of the crewneck shirt he gave me. It's soft and hangs loosely. Next, I throw on the large sweatshirt, grateful he left it for me as I don't have a bra anymore.

Looking at myself in the mirror, I notice I have a few scratches on my face but nothing serious. The wound on my arm appears much better, feeling more like a burn than a bullet wound now.

I take a deep breath and slowly make my way back to the living room.

Owen's in the kitchen, cooking. It smells like bacon and eggs and spices and coffee.

My stomach rumbles of its own accord, and my mouth waters.

"Smells amazing," I say, falling onto the couch and pulling my legs under me.

"It is," he shoots back without facing me.

"Ever the egotist."

"It's not ego if it's fact." He twirls around, holding two plates. Steam rises from both of them.

He places the plate in my lap.

I smile. "Thanks."

"Don't mention it." He plops down on a brown, matching leather chair across from me.

He's silent while I eat, but I can't seem to hold in my questions any longer.

"What the hell, Owen? Why do you have people trying to murder you?"

He wrinkles his nose and looks like this is the last thing he wants to answer, but he doesn't deny me.

"The companies I recently acquired had some nefarious business dealings. When I bought the companies, I terminated those dealings, cutting off the financial ties. Some dangerous people got a little pissed."

This confirms what I already suspected. "What good does it do them to have you dead, though?"

Owen shrugs. "Revenge?"

"So why don't you have private security? Why haven't you contacted the authorities? Seems like common sense to do those things."

Owen sighs. "I had my suspicions about them wanting me dead, but that was truly the first attempt. You're right. I need to hire someone." He pauses and looks away from me. His following words are hushed. "I didn't contact the authorities like I should have because even though I feel like I did the right thing by acquiring these companies and ending those business deals, they could arrest me for the past deeds of those companies, and I could lose everything."

"You really think they could convict you for someone else's business deals just because you acquired the company?"

"It took a few months after the acquisitions to end the business ties with the underground crime syndicates. They could use that against me."

I take a deep breath. This got way more complicated, and all I can think about is how unfair all of this is—how bad people can get away with doing bad things, but if you try to stop it you could be the one to go to jail instead.

What a fucking mess.

I don't respond to Owen and realize I'm blankly staring at him.

"I understand if this isn't what you signed up for. I understand if you want to leave," he says.

It's exactly what I signed up for, but I don't know if I can do what I'm supposed to. Not anymore.

I shake my head. "I don't want to leave."

My response surprises even me. I do want to run, but I find I don't want to abandon him.

"Really?" he asks, and I can't help but hear the sliver of hope in his voice.

"But you're going to listen to me and do exactly what I say."

The fucker has the audacity to smirk.

"You're going to hire a private security team and private investigators. You're going to protect yourself at all costs, and you're going to find out *exactly* who is trying to kill you. When you find out, we're going to put them behind bars. Do you understand?"

I don't think about how my knowledge and presence are suspicious, or maybe I don't care anymore.

Owen looks at me with an expression I can't seem to read. "Why do I get the impression you've done this before?"

Because I have, but I can't let him know that. "Because after my dad died and I found out who was behind it all, I made sure they couldn't get to me." That part is true, but it was only with the CIA's help that I was able to do it.

"You're kind of terrifying, you know that?" he asks with an undercurrent of amusement again.

"You don't want to see the monster I will become if you don't listen to me."

He raises a brow.

"Don't even think about it."

Owen laughs, holding his hands up in mock surrender. "I'll hire private security and investigators. Or rather, I'll have my personal assistant do it." He winks.

I roll my eyes, but I smile, too. "Fine. I'll start tomorrow morning."

"Until then, you'll stay here," he says, rising from the chair and walking over to me.

"Excuse me?"

"I'm not letting you out of my sight until we have better security in place."

I huff. "If I recall correctly, I'm the one who got you out of that mess and saved *your* ass. I can take care of myself."

He sighs. "I know you can. We've been over this already. Humor me, Miss Riley. It will soothe my anxiety to know you're safe."

I search his eyes. The humor and amusement are gone. There's only concern remaining, maybe even a little fear.

"Fine." I concede.

He smiles, big enough that his dimple appears, and I have the stupid urge to keep it there.

"You have to tell Dec," Ella pleads with me over the phone while I roam the desolate woods behind Owen's cabin. I caved and called to tell her everything.

"I can't, Ella. Not yet. I need more evidence than the whistleblower. If I don't have more, then I risk pulling Regenerative Industries under and, with them, everything Owen's worked so hard for."

"This is a fucking mess, Nova."

"I know. To be honest, I don't know what to do. I don't even know what the *right* thing is to do. I'm supposed to put Owen behind bars, but I'm not so sure he's the villain in all this."

She sighs heavily. "Eagan has some info on the second victim. Rape cases. Ten of them. All settled behind the scenes."

"Shit."

There's a long silence while I pace back and forth. My steps are silent beneath the soft bed of pine needles. The smell reminds me of Owen, and my stomach flips at the thought.

Get a grip.

"I'll give you until the gala, and then I'm going to tell Dec if you haven't," Ella says finally.

She's right. I should tell him. He can help. He's not just my boss. He's my friend. So why am I afraid to say anything to him?

"Fine," I answer at last. "You're right. I'll gather what I have, and I'll tell him."

"I know you don't want to know what I think, but I'm gonna tell you anyway. I think you're falling for this guy, and that makes your judgment a little cloudy. I don't mean that as a criticism. I don't want you getting hurt."

I don't mean to get defensive, but I'm so on edge that I snap. "So you think I should just get the evidence I came for and turn him in and leave the rest?"

Ella takes a deep breath. "No, Nova. I didn't say that. I want you to be careful. This is too big for one person to handle. You're attached to him, and I get it. I kind of am, too, knowing what I know now. But you can't save everyone, and you can't do it alone."

"I don't want to do it alone," I whisper back.

"Tell Dec."

I sigh. "I will."

I find Owen in the kitchen again. He has his shirt off. Of course. Music blares from a speaker in the corner of the kitchen, and he hums along.

He doesn't notice me right away, and I pull myself up onto the island counter and pluck a blueberry from the bowl and pop it in my mouth. The muscles in his back ripple as he stirs something and moves along with the music.

When he finally turns and notices me, he jumps and clutches his chest. "Fuck, Nora," he says, breathless.

I can't help the ruthless smile. "Didn't want to disturb your hard work."

He watches my mouth and drops his hand. His gaze narrows. "Or you wanted to enjoy the view for a little while longer."

I roll my eyes. "Why would I have to sneak a peek when you willingly flaunt yourself every second of every day?" He gapes at me, and I laugh. "Two can play this game, Mr. Mills."

He shakes his head, putting down the spoon that appears to be covered in tomato sauce. "Once again, you surprise me, Miss Riley."

Shrugging, I pop another blueberry in my mouth. I go to jump off the counter, but he stops me.

"How's the arm?" he asks, serious now.

"Fine."

He walks to the island, picks up a small tin, and hands it to me. "My grandmother makes it. Helps with healing."

Staring at the container, I twist the lid off. The smell hits me—honey and beeswax and flowers. It's divine.

"Let me help you," he says, reaching for my arm.

I must be in some sort of shock because I do without objection. He pulls my arm out of my sleeve, careful not to expose my chest. Unwrapping the gauze bandage, he dips his long fingers in the balm. The smell of it grows more intense, and I subconsciously inhale deeper. Owen pauses at the sound of my breath.

I halt breathing altogether.

He waits only a moment before carefully applying the balm. I'm surprised at the softness of it. It's soothing, and I almost groan in relief.

He carefully wraps my arm with a clean bandage and helps me pull my arm back through the oversized sleeve of his shirt.

When he's done, he looks at me. I meet his gaze and suddenly realize how close he is. He's pressed against the counter between my legs, and somehow, even sitting on the counter, I still find myself angling my head upward to meet his eyes.

He doesn't move, and I don't make him. I know he'd move away if I asked. I know I *should* tell him to move away, but I find my lips can't form the words.

"I'm sorry," he whispers.

I swallow. "For what?"

"For getting you into this mess. I never wanted to put anyone in danger, least of all you."

"I'm not the one in danger, Mr. Mills. You are. I just happened to save your ass, and I'll likely have to do it again. Over and over and over—"

He cuts me off by placing a finger on my lips, and I freeze. His finger feels rough against my skin, and it makes me shiver.

He doesn't move his finger as he smirks. "I have no doubt, Miss Riley, but regardless, I am truly sorry and understand if you want to resign."

He drops his hand, his face turning serious now.

I cock my head to the side and regard him. "And miss all the fun?"

A hint of a smile turns his lips up as he finally takes a step back. "You'll be the death of me."

He has no idea.

Jumping down from the counter, I grab the spoon next to the stove. I dip it into the tomato sauce and blow on it before popping it in my mouth.

Owen watches me with curiosity, raising a brow when I turn and face him.

"This is really good," I mumble, taking another spoonful.

He smiles, the dimple returning. "Of course it is."

Rolling my eyes, I make my way to the couch, letting him finish dinner.

I stare out the window, knowing I should call Declan. Knowing I need help. Knowing I'm stupidly falling for this guy. But somehow I can't get myself to pick up the phone.

Chapter 17

"This place only has two bedrooms. I'll let you have the master. I'm used to sleeping in my childhood room anyway," Owen explains after a delicious dinner of homemade pizza and salad.

"You actually fit in that thing?" I ask him as I stare at a twin bed that doesn't even look like it'd fit me.

He chuckles. "I'll survive. Your room is across the hall." He motions to a closed door behind me, and I open it to find a large, king bed pushed up against the far wall.

Massive French doors open to a wide porch and the forest beyond. The room has its own fireplace, and the comforter is so large and fluffy that it looks like it'd swallow me.

"Are you cold? Do you want me to light a fire?" he asks.

"I'm fine. Really."

He runs a hand through his hair, once again looking a bit flustered. I almost laugh, and he catches my smirk.

"Well, goodnight then."

"Goodnight."

He nods, shutting the door behind him.

I fall onto the bed and stare at the wooden ceiling, deciding whether I should call Declan tonight. But before I can decide, I'm fast asleep.

We're at my dad's shop in downtown Oakland. His hometown. When he's not on the road with his Formula 1 team, he's here fixing all types of cars. I spend most afternoons after school helping him out. Everyone knows him, and several people pop in to chat. I sit on a tall counter, and my teenage, spindly legs hang over the side while I quickly finish my school assignment so I can help my father with a Ferrari that just came into the shop.

My father clicks the garage opener, and the door slowly squeaks until it's fully open.

"Much better," he mumbles.

The sound of the busy streets fills the space as he lifts the bright red car.

Intending to help, I slam my book shut—

Screaming and gunshots come without warning, and my father's voice shouts at me to run. But I can't. I'm frozen, unable to turn away.

I catch my father's eye and see panic. I run toward him as a bullet passes straight through his head. He lurches forward. I reach out to catch him, and we both fall to the ground.

I'm still in the dream, screaming. Or am I doing so in real life? I can't tell. All I know is that a few seconds later, everything calms down, and my brain goes blank. The darkness consumes me.

I welcome it.

There is light as I wake to the feeling of warmth against my body.

That can't be right.

I jerk awake to find a person wrapped around my waist.

In my half-asleep state, I don't think. I react. My fist swings around and lands on the person's nose. A startled yelp, and the arm instantly disappears from my waist, freeing me.

I spin, ready to attack again, when Owen's voice fills the space. "It's me! It's me!"

Oh fuck.

My brain's awake now, and adrenaline courses through my blood.

I sit up on my knees. "Shit, I'm so sorry, Owen. I didn't…" I reach for his face and finally register the blood. "Fuck. I'll get you something to clean that up."

Jumping off the bed, I race to the bathroom, grabbing a dry towel and wetting another one. I run back to the room to find him sitting up, his head bent back against the headboard. He's holding his nose.

"Let me see it," I say, pulling his hand away.

There's blood coming out, but it's already slowed. I wipe his face and place the cloth against his nose. "Hold it there. I'll grab some ice." I face the door.

"Damn, do you do that to all your boyfriends?" Strangely, he doesn't sound mad. He sounds curious.

I turn back to find him looking at me out of the corner of his eye.

"I don't have any boyfriends. Haven't in a long time. Perhaps that's why I was startled." I have no idea why I would admit that to him. But here we are.

He straightens his head, still holding the cloth to his nose. I can't and don't want even to begin to unpack the look he's giving me.

"Why were you in my bed?" I ask, carefully sitting next to his legs.

"You were screaming in the middle of the night, and I thought something was wrong. I came in to find you thrashing around and covered in sweat, but you were still asleep. I tried to wake you, but I couldn't. So, I wiped your face with a cool cloth and yanked off the blankets. You calmed after that, and when I went to leave, you rolled over and wrapped your arm around my waist. You seemed so at peace…" He trails off for a moment, angling his head toward the ceiling again. "I didn't want to disturb you, so I...stayed."

I blink at him. I don't know how to process all of that.

"Serves me right." He laughs.

I finally look around and realize the sun is already up.

"What time is it?" I ask.

"It's around seven, I think."

My heart practically stops dead. I can't remember the last time I slept until seven.

"We're late," I stutter, because I'm pretty sure I'm in shock.

"You do realize I'm the boss, right?" That familiar arrogance is back in his voice. I ignore it.

"Why didn't you wake me this morning?" I ask instead.

He doesn't say anything right away and looks as though he's trying to figure me out. What he doesn't realize is that I'm trying to do the same. I'm so confused and ungrounded, and everything I thought I knew seems to be going to shit right now.

"I didn't wake you because I was asleep, too. Best sleep I've had in a while, actually. But I could do without that alarm clock of yours." He smirks, and now that the blood's stopped, swelling and bruising inch their way to his green eyes.

He catches me staring. "Finally got a chance to ruin my beautiful face, haven't you?"

I squeeze my eyes shut and drop my head into my hands. "That's not what I had in mind when I imagined it."

Owen laughs, and it surprises me so much that I drop my hands and look at him.

"So you have thought about it?" he asks.

I scoff. "Of course I have. But that was..." I trail off for a moment and look away. "Not what I wanted. I'm sorry."

He surprises me by grabbing my hand. "What do you dream about that makes you scream like that?"

Looking down at his hand covering mine, I can't help but feel small compared to him. What terrifies me the most, though, is that I don't mind it. I feel safe with him. Which doesn't make any fucking sense because he's probably a murderer.

"My father's death. It's on repeat in my dreams. I've struggled with them for fifteen years, but they've gotten worse lately." I still can't understand why I'm telling him so many truths, but in this moment, I realize that I don't care. I *want* to tell him. I want someone to know me. I want *him* to know me. And I'm utterly terrified of that realization.

"Fifteen years is a long time to carry that burden," he whispers, still holding onto my hand.

My eyes suddenly fill with tears that I somehow hold back. Fifteen years *is* a damn long time.

I pull my hand from his and crawl over his lap. His eyes widen when I wrap my arms around his neck and hug him. "Thank you," I whisper, unable to say more than that. Unable to express everything I'm feeling and thinking.

His arms hesitantly wrap around my waist, but when I don't object, he squeezes me tight and takes a deep breath.

I finally allow myself to breathe, too, and we both stay that way for a long time.

The drive to the office is silent, if not awkward. I spend the time rescheduling some of Owen's first meetings since he won't make them. We don't speak, though his attention volleys between the road and me.

Owen drops me off at my apartment and waits for me in the car. I rush up and throw on my standard black suit and heels and race back.

"I've been thinking," I finally say as we make our way the five blocks to the office. "You should borrow someone else's car for a while. This thing is too easy to spot and track."

Owen only nods and doesn't say a word.

We make it to the office, silence still hovering over us. I don't know what to say to him, and he doesn't know what to say to me, apparently. He leaves me there to attend a meeting, and I rush to my desk, eager to hire the necessary security to protect him. It doesn't take me long. I know far more about private security than any normal person should. In fact, the guy I call is the best. He's a former CIA field agent. Most importantly, I trust him with my life.

"Listen, Noah, I need you to pretend you don't know me. Can you do that?"

Noah laughs on the other end of the phone. "Got yourself in a little too deep there, Nova?"

"I'm on assignment and don't want my target getting murdered before I complete it, understand?"

All of that is the truth, but I don't say anything else about it, and I know Noah understands why I can't.

"Understood. As long as I'm getting paid, I couldn't care less what mess you're getting into." I hear the delight in his voice. Noah loves drama and violence far more than any normal person should. He was a reckless agent, but he's a hell of a security guard.

"Thanks, Noah. I'll see you later today to meet with the boss?"

"I'll be there with my team."

"I owe you."

Noah chuckles on the other end. "A date, perhaps?"

I groan. "Not a chance."

Noah barks out a laugh. "It was worth a shot."

I hang up the phone, somewhat relieved that there will be more eyes around that I trust. Now the question is, how much do I tell Declan?

I stare at my phone, at Declan's personal cell phone number on the screen. My fingers shake when I press the call button. I slowly raise the phone to my ear and wait for his voice to pierce the silence.

"About time. I was getting worried you fell off the face of the Earth." His teasing voice relaxes me a bit.

"I'm sorry, Dec. I got into a bit of trouble yesterday and had no way to contact you until today."

"What happened?" His voice is serious now.

I take a deep breath. "This is more complicated than we thought. There are more parties involved. I believe that the companies Owen acquired had some crime going on."

I wait for Declan to say something, but when he doesn't, I continue, "When he acquired them, the money was cut off to these crime groups, and now they're after Owen."

"You have evidence?"

"One witness who used to work for one of the companies."

"How do you know they're after Owen?"

"Because we almost got shot yesterday."

"What?" he roars.

"Someone was trailing him on a hike yesterday morning. They had a gun."

"Wait, wait!" Dec shouts, and I snap my mouth shut. "You were on a hike with him? Alone?"

Shit.

"Yes."

"That's not in your job description," he says carefully.

"I know, but he asked. I didn't want to say no." I cringe, knowing there is far more to the story than I'm telling him and hoping he can't see right through me.

I hear Declan take a long breath. "I'm putting Gray in there with you."

I go to object, but he cuts me off. "No, Nova. I'm giving you a backup. No arguing. This got way more complicated than I expected, and I won't have you getting killed because some idiot got himself involved in something that was way over his head."

I tense, wanting to defend Owen, but I know that will only make things worse.

"I'll post Gray at the coffee shop in the lobby," Declan continues. "He can monitor everyone coming and going and pick up on any gossip."

"Fine."

"Nova, I don't know what's going on with you, and I've given you space and time hoping you'd come back to yourself at some point, but..." He trails off for a moment. "You're getting sloppy. I thought the mess with the trial would make you more careful." He stops and breathes deeply. "Do I need to pull you out?"

"No," I say way too quickly. "I won't fail you. I'll be more careful."

Declan sighs. "You are the best, Nova. I can't imagine this job without you, but I don't know how to help you. I don't know how to get that trial dropped. I know a win on this assignment will help, but now I'm not so confident."

He's right. This assignment could save me. But is it worth damning someone else to save my own skin?

Chapter 18

"Can we get to the security plan, please?" I beg Noah and Owen, who stand facing each other and look as though they might throw punches.

Noah finally breaks his stare and turns to me with a wicked smile. "Of course, love."

I swear Owen flinches, but I ignore him. "You'll have someone assigned to Owen at all times, correct?"

"Yes. A personal guard will shadow him. I will have another guard stationed at the front entrance and the entrance to his office. The last guard will be wherever he's needed."

I nod. That's better than I expected. I turn to Owen, who still looks furious. "Is that ok?"

When he looks at me, his gaze softens a bit. "What about you?"

"What about me?"

"No security for you?"

I almost laugh. "They aren't after me."

"They might be now."

Noah raises a brow. I didn't tell him I was involved in the run-in yesterday.

I shake my head. "As I said before, I can take care of myself."

Owen glares at me, but Noah chimes in. "I'd be happy to watch over you, Miss Riley."

I want to wipe the smirk off his face but hold back. Once again, Owen looks as though he wants to punch Noah. I don't blame him this time.

I grit my teeth. "No, thank you, Noah. I am perfectly fine on my own."

Noah winks at me conspiratorially, but Owen doesn't understand the meaning behind it and only takes it as more flirtation. Not that it isn't, but he doesn't know Noah like I do.

"Is that all?" I ask Noah, trying to push him out the door.

"As long as the plan is satisfactory?" He addresses the question to Owen. Owen clenches his teeth but nods.

"Excellent. We'll have the contract drawn up, and the security team will be in place first thing tomorrow."

"Great. Thanks," I say, now physically pushing him out the door.

Noah turns at the last minute and bends to whisper in my ear. "That one has it bad. I'm pretty sure he wants to kill me."

"You didn't make it easy for him," I reply through clenched teeth.

He chuckles. "See you tomorrow, love."

Noah finally turns and walks away. I shut the door and turn to find Owen watching me. I swear there is fire in his eyes.

"Relax. Noah is harmless."

"You know him?"

"Yes. He worked security at some of the Formula 1 races."

Oddly enough, that isn't a lie. He did work security for Formula 1 before his brief stint with the CIA.

Owen nods and returns to his desk. His silence since this morning has me worried and slightly annoyed. It puts me on edge, and by the time 5 pm comes around and he's still silent, I'm practically sprinting out of the office.

"Miss Riley," he says before I reach the door. His voice is low and gruff.

Turning slowly, I find him leaning against his desk, arms crossed.

"I'd feel better if you weren't alone tonight. Not until security is in place."

"I'll be fine. I'm meeting Jax. He'll make sure I get home safe."

He studies me for far longer than is comfortable. I shift on my feet.

"Fine," he snips.

I want to comment on his shortness. I want to comment on his mood. I want to know what the hell happened since this morning, but I say nothing. Instead, I leave, and a crawling feeling slithers down my spine.

The smile Jax gives me when I enter the bar instantly has the tension melting away, and when he wraps me in a hug, I melt in seconds, letting out a long breath.

He pulls back and looks at me. "Something's happened."

Slumping as if those two simple words took an invisible weight from my shoulders, I take off my coat and sit next to him at the bar.

He doesn't join me right away, waiting for an answer.

"Just work," I reply.

He tilts his head to the side, giving me a knowing smile.

"Work isn't what I expected," I continue.

Jax actually snorts and sits down. "Such as you didn't mean to fall for your boss?"

I scoff. "That's not what I mean at all, actually."

Jax laughs and orders us both a glass of wine. We take a few sips before he speaks again. "I know you probably can't say much about work, but I'm here if you need me. Always."

Reaching over, I take his hand, giving it a slight squeeze. "Thank you. Some complications have me questioning pretty much my whole life."

"Existential crisis?" His eyes flash with amusement.

I nod miserably. "What would you do if you were faced with an impossible decision?"

Jax cocks his head to the side. "You'll have to give me more information than that."

I don't know how to ask without revealing too much, but I desperately need a friend right now. "My heart and head are at war. The line between right and wrong seems to be completely gone, and I have no idea what to do about it."

I don't mean for the tears to come, but they rush to the surface and threaten to fall, stinging my eyes.

Jax squeezes my hand. "I may not be the best person to ask, but I've always found that following my heart has never led me astray."

I stare at him for a long moment. "And if that decision leads to your own downfall?"

He laughs. "Then you have to ask yourself if it's worth the fall."

I don't know how to reply, so I take another sip of wine and wipe at my teary eyes.

"I know I don't know anything about your situation, but I do know you." My gaze snaps to his as he continues, "I know that you have *always* fought for what was right and for those who couldn't fight for themselves. But when have you ever fought for yourself?"

I blink, a tear finally escaping down my cheek. Jax reaches out and wipes it away with his thumb and cups my cheek with his hand. "I love you, Nova. You've been through hell and back, and I think you deserve a little peace. A little happiness."

I clear my throat, my voice shaky. "Even if that happiness is so brief it feels like a blink in a whole lifetime?"

Jax nods. "Even so."

I try to laugh, but it comes out a bit like a sob. "You've always been a softy."

Jax smiles. "And you've always been the tough one."

I'm not so sure I want to be the tough one anymore.

Jax watches me for a few moments, and I take another sip. "If this is about Owen, I want you to know that Evan and I both think he's a really great guy."

"He is." And I mean it. The only problem is, I don't know how to come to terms with the murders he's accused of. Even if I could live with it, how would I even begin to get him out of it?

Jax and I drop the subject, and the night turns into laughs instead of tears. The tension around my heart, that I didn't realize was there, slowly melts. I lay in bed that night and hope that means I'll have a peaceful sleep.

I drift in and out of consciousness. I hear Gray on the phone, somewhere to the left of me. It's pitch black, and I have no idea where we are, but his voice reassures me that I'll be fine.

"She's alive. She'll likely survive."

"We're in a safe location. CIA will be here in a few hours."

My brain registers his words, but I can't seem to stay awake, and I drift off, his voice getting lost in the dark....

I wake with a start and vaguely remember that conversation, but it's still fuzzy. At least the dream wasn't a nightmare, though my body is acting like it was. I'm drenched in sweat as I reach for the lamp and switch on the light.

I sit up, instinctively grabbing my phone.

4 am. Again.

I groan.

There are a few text messages from Owen, and my fingers pause and hover over the notification. I'm afraid to open it, and I don't know why.

I close my eyes for a moment before pressing on the message.

Owen: *You still coming in before work?*

Owen: *I feel like I may have scared you off yesterday.*

Owen: *You don't have to come early. I just wanted you to know that you can if you want to.*

Owen: *I'm sorry.*

I sigh and type back.

Nova: *I'll be there.*

I pause. Not sure it's a good idea anymore.

I hit send.

In the shower, I let my thoughts and feelings wash down the drain. But the shower doesn't really solve anything.

Entering, I'm instantly assaulted by the scent of alcohol. My eyes snap to the bar that's covered in open bottles of all kinds. A half full glass sits precariously on the edge of the counter.

Owen gazes at me and grimaces when my eyes meet his.

"I hope for your sake, there isn't a naked woman in the bathroom," I growl, throwing my bag on my desk chair.

"No. Just me."

The bar has only one used glass, so I know he's telling the truth.

"You could have gone out with Jax and me. You didn't need to drink alone," I say, still angrier than I should be. He's a grown ass man. If he wants to drink alone, then why would I care? And yet, I do.

"You needed your friend," he says.

Though he's right, I still feel like his drinking is somehow my fault. If I'd been here, he wouldn't have done it.

I shake my head to clear my thoughts. I know it's not my fault. "Can you even stay on your feet?"

He nods. "I didn't drink as much as you think I did. I'm not drunk."

I narrow my eyes, assessing him. His eye is now officially black, but all that does is bring out the green more. He is dressed as he usually is in the morning—jogger sweats and no shirt, and he's standing without assistance and not swaying.

Taking a few steps closer to him, I tilt my head to look into his eyes. His mouth twitches up, revealing the dimple, when he realizes what I'm doing.

I step back once I'm satisfied. "Your eyes aren't dilated, and you barely smell of alcohol, so I guess I believe you."

He laughs but steps aside and motions for the gym floor.

I wrap my knuckles and remove my sweatshirt, acutely aware of his eyes as they land on my wound.

"It's fine," I snap before he has a chance to ask. "I can barely feel it."

"It looks angry."

I look up from the task of wrapping my knuckles to meet his eyes. "Have you seen your face?"

Owen laughs, and I find myself smiling despite the pit in my stomach.

"There she is," he says.

My smile fades. I have no idea what to make of that.

"Let's go," I say, raising my fists to frame my face.

Owen nods and does the same.

We spend the next fifteen minutes sharing hits. He's getting better, but he's still not good enough.

"Fuck, Owen! Protect your left side. You have a terrible habit of exposing it after a right hook."

Owen steps back and drops his hands. "Excuse me, Miss Perfect. Didn't realize this was so serious."

My anger rises. "It wasn't until you went and did something that almost got you killed!"

Owen's eyes widen. "How is this my fault?"

"I don't know! How about you tell me because I know for damn sure that there is more you're hiding."

Owen stalks toward me, and I instinctively retreat, my back smashing against the mirrored wall behind me.

He slams both hands on the glass by my head, but I don't flinch. I know he won't hurt me.

"And what about you, Miss Riley? How about you tell me why your friends call you Nova and not Nora?" His voice is a low growl that has goosebumps rising all over my body.

Fuck.

"Nova is my given name. I changed it recently." Not exactly a lie.

He narrows his gaze. "Why?"

"Does it matter?" I ask, exasperated. "It's just a name."

"It's not just a name, and you know it," he says, leaning closer. The whisper of his breath skates over my lips. I shiver against the wall.

Somehow, I know what he means. It isn't just a name. It's the truth of who I really am. A lie I told him to weasel my way into his life. To manipulate him. To take him away from this life and lock him up until his bones turn to ash.

"Nova. Call me Nova." I whisper because, truth is, I want him to call me by my real name, even if I can't give him the reason why I lied. Even if, in the end, I'll never hear it spoken from his lips again.

Owen closes his eyes, and I don't know if he's angry.

When he opens them, it's not rage glinting in them. It's something that scares me even more. Something dark and promising. Something I refuse to name.

"Owen." It comes out breathy and shaky, and I have the urge to either run or pull him closer. My hands tremble with indecision.

Owen's eyes drop to them as if he knows my struggle and is battling the same urges. When his gaze shifts back to my face, they linger on my lips.

He leans closer. So close, I'm pretty sure he can hear my racing heart, and that urge to run disappears.

"Nova," he whispers, low and deep, as if my name is something sacred.

That name. My name. My *real* name.

Something snaps in both of us, and the wall I've put up comes crashing down. His mouth collides with mine.

It only takes a moment, a single sharp breath before I open my lips and his tongue sweeps in, devouring me.

Perhaps it's been too long since I've been properly kissed. Perhaps it's that I've never quite let myself feel much for the people I've kissed. But nothing compares to this one. Nothing compares to the hungry way in which he consumes me or how right it feels despite everything.

If this is how a kiss is supposed to feel, then I never want it to end.

I let out an unintentional moan as my hands reach for him, wanting to fuse our bodies. He releases his hands from the mirror, and they are instantly on me, traveling from my hip to my waist, pulling me even closer.

His responding groan, and his hard body against mine, make me lose myself. All thoughts fall away, and I welcome it. For the first time in a very long time, I simply don't give a fuck. There is only him.

Until the sound of the door opening has my eyes flying open.

Owen immediately releases me, taking two large steps back. His eyes widen, and his breath comes in shallow bursts.

I have no doubt I look the same, but I school my face into one of neutral disinterest and force my breathing to slow.

My head turns toward the door, Owen following my lead, as Parker walks in and freezes, taking in the two of us.

A broad smile spreads across his face, revealing his identical dimple. It comes out more often with Parker than Owen. A thought that leaves me feeling oddly sad.

"Am I interrupting?" he asks innocently.

Owen finally snaps out of it, walking toward his brother. "You know you are, but we were only sparring."

Parker's eyes shoot to me and back to Owen. "Well, if that's all you were doing, I sure hope she kicked your ass. Given your eye, I feel like I may have already missed it." He says the last part with a disappointed pout.

"What are you doing here so early, and what do you want?" Owen barks.

"I could ask you the same question, big brother?" Parker shoots back with a mischievous grin.

"You know I'm always here."

"Sure, but that's usually with a naked woman and cocktails. She's your assistant, and she's fully clothed."

I can't quite gauge what he's trying to get at, so I quickly grab my sweatshirt and throw it over my head before Parker notices my arm or shoulder. That's a whole other conversation I don't want to get into.

Parker looks at me as if he already knows what happened, even if he didn't see anything.

"What's your point, *little* brother?" Owen seethes.

"No point. Just came in to tell you your new security is here." He says it so casually that I almost laugh.

"And you're the messenger because?"

"Because I'm the only one here this early besides the two of you, dumbass. They were hanging around the entrance waiting to be let in."

"Shit," Owen mumbles before racing to his desk and picking up his phone. "Missed messages from Noah."

Parker shakes his head. "Losing your grip, *big* brother."

Owen flips him off and puts the phone to his ear. I chuckle, walking back to my desk. I'm too grateful for the interruption. I'm not sure I'd have been able to stop Owen on my own. I don't think I'd have wanted to.

Parker saunters over to me while Owen says a few words to Noah. He plops on the edge of my desk and looks at me with mirth in his blue eyes.

"Yes?" I ask, though I'm not sure I want to hear what he has to say.

Parker crosses his arms and looks at his brother for a moment. "I'm doubting it was on your job description to come here before sunrise, so why are you here exactly?"

"I don't sleep well, and he doesn't sleep well. We both work out, and this office is far closer to my apartment than the gym. That's it."

He nods his head, but his mischievous grin is still plastered on his face. "Right. So, my brother gave up his one-night flings to work out with you instead?"

I shrug. "Perhaps he kicks them out before I get here. It's none of my business." Parker smirks at my response, which only fuels my fire. "You'd be better off being direct. I don't like to play games, Mr. Mills."

Parker chuckles. "I have no intention of playing games, Miss Riley, especially since I don't want to end up with an eye that looks like my brother's. How, again, did that happen?"

I roll my eyes, desperately wanting this conversation to end. "He startled me, and I instinctively threw a punch."

Parker laughs this time, earning his brother's attention. "Oh, how I would have died to have seen it."

I stand up from my chair, intending to go to the bathroom to shower. "I'll be done in ten minutes and perhaps we can have our scheduled meeting a little early? Discuss charity donations and get it out of the way?"

He nods, still smiling. "It'd be my pleasure, Miss Riley."

I roll my eyes again and shut the bathroom door. It sounds like a hammer dropping. One that may crush me.

Chapter 19

"I have a rather odd question if you don't mind me asking?" I say to Parker after our meeting. He's sitting in a chair in front of my desk that he dragged from his brother's. His feet are propped on my desk, and his arms are tucked behind his head. He looks more like an unruly teenager than a businessman. However, it makes sense, given what I've been told about him. He grew up with his mom, away from the business world. He also got into modeling early, so I doubt he even has more than a high school degree.

"Not at all." A bemused smirk graces his lips.

"Has Owen legally signed over all control of these charities to you?"

Parker cocks his head and doesn't say anything right away. I fiddle with my thumbs, hoping I didn't say too much or step over some boundary.

"We're in the process," he answers. "Why do you ask?"

"Just curious. Seems I'll be your assistant once that's all said and done."

Parker smiles when he realizes it's probably true, even though I'll be long gone by then.

"When do you sign the papers?" I ask, trying to sound as though these questions are innocent.

"Sometime next month. You eager to escape my brother, Miss Riley?"

"You seem far too confident in my impression of you, Mr. Mills."

Parker laughs, and I can't help but love the sound of it. "You didn't answer my question, Miss Riley."

"I am neither eager to leave nor eager to stay."

Parker snorts. "That's a non-answer if I've ever heard one."

I shrug.

We're interrupted by Owen and Noah, who both come barreling through the doorway and look as though they want to kill each other.

Standing, my eyes dart between them. "What the hell happened?" I ask. It's only been an hour, and they are already fighting with each other.

"Mr. Mills here has the impression that he can still do whatever the fuck he pleases without the protection of his security."

I raise a brow at Owen, who shakes his head but doesn't offer any sort of explanation.

"We detected some unusual activity across the street from the office. My men are investigating, but Mr. Mills here thought it would be a great time to slip out the front door and—what?" He turns and addresses the question to Owen. "Get a *better* pastry from the coffee shop down the street?"

This time I laugh, and all three men shift their attention to me, which only makes me laugh harder.

"I'm sorry," I choke out, wiping away the moisture from my eyes. "That is just—"

"The pastry was for her," Owen grumbles. "I couldn't care less about the goddamn pastry."

"Oh, so this is my fault?" I practically shout across the room.

"I didn't say that." He grinds his teeth.

I take a deep breath. "Thank you, Noah. I'll keep him here. Inform us of what you find."

Noah nods and smirks at me before turning to leave.

Once the door shuts, Owen takes the pastry bag and flings it at me. It hits my chest and I fumble with the bag before catching it.

"Asshole," I mumble, but I already have my hand in the bag, pulling out the best chocolate croissant in the entire United States. I take a bite and practically moan at the taste.

Owen and Parker watch me with amused curiosity. I flip them both off but mumble "thank you" to Owen.

He nods and falls into his office chair.

"You know, there are assistants to get you pastries, Mr. Mills. You didn't need to go yourself," I say.

He eyes me over his computer screen. "I wanted to."

Parker finally stands. "I'm sure you don't want my opinion—"

Owen cuts him off. "We don't."

Parker chuckles and walks to the door, stopping before it. "Owen, don't be a dick and just tell the girl what's really going on, will you?" He doesn't give Owen a chance to respond before he's out the door.

I whip my head in Owen's direction and hear him sigh. He stands and makes his way over to my desk.

I ungracefully choke down another bite of my pastry, my curiosity piqued.

"It's not what you think," he says, watching my mouth as I swallow.

"And what am I thinking, Mr. Mills?"

"That I'm some sort of criminal."

Oh shit. "Why would I think that?"

"Because every multi-billion-dollar company is committing at least one crime. More like fifty, though."

I raise a brow. Owen appears nervous, his hands stuffed in the pockets of his sweats. Small motions indicate he's fiddling with something in them.

"Another reason my father hates me. I'm trying to weed out the nefarious activity," he continues.

"Why is that something you needed to keep from me?"

"Because it has created more enemies than I can count. This security team should have been in place a long time ago. I put you in danger. I can't stop thinking about that. My mistake almost killed you."

He's right. This also puts other players on the board, increasing the number of people who may be after him. Too many leads to follow. Too many players in the game. Too many villains.

Instinctively, I reach out and pull his hand from his pocket. He startles and looks down.

"What's done is done. Perhaps it was the motivation to do what was needed," I say.

His green eyes raise and meet mine, and guilt shadows them. "I don't think I want you working for me anymore."

The statement is so unexpected that I yank my hand free.

"You can't mean that." There's a slight wobble to my voice now. A tremor I didn't expect. A tremor that shouldn't be there. Not if I was doing my job correctly.

He shakes his head. "I can't have you be a part of this."

If only he knew how much I already was.

"I thought maybe I could keep this all from you. That I'd have you do admin work, plan the gala. But, but..." He trails off, and I desperately want to pry the words from his beautiful lips. "I need you away from all this. I won't put you in danger anymore."

His words sting more than I want them to. I know him, though. Don't I? This is his fear speaking. His fear for me. His need to protect that which is precious to him. Just as he's trying to protect his brother and the charities.

Have I become that important to him?

I still don't have the evidence I need, but somehow that isn't why I'm upset. Maybe I don't want to admit it to myself, but now that I'm being forced out, perhaps it's time I face it.

He's not the villain. He's not who I'm after. Not anymore.

What's worse is that Ella's right. I am falling for him. I *have* already fallen.

"I'll resign if you want me to, but at least let me finish the gala. You owe me that much," I barely get the words out.

He doesn't say anything for so long, I fear he won't say anything at all. "Until the gala. But I'm assigning you private security until it's over."

I nod, not wanting to fight him on it.

His eyes dart to the pastry bag sitting under my left hand. "You going to finish that?" he asks with a half-smile.

I cock my head to the side. "Why? You want the rest?"

"Only if you don't want it."

I snort. "You're impossible. You're giving me whiplash. One second you're getting me a pastry, then you're firing me, then you're asking to eat the rest of said pastry."

Owen looks at me thoughtfully, and the corner of his mouth kicks up. I can't help but stare. "It's you, Miss Riley, who is throwing me off my game."

"Yes, it's all my fault." I roll my eyes, aiming to stuff the rest of the pastry into my mouth when he swipes it from me. It instantly disappears behind his lips as he jumps up from the corner of my desk and steps back. He dramatically chews and audibly swallows.

"I'm going to kill you." I stand up.

Owen races for the door. "You can later. I'm late."

He laughs and hurries to his next meeting, not giving me a chance to protest or try to catch him.

Chapter 20

We spend the rest of the week focused mainly on work. The last-minute gala prep has me scrambling to complete my tasks. Owen and I barely see each other, his meetings keeping him away as well.

Our early morning sparring sessions are nothing more than that, though they are the only thing keeping us both sane. Owen doesn't try to kiss me again. He barely touches me, only hitting me when needed during our gym sessions. I can't tell if I'm grateful or angry about it. Neither of us has mentioned what happened, and suddenly I'm questioning the whole thing.

Gray and Noah both come up empty-handed on information regarding who is targeting Owen, which doesn't help my frustration. We're getting no closer to finding out what is going on, or to finding the evidence I'm supposed to be searching for. Declan has been nothing but persistent about it every night. I keep deflecting, but I don't know how much longer I will be able to.

My dreams are becoming more vivid but no less confusing. I wake every morning drenched in sweat and shaking from head to toe. The whole incident was a setup, that much is clear. But a setup for who? Was it specifically to attack someone at the market? Me? Someone else? Was it a drug deal gone wrong? Or was it a decoy? A way to keep eyes off of what was really going on?

The latter keeps my brain occupied for hours. There were at least twenty shooters stationed throughout the market. They waited until my target got almost all the way out before they started shooting. The bullets were aimed mainly in my direction.

What was around me? I can't quite seem to remember. There was a clothing vendor, a food vendor, and a jewelry vendor. But what was in the building behind them? The building that was also my rendezvous spot and escape route?

"What the fuck, Owen?"

Noell's angry voice pulls me from my thoughts. Owen's CFO marches across the office and slams her hands on his desk.

Owen casually looks up as though this isn't the first time this interaction has occurred.

"You're sinking the company. You lost yet *another* client."

"I'm weeding out the bad ones, Noell. Not that it's any of your business."

"Not my business?"

I flinch.

Owen sighs. "Noell, I informed you of my plans when I took over this company. You knew what I was planning to do. I gave you the option to leave with a considerable sum of money. You declined."

"I didn't realize that when you said you were going to weed out the clients that were less than savory, you were going to weed out *every single one*."

Owen shrugs. "Neither did I, but I won't have this company representing anything but what the name suggests."

Noell grabs a piece of paper, balls it up, and actually throws it at Owen's head.

I stifle a laugh.

Owen has the nerve to smile at her. "I will give you the choice a second time, if you want it. You can leave with the same offer I gave you when my father handed me the company. If you decide to stay, all I ask is that you trust me. The company will lose a significant amount of money, but it won't be permanent. I promise you that."

Noell takes a deep breath. "Owen, I don't know what you're doing. No one does. You keep saying you're turning the company around, making it a better place to work, making it live up to its name. However, I don't see how you can do that without *profit*. You cannot float the staff we have by losing this much money. You either have to let people go, or you need to cut some of your charities."

"No," Owen growls as he stands. "No one touches the charities, and no one loses their job."

Noell shakes her head. "You have one year, Owen, before this company needs to file for bankruptcy. I certainly hope you have a plan."

With that, she turns and stalks out of the room, slamming the door behind her.

She doesn't so much as look at me.

I stare at the door long after she's gone.

Owen's voice pulls me out of my stupor. "It's 5 pm on a Friday, Miss Riley. Shouldn't you be heading home?"

I glance at him, wondering if he'll say anything about what happened, but when he only looks at me, I answer, "I'm almost done with gala prep, then I'll head home."

We haven't mentioned the gala tomorrow. It is my unofficial last day, and I don't think either of us has wanted to broach the subject. I still haven't told Declan about it, hoping Gray or Noah or I would have found something by now. But as the days ticked by, the knot in my stomach grew. I'm no closer to finding the answers to any of it.

"You bringing a date?" Owen asks, the words suspiciously too calm, and I cannot help but smile.

"Yes," I respond, pretending to type something on my computer.

Before I know it, he's standing in front of my desk, peering down at me.

"Anyone I know?"

"Not that it's any of your business, but I'm taking Jax."

Owen visibly relaxes, and I almost laugh.

"Tell him to bring Evan, too. I'll put him on the list."

"You mean, you'll have *me* put him on the list?"

"Right."

I roll my eyes and stand, still staring up into his green eyes. "And your date, Mr. Mills? It says 'plus one' here."

Owen looks away and runs a hand through his black hair. "Evan can be my date."

An unexpected laugh escapes me. "He'll be thrilled when I tell him."

This time, Owen rolls his eyes. "I like him. He'd be an excellent date."

"No doubt, Mr. Mills. You will certainly turn heads with Evan on your arm."

Owen nods. "You can take my guest off the list. Add Evan to yours."

"If you're sure?"

"I'm sure. Then go home, Miss Riley. The gala will be great. Everything's been set up." He throws a bag over his shoulder and heads for the door.

"You're actually going home?" I ask, curiosity getting the better of me.

Owen turns and faces me with a smile. "Contrary to what you might believe, I do actually love my home."

"I never said you didn't. You usually go out on Fridays."

Owen shrugs. "People can change, Miss Riley."

Then he's gone, his personal security trailing behind him.

Chapter 21

Noah follows me to my apartment, his knowing smirk never leaving his lips.

"What?" I bark as we reach the entrance to my building.

"Does the boss know what you do for a living?"

"Don't ask questions you already know the answer to."

"Fair. Does he know the real thing you've tasked me with?"

That's a much better question, but I'm reluctant to answer. "No."

Noah's smile widens. "Oh, the irony. He hires me to protect you, but you hire me to guard him and save his ass. What a tangled web you find yourself in."

I stop before the door of the building and put my hands on my hips. "I didn't hire you for your opinions, so do you have something actually useful for me?"

Noah chuckles. "Your man seems to have two main groups targeting him. We don't think they're working together, but I can't confirm that."

"Have you caught anyone?"

Noah looks around as people walk by, heading home from work or headed to a bar for happy hour. "We should take this conversation to another location."

"A ploy to get me to invite you up?"

Noah smirks. "Is it working?"

I roll my eyes. "Come on, asshole."

I take out my keycard and let us into the building. We don't say anything until the door closes behind me.

"We haven't caught anyone, but we've intercepted some messages." Noah pauses, and I wave my hand, encouraging him to go on. "Two private assassins have been hired."

"Hired by whom?"

"You know they wouldn't just announce that, Nova."

I huff, frustrated. "When?"

"Tomorrow. The gala."

"But they wouldn't murder him in front of everyone."

"Maybe they plan on poisoning him."

I know Noah is joking. Poison seems like something only kings and queens do on TV shows. But I also know that the three owners of the other companies were murdered that way.

Maybe it wasn't Owen who killed them. Maybe he's the next target on someone's list. But whose list? And why?

"I need you to beef up security," I say. "Can you do that? I need eyes and ears everywhere."

"Already done."

I take a deep breath and pace back and forth.

"Nova?" Noah asks hesitantly. "Who are the bad guys here?"

Isn't that the question of the century?

"Honestly, I don't even know."

"Have you told Dec?"

I nod. Well, I haven't told him everything.

"What does he advise?"

"You know I can't tell you."

"I also know you will."

I sigh. He's right. He's about the only person, aside from Ella and Declan, that I fully trust.

"He wants me to do the job I came here to do."

I know Declan hasn't heard the whole story, but I've never questioned his guidance until now. He's trying to protect me. He's trying to help me win my trial. But at what cost? He knows me better than that. Or he should.

"And you want to lock 'em all up? Every single asshole?" Noah winks as he says it.

"Something like that," I mumble.

"I take it this Owen guy isn't one of the assholes?"

"Honestly?"

Noah nods.

"I don't know."

"Shit."

"Yeah."

"Well, for what it's worth, assholes don't tend to put themselves in danger to get someone their favorite pastry."

I stop pacing and stare at him. I must look shocked because Noah laughs and pats me on the shoulder.

"Get some rest," he says. "I'll take care of the security for tomorrow. Get your CIA team ready. Nothing will happen to your man."

"He's not my man."

Noah laughs and shakes his head. "Sure. Whatever you say. Want to know what I think?"

"No."

Noah ignores me. "I've known you since you were a gangly teenager at the races, and I've never seen you so wound up and protective of any guy. Even the ones you dated."

When I don't respond, Noah gives my shoulder one more pat and closes the door behind him.

He's right. *Damn him*.

"Eagan found the info about the last company, and the whistleblower's testimony lines up. Nova, this company is, or was, in bed with the black snake underground syndicate." Ella speaks like there's a bomb about to go off.

"You're kidding? The largest underground drug operation in the world?" I'm pretty sure my mouth is in my lap. I've been taking out big players in their operation for years. No one has been able to take them out completely.

"Eagan had to dig, but he found anonymous calls, texts, and emails. He traced them to the IP addresses the underground uses."

"Shit. This is bad. Really bad. This has to be who's going after Owen. They are the only ones with the money and resources to risk killing someone as large and influential as Owen."

I run my hands through my hair, my bare feet still pacing back and forth across my apartment. "Human trafficking, rape, and the biggest drug syndicate in the world. None of this was coincidental. Owen must have done it on purpose. He must have killed them."

"But he's smart. He must have known they would go after him?"

"Oh, he knows. And I'm pretty sure he's been preparing for his own death."

"What?" Ella practically shouts into the phone.

"He's slowly signing everything over to his brother. He knows he's not going to be around long. I'd put my money on it."

"What are you going to do?"

"Stop the bastards trying to kill him, then take them all down."

"The whole underground operation?"

"Yes. It's about damn time someone does."

"What about Owen?"

"What about him?"

"Are you going to put him behind bars with the rest of them?"

"No. I'm going to save him."

There is a long silence on the other end of the phone.

"But, Nova... Your trial. Your assignment. What will Dec say?" Ella sounds genuinely worried.

"Fuck my trial. Fuck Dec. I'm not going to sit here and let these fuckers get away. Not this time. I refuse to put Owen behind bars, so I'm gonna go down swinging and take them all with me."

I hear Ella suck in a breath. "Nova." Her voice is wavering, and I know she's about to lose her composure.

"Ella, I'm taking you off my communications. If there's another trial, I don't want caught up in it."

"You can't do that!" she shouts on the other end of the phone, and my heart breaks at the desperation in her voice.

"Ella, you have been the best assistant and, more importantly, the friend I never knew I needed. I refuse to take you down with me. I'm going to recommend to Dec that you be promoted so it doesn't look suspicious and so I don't have to fire you."

"Nova, no. I don't want this! I want to help you!"

"You already have. More than you know." This time, I can't help the waver in my own voice as tears fill my eyes. This isn't what I want, but I don't know how else to protect her. Things are going to get worse, and I'm likely going to jail for a very long time. I can't have her, or anyone else I love, go down with me.

This is something I need to do on my own.

I end the call before she can talk me out of it and text Dec.

Nova: *I think you need to promote or reassign Ella. She's fantastic, and I don't want my trial reflecting poorly on her future at the CIA.*

The text bubble pops up instantly but disappears before popping up again.

Dec: *Ok. I won't fight you on that, but I'm not sure I'll be able to find you anyone near as good as she is.*

Nova: *I know. But my mistakes aren't fair to her.*

Dec: *When do you want her reassignment?*

Nova: *Immediately.*

Dec: *Have you told her?*

Nova: *Yes.*

Dec: *Ok, then it's done.*

Nova: *Thank you.*

I stop typing and throw my phone on the bed and tunnel under the covers in my work outfit and let myself cry until I fall asleep.

The screaming—I can't get it out of my head. Everything happens so fast. The jewelry stand is now knocked over, and the colorful trinkets are scattered across the street. I look behind the stand to find a frightened child, but there's nothing I can do to help him.

I glance at the building behind the child, and an open door catches my eye. "Go!" I shout in Italian and point to the door.

The child looks behind him and back at me, shaking his head vigorously.

A series of shots brings me back to my goal: get to the rendezvous spot.

Reluctantly, I leave the child.

I wake drenched in my usual sweat. This time, though, something sparks in my brain—the door in my dream. The boy was more afraid of that door than the bullets flying all around him.

The sign above the door is blurry in my vision, but I recognize the word. *Vivario*—or Vivarium in English. A reptile store.

Chapter 22

My head is pounding from a long night of little sleep and spent emotion.

I don't regret my decision to reassign Ella, but it still hurts. I want to call her, but I know it will only make it worse. I need to give us both time. At least, that's what I tell myself.

"You set up the extra surveillance?" I ask Gray through the phone, stuffing breakfast in my mouth and trying not to think too much about the lack of texts from Owen.

"Yup. All done. I have your comm, and I'll be at the bar. Backup will be right outside."

"Good."

Though I know everyone is prepared, I still can't help the sinking feeling in my gut. It's like I'm missing some significant piece to the puzzle.

"You're covered, Nova. Don't worry. Nothing will slip by me."

"I know. I know. But I have this feeling that something's not quite right. I can't shake it."

"You've always had great instincts, but don't let your trial make you suddenly question yourself."

Is that what I'm doing? Is this assignment going to shit because I don't trust myself? Or is my gut correct in telling me I'm missing something?

I don't voice the questions and thoughts rolling through my head, but I do admit something to Gray, needing to tell someone. Someone has to be on my side. "I haven't told Dec yet, but technically Owen fired me. This is supposed to be my last night."

"Shit, Nova. But you don't have the evidence, do you?"

"No. I'm going to get it tonight, though. I have to."

There's a long silence on the other end.

"Gray?" I ask, concerned.

"You should tell Dec."

Oh. Of course. I should have known he didn't really trust my judgment after what happened in Italy, even if he said the opposite.

"I'm about to call him. Don't worry."

"I trust you, Nova, but I'm concerned about the trial. This assignment has to be by the books."

"I know."

His career is on the line, too, and I feel like shit for what I'm about to do, but hopefully by sinking myself, he can further throw me under the bus and blame me for everything. He doesn't even have to accuse me. It *is* me. All of it is my fault. Hopefully, the judge will see that.

Gray pulls me out of my thoughts. "Niki will be by with your comm later today. I'll see you at the gala."

"Yeah, ok. See you there."

When he hangs up, I slam my fist into the wall next to the fridge. The sheetrock shatters and pain spreads across my knuckles.

I feel the blood—I reopened the scabs on my knuckles, but I can't seem to find the energy to care.

It's so much less than I deserve.

"Red. I'm shocked," Jax says with a smile when I open the door later that evening.

"Don't be a dick," Evan says, pushing past both of us. "You look stunning, Nova. You always do. I hold to my previous opinion. You're definitely the only girl I'd fuck."

Jax feigns surprise. "I'm sure that's meant to be a compliment, but somehow it doesn't sound like one."

I offer a small smile. Evan's comment was one-hundred percent in jest.

Evan waves off Jax and motions for me to spin around so he can get a good look at my dress. Jax is right, though. Red seems to be the only color that I wear other than black. I chose a tight-fitting, satin, red dress with a plunging neckline and a low back. It falls to the floor and has a thigh-high slit on the right side. Aside from the cut, it is relatively simple.

When I make a complete turn, I find Evan scowling at me.

"What? Did I get something on it?" I ask, concerned.

Evan laughs. "No. I was just thinking if you were going for subtle with that dress, you are going to be sorely disappointed." I scrunch my nose, and Evan steps closer to flick it. "You look beautiful, Nova. Unfortunately, you could wear a T-shirt and people would still look at you."

This time, I scowl, and it makes Evan howl with laughter.

"Ignore him. He's just jealous there is someone who looks better than him," Jax whispers in my ear.

"I heard that!" Evan hollers as he heads to the kitchen.

Jax chuckles, pulling me into a hug. "You didn't tell me you fired Ella," he whispers into my hair.

I pull away so I can observe his face. "I didn't fire her. I reassigned her."

Jax studies my face, and I push the emotion deeper into myself.

"She's really upset," he says.

"I know. I am too."

"I don't know much about your career, but I don't want this to ruin your relationship with her."

"I don't either."

"You need to call her."

"I know. I will." Jax gives me a knowing look, and I step back. "I promise. First thing tomorrow."

Jax nods as Evan comes back in with champagne and three glasses. I give him a suspicious look.

"What? I've never been to such a fancy party. It calls for some champagne!" Evan beams as he pours us each a drink.

We clink our flutes, and Evan declares, "To the fiercest woman I know."

"And the only woman you know," Jax adds with a bit of mischief.

Evan glares at Jax but yanks him into a fierce kiss.

"Let's go. The limo is waiting," I say when they finally pull away from each other.

The men both down their champagne in one large sip, and I place my mostly full glass on the counter. With what I might have to do tonight, the alcohol would only hinder my ability.

Evan and Jax don't say a word as we make our way to the limo, but Evan is practically exploding with excitement, and I can't help but soak up some of it myself. Even though this is my last night as Owen's assistant.

And possibly my last night as a CIA agent.

We make it to the Cal Academy of Sciences and wait in a long line of fancy cars unloading their rich guests on a red carpet. There's a wide staircase that leads to many glass doors at the top. Cameras click all around us, trying to get photos of the rich and famous.

All the commotion, bright lights, and fancy people make me feel a little queasy. I may have always stood out and attracted attention, but this has never been my scene.

"We got you," Jax says, likely noticing the look of anxiety on my face.

I nod, still a little anxious despite his reassurance, as the limo comes to a stop by the carpet and the driver gets out to open our door.

Evan and Jax exit first, and each holds out a hand for me. I grab onto them and let them lift me to my feet, snaking my arms through theirs as we walk together down the carpet.

Plastering on a fake smile, we pause for a set of pictures. I cross my fingers that these will be the only photos of the evening.

As we continue at a glacial pace, my anxiety rising again, I look up the stairs to find Owen at the top. He's dressed in a tux that fits him like a second skin, and he's looking at me as if I'm the only one made for him.

Shivering at the way his eyes pierce through me, Jax immediately catches on to my line of sight. He inclines his head in Owen's direction, and Evan winks at him.

"Could you two be more obvious?" I grumble. "I feel like we're at high school prom again."

Jax and Evan both laugh, the sound easing my jitters a bit.

"He's hard not to stare at," Evan comments as we make our way up the stairs. The guests ahead of us stop to chat or take pictures, so our ascent is excruciatingly slow.

"So you've said," I mumble.

"Too bad he only has eyes for *you*," Jax comments.

"Shut it. Both of you," I whisper at them. Only two groups now separate us from Owen.

Evan dramatically pretends to zip his lips, and Jax chuckles, his body vibrating against mine.

I smile despite it all. Somehow, their ridiculousness has calmed the pit in my stomach.

When the final group ahead of us disappears into the building, Owen's voice is deep and low as he addresses me. "How come I'm not surprised you're wearing red?"

"I guess I'm predictable."

"May I?" he asks Jax and Evan, holding out his hand.

The two of them give each other a knowing look before shoving me toward Owen. The next thing I know, my hand is tucked into Owen's elbow, and Jax and Evan are trailing behind us, arms locked and wide grins on their faces.

Owen leans down and whispers in my ear. "You were right."

"About?"

"The venue. It's the perfect spot, and the perfect surprise."

I angle my head toward him and smile at the compliment. He pauses, and his green eyes lock onto my lips, which are painted the color of my dress.

"It is, isn't it?" I don't hide my smugness, and Owen's lips turn up, his dimple making an appearance.

"You know, brother, she's soon to be mine." Paker's voice pulls us away from our silent trance, and Owen's smile turns into a frown.

I'm taken aback for a moment. Owen must not have told Parker about firing me. But why?

"Where's your date?" Owen growls.

"Parker's slept with all the eligible women in the Bay Area, and no woman has come back for seconds." I hadn't seen Noell come up beside us until those words stole everyone's attention. She is dressed in a plain black dress. The only eye-catching part of it is the low neckline that shows off her incredible chest.

Evan and Jax try to hide their chuckles at her comment, and I feign a yawn to cover my mouth.

"Pleasure, as always, Noell," Parker drawls, though his eyes catch on her chest for a brief moment.

She waves him off and continues into the building without another word.

"I hate her," Parker mumbles.

Owen laughs. "Because she's right?"

Parker looks at his brother and flips him off. Owen ignores the gesture, and to my surprise, Parker takes my other arm. I'm now sandwiched between them. I almost miss Owen's eye roll.

"I feel like Nova just upgraded her dates," Evan interrupts far too loudly, but he doesn't sound very disappointed.

Owen's smirk returns at Evan's comment, and Parker glances behind us.

In the chaos of the moment, I forgot to introduce Parker to Jax and Evan. I stop, halting our entire party right outside the doors to the venue.

"Evan and Jax, this is Parker, Owen's brother. Parker, Jax is my oldest friend, and this is his boyfriend Evan, who has no filter, especially after an entire bottle of champagne in the limo."

Evan takes Parker's hand and raises it to kiss his knuckles. Lingering too long.

Parker freezes but does not attempt to pull his hand away. Jax appears amused by Evan's overly enthusiastic greeting.

"Nice to meet you. It should be a crime for there to be two of you," Evan comments, finally releasing Parker's hand.

I shake my head but can't help my grin.

Color rises to Parker's cheeks at the compliment, and Owen claps him on the back, a low chuckle rumbling through his chest.

Parker swats his brother's hand away. "It's a pleasure to meet you both."

"Now that we've all been introduced and properly embarrassed, can we move inside?" I ask them all.

Evan chuckles, but no one objects, and we enter the building.

The party planners I hired outdid themselves. The central atrium, a glass dome located inside the building, is adorned with stunning art and photography that showcases the various charities and their respective work. There is a temporary, wooden dance floor set up, and a string quartet is playing a beautiful melody at the far end of it. They will be replaced by a DJ later in the night. Cocktail tables are set up around the perimeter with long, white tablecloths and vases of native wildflowers in the center.

Beyond the atrium is another glass dome, holding the rainforest exhibit. Large trees reach from floor to ceiling, and tropical plants fill in the spaces between them. I can just make out the fluttering of butterfly wings and hear the calls of the macaws. The rainforest exhibit has always been my favorite, and I make a note to take Owen there sometime tonight.

If I have the chance.

Owen looks around, taking it all in. All three of them do.

Parker is the first to speak. "I'm blown away, Miss Riley. I have no words."

"Thank you, but I can't take all the credit. I gave my ideas, but the party planning team did most of it."

"Stop giving everyone else the credit, Barbie," Evan says.

"Barbie?" Parker asks, and I groan.

"A dumb nickname I had in high school that Jax and Evan won't let go."

Parker looks me up and down and nods. "Switch the red to pink, and I'd say they're spot on."

I roll my eyes. "That is very stereotypical, Mr. Mills. Doctor Barbie was my favorite, and she definitely didn't wear pink."

"Runway Barbie," Evan chimes in, and Jax chokes on a laugh.

Glaring at both of them makes them laugh harder.

Suddenly, my hand is swept up, and Owen's voice pierces the laughter. "Excuse me, but I must steal her away to meet a few people. Please enjoy the party, gentlemen."

Without waiting for a response, he pulls me away, and I let him. A few steps out of the central atrium, heading toward the rainforest, Owen lifts my hand up to eye level and studies it.

I instinctively yank it away from him, wincing, and he stops.

"What happened to your hand?" he asks, concerned.

Rubbing at my raw and bruised knuckles, I don't really want to admit anything, but he waits for me to answer, unwavering in his stare.

"I had an unfortunate incident with my kitchen wall. It got in my way."

Owen surprises me by laughing. "I feel bad for your wall. I know what it feels like to get in your way."

I go to open my mouth, but the way he's gazing at me makes me pause. There is nothing left of the black eye I gave him a week ago, and somehow that makes me oddly disappointed.

Owen bends over, his breath tickling my ear. "I was worried you'd look amazing tonight, but I was wrong. You look absolutely devastating."

Angling my head, I extend my chin to get closer to his ear. He doesn't move. With the heat of his body against mine, all I want is to curl up in him and get lost. I don't want to face any of what's ahead. The fear that I've held back is suddenly way too close to the surface.

Jax's words echo in my mind, and even if this is the only moment I have, I don't want to waste it.

"I'm not the only one. You have destroyed me, Owen," I whisper back. It's the truth. He's wrecked everything I thought I knew about the world—about villains and heroes and everyone in between. He's ripped me wide open, and I don't know how to put myself back together. I want it to be him who does, but I know there is no path for us to be together. Even if I save him, he won't choose me after he finds out I've been lying to him since the day we met. After he finds out who I really am.

"Nova..." There's a hint of desperation in his tone, but he doesn't finish as a voice interrupts.

"This must be the woman who organized the event?" The male speaking sounds neither impressed or disappointed.

Owen takes a large step back from me and practically stutters, "Father. Yes. This is Nova."

Father. *Oh*.

I extend my hand. "A pleasure to meet you, sir."

He takes it and shakes firmly. "I've heard good things about you but was wary of them since it was my son who hired you."

My eyes widen, and I have the sudden urge to hurt this man.

Owen flinches beside me but doesn't respond to the dig.

"I am pleasantly surprised with your work, Miss Riley," Owen's father continues. "Wonderful to have a competent employee at Regenerative Industries, even if you are only assisting with the charity work."

Plastering a fake smile on my face, I grit my teeth. "Thank you."

If he continues with the passive-aggressive insults, I'm not sure I'll be able to hold myself back.

Owen either senses it or sees the balls I've formed with my fists, and he grabs onto me, prying my fingers apart until his are wrapped between them.

"As for you," Owen's father turns to him, "Noell tells me you're going to have to file bankruptcy soon." If his tone was even before, it now sounds downright lethal.

I overlooked Noell until this moment. She stands behind Owen's father. There's a grimace on her face as her name spills from his mouth.

Owen glances briefly at Noell before addressing his father. "She's correct."

His father clenches his jaw then spits, "You're a disgrace. Your mother would be so disappointed."

Owen tenses. "This isn't the time nor the place to be discussing this."

Owen's father stands at the same height as his son. Like with Parker, they all share a similar build and bone structure, but Owen's father is pale with dark brown hair and dark blue eyes.

Those eyes stare at Owen with such disdain that I almost say something, but Noell beats me to it.

"Shall we get a drink, Mr. Mills?" she offers to Owen's father.

He gives Owen one more seething look before stalking after Noell, heading for the bar.

Owen stands stiffly beside me, his hand trembling in mine. I squeeze in silent support. His green eyes are shiny with unshed tears as they meet mine, and my heart breaks as I stare at them.

"Dance with me?" I offer.

He suddenly comes back to the room and looks toward the atrium and string quartet in the corner. When his eyes meet mine, they've brightened. "This is not dancing music, Miss Riley. This is a waltz."

I cock my head to the side and give him a challenging grin. "The waltz is a dance if I'm not mistaken."

He smirks, and the sight allows me to breathe for the first time in minutes.

"You know how to waltz, Miss Riley?"

The odd thing is, it was a skill that was taught during my field training with the CIA. Apparently, influential people still waltz.

"I do," I reply.

Owen shakes his head. "Of course you do."

"I take it you know how, too?"

He nods. "My mother taught me."

"Then shall we?" I ask, even though I'm trembling with nerves and all I want to do is pry information about his mother from him. I hate being the center of attention, and we surely will be if we're the only ones dancing a waltz in the middle of a crowded room.

Owen looks at me as though he isn't quite sure if I'm serious, so I tug him back to the atrium and onto the dance floor. He doesn't fight me.

When we reach the center, he pulls me close and places his hand on my lower back. His calloused palm scrapes against my exposed skin, and I close my eyes for a moment to compose myself. When I open them, he takes my hand in his other and expertly leads me into the steps.

I haven't danced a waltz in a decade, but Owen makes it feel effortless. I'm soon lost to our moving bodies perfectly in sync with one another.

"Once again, you surprise me," Owen whispers as we turn together.

"I think I may be the one who's surprised this time," I whisper back.

Owen pulls me closer as we move faster with the music filling the space around us.

I don't register the crowd gathered around, watching, but when Owen spins me toward the bar, one person catches my eye among the myriad of faces.

Owen grabs my waist again, gracefully, as my heart rate speeds up.

I know that face. I've stared at it so many times in a CIA file recently that I've almost memorized the slope of his nose and the lines around his wide-set eyes.

It's the assassin from the Post-it beside Owen's computer.

Peyton Radd.

Chapter 23

When the music stops and the crowd cheers, I don't hear them. I don't even feel Owen's hand as he leads me away.

My eyes scan the crowd for Peyton. Even though I knew there would likely be assassins here tonight, for some reason, I didn't expect him.

"Is something wrong?" Owen leans over and whispers so no one can hear us.

I shake my head. "I just need to use the restroom. Will you excuse me?"

Owen looks disappointed at my sudden change in mood, but I need to get away. I need to find Peyton. I need to find out who he's working for.

Owen nods and releases my hand, watching me walk away. I don't want to. I want to stay and make sure he's okay. Make sure he knows I'm on his side. But this is the only way I know how to do that, even if he isn't aware.

I practically sprint from the crowd now closing in around Owen. I don't turn to see his face. I focus on what I'm supposed to be doing: finding the assassins and finding out who is pulling their leashes.

"Gray," I whisper into my comm, exiting the atrium and scanning the crowd by the entrance. "Peyton Radd is here. I need to know where he went."

"Last location?"

"Exiting the atrium toward the back exit."

"On it."

As Gray searches the cameras, I wind my way around the outside of the crowd, searching for Peyton's dirty blond hair among the commotion.

"Got him," Gray's voice comes through the comm. "He's headed down to the aquarium."

The aquarium is on the floor below the atrium, displaying creatures from all over the world in beautifully designed tanks. From tropical waters to the deep sea, there are a myriad of exhibits. The problem with the aquarium, though, is that it's dark, and there are many places to hide.

"Shit," I mumble into the comm.

"You want me to send backup?" Gray asks.

"No. I'll handle it. Keep eyes on him, let me know if he leaves the area."

"Will do."

I quickly walk to the stairs that descend into the aquarium. The sound of my heels is drowned out by the number of people talking and laughing around me.

When I reach the bottom, the crowd disperses, and all that's left are small groups scattered around the exhibit. Many of them socialize around a temporary bar set up in the middle.

Walking to the tank of sea anemones to the left of the bar, I pretend to study them as my eyes travel around in search of the familiar face.

My heels click along the floor, audible now. I make my steps slow and purposeful as I round the corner into another section of the aquarium. The deep-sea exhibit. There is almost zero light.

I know he's here before his snakelike voice sounds over my shoulder. "I know who you are, Miss Riley. The question is, does Owen?"

Turning slowly, I find Peyton Radd standing close. Too close. He presses a blade lightly into my side.

"Does he know who *you* are, Mr. Radd?"

Payton laughs, but it's humorless. "That's not my real name."

"Nor is Miss Riley my real name, but you already knew that. Why don't you get to the point?"

Peyton laughs again, and the sound grates against my nerves. I've encountered many men like him. Too many. But the visceral reaction I still have to them never ceases to amaze me. My brain wants me to run, but my body wants me to fight. It wants me to eliminate every single one of them.

"He thinks he knows who I am," Peyton says. "Just as you think you know who I am."

"So he didn't hire you?"

"I didn't say that." He pauses for a second, changing the subject. "I've been keeping an eye on him for a long time, Miss Riley. I know more about his life than anyone actually in it. I know what makes him angry, what makes him happy, and what he desires." Peyton leans in and licks up the side of my ear.

It takes all of me not to kill him. I clench my fists and grit my teeth. "You speak in riddles. Who hired you?"

Peyton pulls away, but only slightly, and laughs again. "One favor for another, Miss Riley. You know how this works."

"What do you want?"

"You see, I know far more than you probably do. So I'm not sure what you can offer me."

"How about I don't kill your ass or put you in jail?"

"You amuse me, thinking you have any power in this situation. You are sorely outmatched, and you have a little rat in your midst."

That information should surprise me, but somehow it doesn't. My gut has been telling me something isn't right for a while. This only confirms what I feared.

"What do you want?" I ask again, this time ready to put him on his ass regardless of the people and the charity event going on around us.

"Five minutes alone with Mr. Mills."

"So you aren't working for him, then?"

"Once again, I didn't say that. I only asked for a meeting with him. Alone. Tonight."

"And you think I have the power to give that to you?"

"You may be the only person in this building who holds any sort of power over Owen Mills."

"What's that supposed to mean?" I hiss.

Peyton chuckles in my ear. "Oh, I think you know what that means, Miss Riley."

"Tell me who you're working for, and I'll *try* to get you what you want."

"Are you sure that's the question you want answered, Miss Riley? Not who the rat is?"

Though I'm not really sure, I nod. "Five minutes alone with him. No weapons allowed in the room, and security will be stationed outside the door."

"Fine," Peyton growls.

"Who is paying you?"

Peyton leans down and whispers so quietly I almost miss it. "Vivario."

"What?" I stammer. The word catches in my memory. The little boy. Italy. But how?

"You have thirty minutes to secure the meeting before I decide to kill him."

He disappears around the corner, the shadows swallowing him.

"You want me to keep eyes on him?" Gray asks through my comm, having heard the entire conversation.

"Yes. Where's Mr. Mills?"

"Right in front of me. The bar."

I groan, and Gray chuckles.

"I'm guessing you don't want to know how many drinks he's had since you left his side?"

"No."

Gray laughs again. I stomp back up the stairs.

I'm intercepted by Parker, who steps to my side while I continue toward the bar. "I take it my father got hold of him?"

I nod. "He's a real piece of work."

Parker chuckles nervously. "That he is, and he's unnecessarily cruel to Owen."

"Why?" I dare to ask.

"He blames Owen for her death."

I halt my steps, and Parker faces me.

"He blames Owen? But Owen was a child."

Parker nods and nervously runs a hand through his hair. "It was a car accident. No one knows what happened, but Owen's mother took him in the car because he was throwing a tantrum. His father believes he was the distraction that caused the accident."

"The scar on his chest..."

Parker nods again. "He almost died, too."

I don't know what to do with this information. It all adds up, though. His desire to follow through with the charities. To do what his mother wanted. His father's treatment. His obsession with defiance, and yet he seeks his father's approval.

"He was a child," I say again.

"I know. He doesn't deserve our father's cruelty. But at this moment, I need your help. Owen is already too deep. Had too many in a short time. I'm not sure he'll be able to make his speech. Do you have his notes for it?"

I nod.

"I'll do it for him, but I need what he wrote, and I need you to get him out of here before the alcohol hits for real and he decides to do something stupid, like bait our father into a fight in front of everyone."

Shit. This is not the night for Owen to get piss drunk.

"Okay," I concede because I don't know what else to do. "Where do I take him?"

"Home."

"I don't know where he lives."

Parker sighs. "No one does except for me. I'll program directions into his car."

Another odd piece of information that creates more questions than answers.

"Thanks. I'll get Owen."

Parker puts a hand on my shoulder before I can slip away. "He likes you. I dare say he probably loves you. And anyone with eyes can see you feel the same way. Just don't hurt him. I don't think he'd survive it."

Tears fill my eyes, but I don't let them fall. He's right. I do feel the same, but how I feel about him won't save either of us when the truth is finally revealed. We're both going to fall, and we're both going to lose each other.

"And thank you, Miss Riley," Parker continues. "There's no one else I trust to make sure he gets home safely."

With that, he disappears through the doors to the atrium, and my heart cracks in my chest.

I take a heaving breath before composing myself and dialing Noah. "I need you. Second floor outside the dinosaur exhibit. Fifteen minutes. Bring two other guys."

"You find the people you were looking for?"

"One of them, and I made a stupid bargain with him. Now I'm going to pay the consequences."

"I hope it was worth it."

"It wasn't."

Noah sighs on the other end of the phone. "Whatever you need, Nova."

"Thanks, Noah. I mean it."

"We'll make sure he gets out of there in one piece."

"He's already not in one piece."

Noah chuckles. "I can see that."

Now it's my turn to sigh. "Fifteen minutes."

"I'll be there."

I hang up the phone and race to Owen. Already afraid of what I'll find.

Chapter 24

He's leaning against the bar. Not surprisingly, he's surrounded by five women, a drink in hand. Stopping outside the little circle of women, I place my hands on my hips. I can't help but glare.

When he finally spots me, his mouth falls open dramatically, and he carefully places his glass on the bar before muttering, "Uh oh."

All five women turn toward me, but I ignore their stares.

"That's all you have to say?" I ask a little harsher than I probably should, but I'm pissed. The fucker's life is in literal danger, and he goes and gets himself drunk in the span of thirty minutes.

"You left." Instead of sounding accusatory, he sounds devastated.

"I went to the bathroom," I explain. "And then I got caught up chatting with a few people on my way back. I didn't realize I'd need to stick to you like glue."

"Will you?" I give him a questioning look, and he clarifies, "Stick to me like glue?"

"Come on, Mr. Mills. You're needed elsewhere," I say, motioning for him to step away from the bar.

When he does, he almost stumbles. The women hurry away from him as though he might fall on top of them. I, on the other hand, rush to him, grabbing his arm to steady him.

"I'm fine," he mumbles. "I can do it."

"I know you can. What if I *want* to hold your arm? Glue, remember?" I whisper.

He smiles, and I almost trip over myself at the sight of it.

I want to smile back, but I'm too afraid of what I got us into. Too afraid to lose him. Too afraid of the truth. Too afraid he may not walk out of that room with Peyton Radd.

"Why so somber, Miss Riley?" he asks, noticing my frown as we make our way toward the door.

"I fear you and I are too much trouble for one another."

He shakes his head vigorously. "No, *I'm* too much trouble for *you*. You're perfect."

I snort. "You're drunk."

"Maybe, but it doesn't make that statement less true."

I pull Owen through the door and corner him against the wall, somewhat away from prying eyes. "Listen to me carefully, Owen."

He sucks in a surprised breath. "You used my first name. This must be serious."

His joking tone only frustrates me more. "Does the name Peyton Radd mean anything to you?"

Owen's eyes widen. "You saw the sticky note on my desk the day you cleaned."

It's not exactly a question, but I nod anyway.

"I should have hired security the moment his name crossed my path," he says.

"What do you mean? How do you know him?"

"I don't know him personally, but he worked for one of the companies I acquired recently."

Confirmation he *wasn't* hired by Owen. But why would Peyton be so reluctant to admit it? And why is Peyton still being so secretive?

"What did he do for that company?" I ask.

Owen looks as if he doesn't want to tell me, so I decide to give him some incentive. "He's here. He cornered me and wants a private meeting with you. Right now. He didn't seem very friendly, so you'd better tell me what you know."

"Fuck," Owen mumbles. "He touched you?"

"Yes. No." I shake my head. "That doesn't matter right now! What matters is what you know about him and why he wants to meet with you alone."

Owen looks like he wants to murder someone, but he answers. "I believe he is some sort of hitman. Someone hired by the drug cartel and then later by the company I acquired. The drug cartel had some business dealings with the company that I ended when I bought them."

"What do you think he wants?"

Owen shrugs, and the movement is slow and sloppy. The alcohol is starting to affect him more than I'd like.

"I don't know. Money? To kill me?" he answers.

"You aren't serious?"

He shrugs again.

"Noah and two others are stationed outside the doors to the education center office, where you're meeting him. He will be searched and stripped of all weapons before you go in there with him. And Owen?"

"Yes?" he asks, eyebrow quirking.

"If everything goes to shit, protect your goddamn left side."

With that, I practically drag him up the stairs.

Noah's waiting for us. The scowl on his face says more than his words ever could. He doesn't trust Peyton, and he doesn't like this situation one bit. I don't blame him, but I made a deal. A rotten one.

"I take it he's already in there?" I ask.

Noah nods, picking up a bag and shoving it in my arms. "This is what we found on him."

I open the bag, and Owen leans over to peer inside, too.

"Fuuuck."

"What he said," Noah chimes in.

The bag is full of weapons. A gun with a silencer, two daggers, another handgun, and...

"Are those position darts?" I ask Noah.

He nods.

Taking a deep breath, I take Owen's hand and pull him to the door of the office.

I open it to find Peyton sitting, his hands behind his head and ankles crossed on top of the round table in front of him. Books are haphazardly stacked in the wooden shelves behind the table, and children's toys and replicas of animals fill plastic bins on the floor.

Peyton wears a cynical grin. "You're late," he says as his gaze lands on Owen.

I don't acknowledge his comment. "You have five minutes, Mr. Radd. No more. If you touch a hair on his head, I'll make you wish you never even heard the name Owen Mills."

Peyton chuckles. "Oh, I have no doubt, Miss Riley." He pulls his hands from the back of his head and holds them up. "I have no desire to get on your bad side. I've seen what you do to men you don't like." He winks for emphasis.

"What does that mean?" Owen asks innocently.

"Nothing," I growl. "Seems he has a flair for the dramatic. You have five minutes, starting now."

I reluctantly drop Owen's hand and storm out of the room, shutting the door behind me. I know what I said to Peyton was risky. I know I'm treading a fine line and that my little act won't hold up much longer, but all I can think of is Owen. I cannot lose him.

The next thing I know, my legs give out, and I collapse against the door. Noah is instantly at my side. He doesn't say a word but sits next to me. A steady shoulder to lean against.

It's the longest five minutes of my life, and all I can think of is: I may have just killed Owen.

When the timer goes off, I'm on my feet and through the door before anyone blinks. Peyton swivels his head to me and grins, though I hardly notice because slumped over the desk is Owen.

I'm on Peyton in an instant, pinning him to the wall, my elbow collapsing his trachea. He chokes for air, clawing at my arm.

"Nova," Noah's voice comes from behind me. "He's fine. Just unconscious."

I let up only enough to let Peyton speak.

"What did you do to him?" I shout.

"I knocked him out for a bit. It won't last," he wheezes.

"What did you say to him?" I slam him against the wall even harder.

Peyton has the nerve to smile. "I'm sure he'll run right to you and tell you everything when he wakes. Don't worry, sweetheart. I didn't spill your secret."

"I wasn't worried about that, asshole!"

"Oh I know you aren't, but you might be once he knows."

"You're a real piece of work, you know that?"

His grin grows. "I'm aware. And now that my business is done here, I'd like to leave, per our agreement."

"Our agreement was you wouldn't touch him."

"Oh, but I didn't. Not without his consent."

"Bullshit."

Peyton shrugs.

"Nova, we have no reason to hold him here. He stuck to the agreement," Noah says behind me.

"You should listen to him," Peyton comments.

"Shut up and get the hell out of here," I say, releasing him.

He smiles again and bows. "As you wish, Miss Riley." He heads for the door, and when he reaches it, he turns one last time. "Oh, and Miss Riley? When shit hits the fan, come find me, will you?"

He's gone before I can respond.

"What the hell?" Noah asks, staring blankly at the door Peyton exited through.

"Your guess is as good as mine. We've learned absolutely nothing, and Owen is out for who knows how long. And he might not even remember this meeting." I pause, pacing the room.

"Gray? You got eyes on Peyton?" I ask into my comm.

"Yes, he just left the building. Out the front door."

"Left in a car?"

"Yes."

"Did you get the plates?"

"Yes, but it looks like an Uber."

"Can you hack the destination? Or trace the car?"

"I'll try."

"Thanks."

I turn my attention back to Noah. "I need to get him home. Can you bring his car around?"

Noah nods. "You want a team to go with you?"

"That would probably be wise, but no. According to Parker, no one even knows where he lives. Plus, I think this meeting with Peyton Radd gave us a few more days."

"Nova, I have to say I don't think it's wise."

"I know it's not!" I snap. "But I need to talk to Owen. Alone. And I don't think he'll say anything with anyone around. Trust me."

Noah nods. "You're bringing weapons at least?"

"Yes, of course."

"Let's get him to the car," he says, coming over to help me lift Owen out of the chair.

"We bring him out the back way. I don't want anyone spotting him."

Noah nods, and we drag Owen down the back steps and out into a back alley. The car is waiting, and Noah helps me strap Owen into the passenger seat.

As promised, Parker typed in Owen's address.

"Be careful, Nova. Call me if you need help. We won't be far." Noah's voice is soft and filled with concern.

I nod, trying to hold back the moisture gathering in my eyes. I look over at Owen's motionless form.

"He'll be fine," Noah reassures me.

"I know, but it's all my fault." I let my head fall onto the steering wheel.

Noah puts a hand on my back. "None of this is. Though I don't know much, it seems to me that Owen got himself in this mess, and it's only because of you that he's still alive."

I pull my head up and stare into Noah's dark brown eyes. "Why does this have to be such a mess? And why does it feel like it's something I cannot fix?"

"If there's one thing I know about you, it's that you can fix almost anything. I've never met a smarter, more determined, and fiercer woman. So many people would follow you to the ends of the Earth. I hope you know that. You're not alone in any of this, and I'll still be here to help you pick up the pieces if everything falls apart."

"You're actually a decent guy, you know that?"

Noah chuckles. "Don't tell anyone. That'd ruin my reputation."

I give him a soft smile. "Thank you. I'll keep you updated."

Noah steps away from the window and pats the top of the car. "Drive safe, and take care of him. And yourself."

"I will."

With that, I pull out of the alley and onto Main Street, heading north toward the Golden Gate Bridge.

My phone buzzes, and Gray's voice comes through the line. "Traced him to a hotel downtown. Near Regenerative Industries."

"Okay, thanks. Will you station someone there to watch him?"

"Already have."

"You're a lifesaver. Go home and get some rest. I'll call you in the morning."

"Will do. Did you find any evidence?"

I glance at the bag on the floor, the one with all Peyton's weapons, and think of the poison darts. I'd have to test them to determine if the position matches the autopsies, but it's a lead, however small.

"I have something. Whether it turns out to match what we're looking for, I have no idea. I'll send it to the lab first thing in the morning."

"That's good to hear. Oh, and Nova?"

"Yeah?"

"Good work today."

"Thanks, you too."

"It feels like things are finally returning to normal," he says cheerily.

Guilt twists my gut. Nothing about this assignment is normal, but I can't tell him that. I can't even tell Declan or Ella, despite my gut telling me to.

"Yeah," I say. "I'll be in touch once I get to Owen's."

"Copy. Drive safe."

With that, I hang up the phone, my hands shaking on the wheel. How did I fuck this up so badly? I've never felt so out of my league before. The trial, Gray, Owen—all of it is a mess. A mess I cannot seem to fix.

And I've always been able to fix problems. It's what I do.

Not this time, though.

Crossing the bridge to the North Bay, the drive is longer than I expect and brings me into a remote area. I'm anticipating a big house with a gate and many cameras and security, but when I pull into the dirt driveway, there is a field of wildflowers on one side and a forest of redwoods on the other.

The gravel driveway is long and winds away from the road. When the house comes into view, I'm pretty sure my mouth drops into my lap.

It's a small stone cottage no larger than my apartment in the city. It's surrounded by what looks like a vegetable garden and a flower garden, but it's hard to tell in the dark.

The house has no lights, no gates, and definitely no cameras. I'd be surprised if it even has central heating.

Stopping in front of the house, I walk around to the passenger's side in my bare feet. When I open the door, Owen groans. My relief is visceral. Grabbing his arm and waist, I somehow hoist his large body over my shoulder.

I grunt, standing. Owen lets out another moan.

"Almost there," I say as if he can hear or understand me.

Taking the two stone steps up to the front door, I try the handle and find it isn't locked. I step through, angling my body so I don't smack his head against the door frame.

The entryway has a small wooden bench, and hooks above it hold various jackets. An array of dirty shoes and boots sits atop the wooden bench, all lined up neatly. The entry opens to a small country kitchen on the left and a cozy living room, with a small wood fireplace, on the right. Lining every wall space in the living room are shelves. Books bleed from them and spill into organized piles on the side table next to a brown leather couch. A large coffee table stands in the center of the room. There's no television.

I walk to the end of the hallway, where there is a single bedroom. It's a large room with tall French doors leading outside. The bed is against the far wall. A relatively big bathroom is connected to the bedroom.

Walking quickly to the bed, I deposit Owen on top of it. He lets out another soft groan but doesn't move or open his eyes. I tug off his shoes and wrestle him out of his tux jacket. Then I take off the vest and unfasten the top two buttons of his shirt. The rest of his clothes I leave on. Pulling him further up the bed, I let his head rest on his pillow.

By the time I'm done, sweat is pouring down my forehead and chest, and I'm exhausted and out of breath. All I have to wear is my red dress, which is now soaked and doesn't seem appealing to sleep in, so I go in search of a shirt.

Pulling open Owen's dresser drawers, I find mostly T-shirts and sweats. I opt for a simple white T-shirt and grey sweatpants with a drawstring. I'm too hot to put the sweats on, so I lay them on the bedside table.

Owen hasn't moved by the time I finish, and I debate calling Declan and telling him everything. Hell, I'm even thinking of calling Ella, though I know I shouldn't.

Deciding my exhaustion is clouding my judgment and I'd be better off telling Declan everything after I speak to Owen about what Peyton said to him, I climb into bed. I'm not sleeping on the couch because I want to keep an eye on Owen's health. His chest moves up and down in a steady rhythm, while I try to ignore the nagging thoughts in my head. Before long, I'm asleep.

Chapter 25

Surprisingly, I don't dream, and the soft light filtering through the doors and windows pulls me from my deep sleep. Warmth and a solid weight wrapped around me pulls me from my slumber, and I instantly panic.

Owen has somehow tangled himself so completely around me that I don't think I'll be able to get out without waking him. And that's a problem because I completely forgot to put on the sweatpants I left next to the bed, and I'm not wearing any underwear under the T-shirt.

He has his head buried in my hair while one arm is draped over my waist. His legs are twined through mine so intricately that it's hard to tell where I begin and he ends.

How did we even end up like this? And how did I not wake up?

Sucking in a large breath, I start pulling the T-shirt over my exposed ass that is plastered to the front of him. Luckily, I kept all his clothes on.

Once I shimmy it down enough to provide at least some coverage, I push the arm around my waist off of me. He makes a slight noise and shifts but doesn't wake.

At a painstaking pace, I slide my top leg out from under his until only my ankle is tangled up with his calf. Another deep breath, and I brave the last tug, and his leg falls on my other one, wedging my limb between both of his.

I'm now awkwardly on my stomach, ass once again exposed, and I have no idea how to get my other leg free.

My body trembles with suppressed laughter at the absurdity of the situation—which, of all the things, is what wakes Owen.

I'm so worried about my exposed ass that I jerk off the bed and tumble ungracefully onto the floor, yelping in the process.

I scramble to pull the shirt down before I sit up and raise my head to find Owen peering over the edge of the bed, a large smirk plastered on his way-too-pretty face.

"Everything all right, Miss Riley?" I can hear the laughter in his voice.

"Fine." I scowl as I stand, satisfied that the shirt covers everything.

Owen looks me up and down, and I shift uncomfortably on my feet.

"Interesting choice of sleeping attire," he comments, the grin still there.

"It was a little hard to find something to sleep in when I had to carry your ass inside in the dark, and I wasn't sleeping in that thing." I motion to the discarded gown I threw onto a chair next to the dresser.

Owen's eyes shoot to the dress and back to me. Still, his smile doesn't disappear. "It's not like me to point this out. In fact, I'll probably kick myself later, but that shirt and the light filtering in from the doors behind you probably reveal more than you want them to."

I instinctively wrap my arms around myself, mortified.

Owen laughs and stands, opening a drawer. He tosses me another shirt—this one is black—and points to the sweatpants by the bed.

"That might be more to your liking," he says, holding back more laughter. "However, I'd be fine with you wearing what you are now."

"Get out!" I shout, wanting to punch the grin off his face.

He holds up his hands in mock surrender and inches toward the door. Stopping at the entrance, he looks back. I'm still awkwardly trying to cover myself.

"You know—"

"Get out!" I shout again.

He laughs again, and the sound does something to me that I don't even want to begin to unpack, but he obeys and slips out the door, closing it behind him.

I drop my arms and breathe deeply. I have no idea why my heart is racing or why I'm practically shaking.

After stuffing myself into the shirt and pants, I open the door and am hit with the scent of coffee. I almost moan.

I find myself content as I enter the kitchen, which is a rare feeling for me.

Owen has also changed, and he's in his usual morning attire: joggers and no shirt.

He doesn't notice me right away as he moves around the kitchen, grabbing mugs and plates. I observe for a moment, admiring the way the muscles in his back flex and move, the jaw-dropping beauty of him.

"Enjoying the view?" Owen chuckles, and I realize I've been staring and hadn't noticed his attention.

I deflect the question. "I have to admit, this is not what I expected when I was told to take you home."

"No? And what did you expect, Miss Riley?" He crosses his arms and leans casually against the counter behind him.

I try not to look at his abs or the muscles in his arms. "You're a billionaire, Mr. Mills. What do you think I expected?"

"Fancy gated house, fancy cars, and way too much house for one person?"

I laugh. "Well, yes. That seems to be the standard with billionaires these days."

"I'm not your average billionaire."

"No, you're not." I don't know why it comes out all breathy.

Owen studies me for a moment until the coffee maker beeps, and his attention returns to his task.

"Do you want some?" he asks.

"Yes, please," I mumble, heading for the kitchen table.

Owen stops me with a hand on my arm before I reach the chair. I lock eyes with him.

"You seem a bit off this morning." It's more of a question than a statement.

"Now, why would you say that?" I ask sarcastically, stepping into him so I can shout in his face. "First, long before I came to your company, you get yourself into some huge mess that involves *criminals*, then I get shot in the woods on a hike with you, then you decide to get piss ass drunk at your own charity gala that happens to have a notorious assassin looking for you! And then I find you completely unconscious and have to drag your ass home to your cottage in the woods that no one knows even exists. I put you to sleep, and then lay there, not knowing what the hell is going on!"

I keep rambling, unable to stop myself. "And on top of that, I wake to you tangled up with me, and I was half-naked, and somehow I actually slept without a nightmare, and you wake up, acting like nothing happened!"

I didn't intend any of it as an insult, but my brain doesn't know how to process what I'm thinking and feeling, let alone the half-naked man standing in front of me, looking as though I just punched him in the gut.

"I'm sorry, I—"

My brain seems to glitch, and my mouth instinctively crashes into his.

Weeks of tension finally snaps as Owen wraps an arm around my waist and pulls me closer. With his other hand, he grabs the hair at the base of my head and tugs so that the angle of his mouth fits perfectly with mine.

His tongue sweeps in. Before I know it, he's kissing me as if he'll never get the chance to taste me again.

I moan into his mouth, and he grabs my hips and spins us, never breaking our contact. He lifts me onto the counter, nudging my legs apart so he can settle between them.

Owen pulls away. His chest rapidly rises and falls in sync with mine. My fingers trace his torso and move slowly down his abs.

He shuts his eyes for a moment, as if he's trying to compose himself. I smile at his body's reaction to my touch.

"I'm beginning to think your sleep attire was by design," he whispers, his voice so deep and rough that it sends a spark right through me.

"If it were by design, I would have stayed tangled up in you," I whisper back, my hands now tracing the edge of his pants.

He sucks in a sharp breath and replies through gritted teeth, "Why didn't you?"

My fingers stop their back-and-forth motion. "Because I was afraid."

Owen's hand lifts, and he runs his thumb across my bottom lip. I swallow the sound gathering in the back of my throat.

"What are you afraid of?" he asks.

"That this is all we get."

The devastating truth. The reality I don't want to admit to myself.

Owen's thumb stops its movement, and I want to take back the words. I want to take it all back so I don't have to watch his green eyes melt into sadness.

Grabbing the edge of his pants, I pull him back to me, wanting—*needing*—to fuse our bodies.

"If this is all we get," he whispers as his lips hover over mine, "then we'd better make it count."

I should be thinking about what he means and how he didn't contradict me, but his words go straight through me, and I let go of his pants. My hands reach for the bottom of my shirt, and I pull it straight over my head.

Owen's gaze slowly roams over my body, and I react as if he's actually touching me. I swallow hard.

"Fuck, Nova," he whispers, and I swear his voice wavers a bit.

I reach for his chin and guide his eyes to mine. "Touch me, Owen. Please."

There's no hesitation as his mouth finds mine again and his hands trail up my bare skin, leaving searing heat in their wake.

His fingers find my peaked nipple and swirl around it. I finally allow a breathy moan to escape my lips. I arch my back, needing more.

His mouth leaves my lips and trails down my neck. I wrap my legs around his waist and pull him even closer.

He lets out a chuckle at my impatience as his tongue finds my nipple. I claw at his back, and my toes curl around the rim of his pants and push them down as far as I can manage. He backs up a step, watching me.

I growl at the separation but am silenced when he steps out of the pants I half-removed.

I'm shamelessly staring when he laughs. "Like what you see?"

My eyes travel to his, and I'm so far beyond embarrassed that I nod.

His smile is so broad that his dimple appears, and I have the strangest urge to kiss it. I beckon him forward again, and he obliges. He steps between my legs, and I grab his chin and plant a soft kiss in the corner of his mouth.

"That fucking dimple of yours is going to be the death of me."

"Really? That's what you find so appealing?"

"Among other things," I smile seductively.

Owen cocks his head to the side. "What other things?"

I trace the outline of his green eyes with my fingers. "These." I move my fingers down his cheek and trace his lips. "And these." My fingertips roam over his chin and down his neck, running along his collarbone. I move them further down, tracing the outline of his abs. "And these." My breath gets shallower the lower I go, and it takes all of me to finish what I started.

Circling my hands around his back, I grab his ass. He lets out a low chuckle.

"And this." I squeeze slightly for emphasis before my hands circle back to the front of him. I let them slide over the hard length of him. "And this," I whisper shakily, scooting closer to him.

He lets out a low rumbling noise in the back of his throat. "Nova," he warns, grabbing my hand and pulling it away from him.

I growl at the separation, and once again, he laughs at my impatience. "I'll give you what you want. I promise. Just let me...let me touch you first. Please, I need to."

The sheer desperation in his voice has me easily conceding to his wishes. I couldn't deny him even if I wanted to.

He runs his hands down the sides of my waist and around the band of his sweatpants until he reaches the strings holding them up. He slowly unties them in a way that makes me want to push him to go faster, and yet, I want to savor the way his face is hungrily taking in every inch of my exposed skin.

I've never felt this kind of attention from anyone, and it sends a wave of pleasure right to my core. He doesn't even have to touch me to get a reaction from me, and that realization has me squirming with desire.

His lips find my stomach, and as he slowly kisses downward, he tugs my pants even lower.

Raising my hips, I let him pull them off completely. He lets out a satisfied groan as they fall to the floor, his lips never leaving my skin.

He grabs my ankle gently, pushing up so I'm forced to bend my knee. He places my foot on the counter, giving himself more room and a better angle.

I snake my fingers through his hair as his mouth travels ever lower. He nudges my legs further apart, and I let him. His mouth and tongue trace my inner thigh, and I shudder.

Every nerve ending in my body seems to light up the second he grazes my center, teasing lightly. I let out a breathy moan. Owen's answering one vibrates through my entire body.

I edge further off the counter, seeking more friction. Owen doesn't give it to me, making another light pass with his lips and tongue.

When I let out a frustrated hiss, Owen chuckles against me, but he gives me what I want. His fingers brush against my entrance as his tongue circles my center. The sound that comes out of me probably reveals how long it's been since I've been touched.

"Fuck, you're so wet," Owen says against me.

All I can manage is an incoherent mumble of agreement, which has Owen laughing. The sound becomes muffled and dies when his tongue lands back on the most sensitive part of me, and his fingers plunge inside.

I arch my back, and suddenly my whole body feels like it's on fire. I squeeze my eyes shut as the heat builds. I now have a death grip on Owen's hair, but he doesn't seem to notice.

"Owen," I warn him, his movements not letting up.

The intensity grows. There's no controlling the ascent. I give into it. When the orgasm crashes through me, I'm pretty sure I'm screaming.

"Beautiful," Owen growls as he stands and trails kisses up my stomach.

Finally opening my eyes, I find him watching me.

"I think you killed me." My chest is rising and falling in rapid succession, my heart beating so fast.

Owen only smiles. "I'm not done with you yet." He grabs my limp body and lifts me off the counter. I wrap my legs around his waist and bury my head in his neck. I inhale the scent of him, trying to memorize it. Trying to memorize *him*.

I'm acutely aware of how close he is to my entrance. How easy it would be for him to slide into me.

He carries me to the bed and drops me on it. I giggle as his body crawls over me, caging me in.

My laugh stops the moment I notice his face. He looks pained.

"What's wrong?"

He shakes his head, his eyes never leaving my face. "You have completely ruined me. You have consumed my every thought since I met you. And the craziest part about all this is…" He pauses, but doesn't pull back or break his gaze. "I feel whole when you're with me. Complete. Like my body has been searching for you. And now that I've found you, I don't know how I'm going to let you go."

I don't say he's not going to lose me, because it's a lie, and we both know it. Instead, I pull his mouth to mine and consume him. I speak the words through my lips and my body. The ones I can't say. The ones I won't admit.

He groans and lifts my hips with one of his hands, pushing into me as I arch my back to guide him deeper.

"Fuck," he murmurs against my mouth.

He moves slowly at first, trailing kisses along my neck and jaw until he finds my mouth again.

As the tension starts to coil, I grab his ass and force him even deeper.

"Nova," he growls a warning.

My only response is a satisfied moan. That seems to trigger something in him as his movements become more frantic.

He reaches between us, and his fingers find my center again.

That's all it takes, and I tumble over the edge a second time. I cry out, his name on my lips. He follows me shortly after.

We're both trembling when he collapses on top of me, burying his head in my tangled hair. I wrap my arms around him and close my eyes, trying to catch my breath. Trying to somehow piece myself back together because, the truth is, he's shattered me, too.

It's a strange feeling not to want to be anywhere else but right here with him, and yet at the same moment, all I want to do is run.

Chapter 26

"**A**re you going to tell me what Peyton said to you, or are you going to make me guess?" I say as we're both lying in bed. Owen's arm is thrown over my stomach as I stare up at the ceiling.

Owen takes a deep breath, and I'm too afraid to look at him. Too afraid of what I'll find in his face. Too afraid of what I know is coming.

"He wants a job."

My head snaps in his direction. "Excuse me?"

I must have heard him wrong.

Owen laughs a bit awkwardly. "He wants me to hire him."

"As an assassin?"

Owen shakes his head, laughing in earnest now. "No. That's the craziest part. He wants a real job."

I don't know how to respond to that, so I simply stare at him.

"I told him I'd think about it." Owen seems almost embarrassed.

I blink a couple of times. "You're seriously considering it?"

Owen shrugs. "Isn't there that saying about keeping your friends close and enemies closer?"

I blink again. Maybe I'm in shock.

Owen laughs. "That wasn't all he said, though. He told me he has information I might need, and if I give him a real job, he'll reveal the information and do his best to help me."

"Why would he help you?"

"I asked him that, and he said because he only likes to work for people he knows will win."

I scoff. "That bastard likes to speak in riddles. I don't trust him."

"I don't either, but I'd rather have him as an ally than an enemy, and he seems to know information that may help me get out of this mess."

"You going to hire him in my place?" I ask, mostly joking.

Owen's face falls.

"Did you forget you fired me?" I keep my tone light, but the question is sincere.

Owen looks away from me and runs a hand through his hair. "I didn't forget. I'm just not sure about anything anymore."

My heart skips a beat, and I sit up, aware I still don't have any clothes on. I know Owen is listening to me, but his eyes wander to my bare chest.

"How do you know Peyton won't get on the payroll, steal all your secrets, put a bullet through your head, and then sell your secrets to the highest bidder?"

Owen's eyes widen. "I don't have any secrets."

I cock my head to the side and smile. "Bullshit."

The corner of his mouth kicks up, and his eyes sweep my body again, sending an involuntary shiver through me.

"Will you focus, please?" I ask him.

"A little hard when you have no clothes on."

"Fine." I stand up and cross the room, opening a drawer full of shirts. I grab one that is big enough to fall halfway down my thighs. "That better?"

Owen pouts like I ruined his day, and I resist the urge to roll my eyes. Instead, I pointedly glare at his still naked body, but he ignores me completely.

"You seem to trust Peyton," I say, taking hesitant steps back toward the bed. I'm not sure if it's a question or if I need confirmation.

"For some odd reason, I do."

That doesn't ease my fear. Owen trusts me, after all.

"He knocked you out after your little conversation," I remind him.

"I let him."

"What?"

Owen laughs at my shock and beckons me back to the bed. I finally sit, folding my legs under myself.

"He didn't trust me not to tell you about our conversation before he left the building."

"And what did he think I was going to do?" I realize it's a dumb question. I know why Peyton didn't want me knowing, because I'd have put his ass in jail, but Owen doesn't know that, so I play the part I'm meant to.

"Knock him out," Owen says like it's obvious.

I narrow my gaze, and Owen reaches out and brushes his fingers along my jaw.

"You're distracting me," I hiss.

Owen's laugh is deep and far too seductive, but it's gone quickly. "Peyton seems to know you."

Fuck.

"I hadn't met the man until our conversation at the gala," I say. "He does seem to know far more about you, me, and the company than he should."

"You think he's the one that's been on Noah's radar?"

"I want to say yes, but you have so many other enemies. I wouldn't rule out any of them until Peyton confirms it."

"He says he knows *exactly* who's after me."

"He's either an extremely convincing liar or an exceptional puppet master. I feel like our strings are being pulled without our knowledge. Like he knows everything, and we only have a single piece to the puzzle."

Owen looks thoughtful for a moment. "Maybe I should hire him."

I'm leaning toward that same conclusion. I think Peyton knows far more than either of us. The problem is: I don't trust him one bit. He has no loyalty. He only wants the side where he comes out on top.

I drop my head in my hands, confused and ungrounded.

When I finally look up, Owen is watching me. A deep wrinkle takes up space between his eyes.

"If I hire him, I can't take you back," he says miserably.

"Why?"

Owen doesn't speak right away, his features twisting into silent rage. "He touched you."

It wasn't a question, and it wasn't what I was expecting. I let my face soften and inch closer to him. "Owen, I can handle that. You know I can."

Owen shakes his head, his rage turning into something resembling sadness. "You shouldn't have to."

I don't know why, but I laugh. "You're right. I shouldn't have to deal with unwanted advances or touching, but I can't change others. All I can do is keep fighting."

Owen grabs my chin and rests his forehead against mine. "Has anyone ever fought for you?" he whispers against my lips.

I squeeze my eyes shut as a lump forms in the back of my throat. "No."

Owen inhales, and I cannot tell if he's angry or surprised by my answer. "Let me fight for you. Please."

It's a broken plea, and I want to say yes. I want to let him in. I want to give in to this beautiful illusion we've created.

I abruptly pull back, and Owen drops his hand to his side.

"You have to fight for yourself first," I choke out. It's the truth, and he must realize that.

Owen shakes his head. "I'm already a lost cause, Nova."

I want to ask him what he means when there's a loud knock on the door. We both jump at the sound, and Owen swears under his breath. He gets up quickly and pulls on his sweatpants before striding for the front door.

Tiptoeing behind him, I grab a knife off the kitchen counter and keep myself hidden behind the kitchen wall.

"Noah." Owen's voice sounds relieved.

"I didn't hear from either of you, so I forced your brother to give me this address." Noah sounds furious.

Stepping out from the doorway, I lower the hand holding the knife.

"Morning, Noah. We're fine," I say as Noah's eyes drop to the weapon and my bare legs.

He raises an eyebrow, suddenly amused.

I point the knife at him. "Don't tempt me this morning. I'm not in the mood."

Noah laughs. "In that case, I'll talk to the boss while you go get yourself a cup of coffee. You look like you need it."

I scoff but storm back to the kitchen. The two men step outside into the garden, and I watch them for a while from the kitchen window.

Noah's features soon melt from anger to something resembling joy, and it's not hard to imagine what Owen is saying to him. It's easy to become enraptured with Owen, and I realize now that's part of the reason why he's so successful at what he does. It's also why I've been so drawn to him since the moment I met him.

Once they both realized neither of them was a threat to me, it appears they've developed an unlikely friendship. A friendship that will likely be ruined by all my secrets.

I'm not only lying to Owen. I'm lying to Noah, too. And though Noah understands a little more about why I need to, it still leaves me feeling defeated.

As their conversation drags on, I finally pull away from the window and decide to take a look around the house.

There isn't much, but I start in the living room and scan the shelves of books. Most are on topics such as botany, herbalism, regenerative agriculture, and permaculture. There are a few on business and a few suspense novels, but that seems to be all.

I make my way to the couch and plop down on the soft leather, taking another sip of coffee. My eyes catch on the stack of books on the side table, and I cock my head to read the titles.

One of them has my heart stopping in my chest.

Nature's Poisons and Their Ecological and Biological Uses.

With a shaky hand, I set down the coffee cup and carefully pull out the book.

Flipping through the pages, I find highlighted lines and notes in the margins. Owen focused on plants that grow in California, highlighting their properties, where they are found, and the potency of the poison. There are calculations of doses in the margins with question marks.

Fuck.

This is the evidence I've been looking for. It's staring me right in the face, and I suddenly find myself shaking so hard I cannot even turn the pages.

As if the book burned me, I chuck it on the couch, staring at the open page it landed on. After what feels like minutes, I force myself to grab my phone.

I have no intention of sending anyone photos of the book or Owen's notes, but I realize if I'm going to fight for him, I have to know what I'm up against. I snap the photos, hoping they don't turn out blurry because of my trembling hands.

When I'm done, I put the book back where I found it and pull on shoes and a jacket and trudge outside. I need air.

I walk around the garden, hardly noticing the beauty and wildness of it. The light reflects off dew drops, creating the illusion that the flowers' petals are actually glowing. I can hear Noah and Owen talking, but their voices are distant and muffled.

Turning around to the southern side of the house, my feet crunching lightly on the stone path, my eye catches on a familiar plant. I bend down to study it. Foxglove. It was one of the poisonous plants highlighted in Owen's book. It can cause irregular heart function and even death—the cause of death of the first victim.

I can't help but notice how beautiful the flowers are, but the thing that causes tears to sting my eyes is what's next to the plant. There are obvious cuttings and evidence that a significant amount was taken away.

Snapping a few more photos, I still don't want to believe what I'm seeing, even if I knew the truth long before this. Even if I ignored it.

I lazily make my way around the rest of the house, my trembling never slowing. Owen and Noah's voices long ago faded as they went inside for more coffee.

Seeing more evidence, I take photos of all of it. I don't remember the other poisonous plants or how they kill their victims. At this point, it doesn't matter.

Part of me wanted to believe he was innocent. That I'd never find anything, because there wasn't anything to find.

I knew better.

I'm completely numb when I reach the front of the house again, but before I can enter, Owen's laughter greets me at the door. The numbness fades, and my heart shatters into a million pieces. I clutch my chest, the unshed tears finally spilling down my cheeks.

Chapter 27

I want to call Ella. I want to tell her all that's happened and have her tell me that everything will work out. That this won't end the way I know it will—with my heart shattered and my ass in jail. And Owen in prison, broken by my lies and betrayal. Or worse, dead.

But I can't call her. I can't drag her further into this. Plus, she probably wouldn't even pick up the phone.

I consider ringing Declan and revealing everything, but the same thoughts float through my head. I'm already threatening his position as director with my trial. He doesn't need to be an accomplice to the mess I've gotten myself into.

I find myself sitting on the front porch, unable to go inside. Unable to do anything. Not sure what to do.

The voices of Noah and Owen talking and laughing drift through the open kitchen window. I don't know how to go in there right now. I don't want to pretend, and they will both know something's wrong.

Not a moment after those thoughts, Noah stumbles through the front door and finds me. His smile is broad, and suddenly my chest aches even more.

"Wondered where you wandered off to," he says, taking a seat in the wooden rocking chair next to me. It creaks under his weight.

I take another slow sip of coffee, not sure I'm ready to speak.

"Owen told me everything."

I raise a brow.

Noah chuckles. "Well, probably not everything, but most of it."

I return my gaze to the wild garden in front of us, and the words still won't come.

"I may not be the smartest guy, but it's obvious you care for each other." Noah's words are soft.

"Caring for someone, even loving them, won't save them."

Now it's Noah's turn to raise a brow. "I don't know what your assignment is. I only know what Owen told me, but I do know you. I know it takes a very special person to break down your walls. You don't just do it for anyone, and I know that's what he's done."

Taking another slow sip, I squeeze my eyes shut. "And would you fight for that person even if it might ruin both of you?"

There's no hesitation with Noah's answer. "Yes."

I open my eyes and look at him. "Why?"

"Because I'd rather die knowing I tried than live with the regret."

It sounds as if Noah is speaking from experience. What have I missed? I've known him since I was a teenager, but he'd always been the guy making jokes. I'd assumed he'd led a relatively easy life. But, I notice it now—the hurt, the pain.

But I see something else, too: resolve.

At that moment, the decision I knew I'd make is solidified by his words. So, I stand, finding my own determination under layers and layers of fear. "So then we fight."

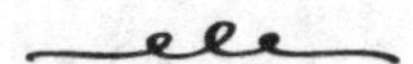

Owen turns out to be a major distraction, so I make a lame excuse about going home and changing my clothes. He begrudgingly drives me back to my apartment and leaves Noah with me as an extra set of eyes.

I station Noah outside my door and get to work.

I pull up the photos I took at Owen's and put them into a folder labeled *Evidence*. I compile everything Ella's boyfriend, Eagan, collected on the companies: rape, human trafficking, and drug cases. Two of the three companies are linked to the black snake crime syndicate, which is the largest worldwide to date. It is so big that it doesn't seem like their involvement in the two companies is related, but I don't rule it out. Lastly, I include the verbal testimony from the whistleblower, implicating the third company and linking it to the crime syndicate.

Pulling up Peyton's file, I scan it. There are loose threads that suggest he may have also been involved with, or worked for, the black snake crime syndicate, but there's no hard evidence.

That can't be a coincidence.

If Peyton is not the one trying to kill Owen, and Owen didn't hire him to kill the three CEOs, then who the hell is he working for? Or against?

I scan the evidence over and over again, trying to find some link in all this.

When I come up empty-handed, I call Gray.

"Can you hack Regenerative Industries' main drive and search for the words 'black snake?' And if anything comes up, anything at all, I don't care if it's a reference to a children's story, can you send it?"

Gray doesn't say anything right away. "Why is that relevant?"

"Just a hunch that the black snake crime syndicate is somehow involved in all this. I'm trying to figure out the link. Were they were the ones who killed the CEOs, or are they somehow after Owen?"

I know they weren't involved in the deaths of the CEOs, but I don't want Gray to know that. Not yet, at least.

"So the poison darts found on Peyton came back negative?" he asks, sounding almost disappointed.

"Haven't gotten the results, but I'm covering every base."

"Got it. I'll see what I can find."

"Thanks."

After I hang up the phone with Gray, my phone suddenly beeps with a hundred messages. They're all from Jax and Evan.

Shit.

I left them at the gala last night without saying anything.

Jax: *Where did you go last night?*

Evan: *YOU LEFT US!*

Jax: *Please tell us you're ok*

Evan: *Maybe she went home with Hot Boss Man....*

Jax: *Can't believe you Irish Goodbyed us!*

Evan: *Perhaps she's still in bed with Hot Boss Man*

Jax: *Evan! You aren't helping!*

Evan: **shrugging emoji**

I can't help the smile, despite the evidence I found this morning.

Nova: *I'm fine. I did go home with Owen last night, actually. He was so wasted, he passed out with his clothes on.*

Evan: *Oh man! I so hoped you'd get into those tight pants of his!*

I laugh this time.

Nova: *I did. This morning.*

Jax: *Oh Fuuuuuck!!!*

Evan: *YES!!!! FINALLY!!!!*

Everything may be going to shit, but at least I can savor these ridiculous moments before my reality changes.

Evan: *Was it good? Wait, don't tell me. I don't think I could handle it if you said no.*

I send a few fire emojis and nothing else.

Evan: *DAMN GIRL!!!*

My phone buzzes with a new message.

Owen: *You dressed?*

Nova: *Yes.*

Owen: *Can I take you to lunch?*

Nova: *Yes.*

Owen: *Pick you up in 5.*

I decide to take Noah's advice. I'll take whatever time I have with Owen, no matter how short. No matter what happens.

Chapter 28

I spend all of Sunday with Owen. He takes me out to lunch by the beach, and we talk and laugh. I almost believe that this could be our future.

Almost.

He gives me back my job, telling me it's to keep an eye on me. Whatever his reason, I'm grateful. It means I can continue figuring out how to save him.

Owen relents when I beg to help him. He gives me access to his company account. That's where I start, hoping that both Gray and I can find a lead somewhere in this mess.

"I think I'll keep you, Miss Riley," Owen says, leaning against my desk with two cups of coffee in hand on Monday morning. Having spent the night together and not wanting to come in early to work out, we find ourselves starting the morning a little later than usual.

I smirk, keeping my focus on my research, combing through company documents and emails from the first victim. "Why's that, Mr. Mills?"

"Because I actually sleep with you around."

I finally turn away from the computer and reach for the cup. "Shockingly, I do too."

Owen winks. "I tire you out."

I roll my eyes at the insinuation, but this time I'm smiling. Instead of playing into his hands, I switch tactics. "That's because you don't protect your left side, so I have to hit you over and over again just to get it through your thick skull. It tires us both out."

Owen lets out an exasperated sound, but I catch his dimple staring at me over the computer screen. "Perhaps that's why my skull is so thick. Been hit too many times."

Shaking my head, my gaze catches on a company email from the first victim. Opening it, I scan the contents, and my eyes snag on a few select phrases—unauthorized funds and shady business dealings.

I'm about to read the whole email in detail when we're interrupted by the office door swinging open and Noah yelling something from down the hall.

I can't hear what he's yelling as a dozen CIA agents swarm the office, guns raised and aimed at Owen.

Shooting to my feet, I instinctively put myself in front of Owen. He clutches my arm, and I back up into him until my spine is plastered to his torso. He's tense but oddly steady.

Declan walks in a moment later and notices me first. Surprise briefly crosses his face before he schools his features.

"Don't do this, Dec," I plead, staring only at him, shaking so hard I might collapse.

Declan's face falls when he hears the raw desperation in my voice. "I have to, Nova. I'm sorry. We have the evidence. It's over."

What? How?

"I didn't send the evidence!" I scream. "Give me more time!"

Declan shakes his head sadly. "You don't have more time, Nova. The success of this mission will help the vote go your way in your trial. The panel will look the other way."

"I don't give a shit about my trial!" My voice is breaking now. All my hopes fall with his admission that I'm out of time. That I failed—not the assignment but Owen.

I wanted to save him. I wanted to prove that he isn't the one who should be behind bars.

Everyone wants to capture the villain. No one understands that sometimes the villain isn't the one who should be locked up.

This is not how I imagined my secret being revealed to Owen. I wanted to tell him when I had all the information I needed to get him out of this mess, when I had something to save him with.

I realized my mistake too late.

"I care, Nova." Declan sounds almost as broken.

Declan knows. All it took was one look at Owen and me. How easily I forget how well he knows me.

"If you take him, Dec, I'm going down with him. I don't care what you say. This is wrong!"

Declan's gaze falls to his feet, unable to look me in the eye as he gives the signal.

The agents surround us, prying me from Owen. I shout, or I think I do. I claw at the hands separating us, desperately reaching for the man I've come to love.

They pin Owen's hands behind his back and cuff him. He doesn't struggle like I do.

I want to shout at him to fight, but he won't. I know he won't.

Owen finally turns his head to look at me. He gives me a sad smile, before turning away as the agents lead him out of the office.

He doesn't say a word, his silence hurting more than his anger would.

As the door shuts behind them, the remaining agents release me, and I drop to my knees. The tears I held back begin to fall from my eyes.

A warm hand presses on my shoulder. I look up to find a concerned Declan.

"You got the wrong bad guy, Dec," I say through my sobs.

"He committed murder, Nova."

"And how many people did those men kill? How many humans did they traffic? How many died indirectly as a result of their dirty businesses?" I want to shout, but it comes out as a croak, my voice dry and spent.

"I can't change the laws." Declan sounds defeated as he crouches beside me, hand still on my shoulder.

"I didn't send the evidence, Dec. I wanted more time to figure out how to get him out of this. I've learned too much. It isn't fair."

Declan stands and takes a few turns around the room before stopping. "The evidence came from your channel, Nova. If you didn't send it, whoever did knows how to access your network."

"There are only two people who have access to it."

"Ella and I," he says before I can.

"She wouldn't." I shake my head.

"Nova, I know you won't take my advice, but you need to let this go. It's a dead end. You can't get him out of this, and you risk not only your career but also jail time. As a friend, I'm asking you to please not pursue this." His voice is now the one that's pleading.

I stand, already knowing what I have to do. "No, Dec. I've seen the bad guys. The true bad guys, and he's not one of them."

With that, I walk out of the office. I don't look back, and Declan doesn't follow me.

The instant I'm out the door, Noah falls into step with me. "What do you need from me, boss?" he asks, his voice laced with concern and defeat.

"Find Parker. I need to speak to him. I have to make sure the company and charities have been transferred."

Noah nods. "Anything else?"

I stop abruptly before the elevators and face him. I know my cheeks are red and streaked with tears, but I don't care. I meet Noah's narrowed gaze and instantly fold myself into his arms. "Someone sold me out."

Noah nods again, lightly stroking my back.

I pull away and steel myself, wiping away the last of the tears.

"Oh, and Noah? Find me Peyton Radd. He has some explaining to do."

With that, I turn and head for the elevator, dreading the call I know I have to make. Afraid that my best friend may have stabbed me in the back.

Ella picks up immediately.

"Nova!" she shouts. "Are you ok? I saw Dec leave the office with a dozen agents. Rumors are that they got the evidence needed to arrest someone. I feared it might have been Owen."

I can't help the accusation that spills out of my mouth. "So you know nothing about it?"

There's a long pause on the other end of the phone. "Why would I know anything about it?"

"I think you know."

"If you're accusing me of something, Nova, just say it!" she shouts.

She rarely gets angry.

"I trusted you!" I yell back. "You're the only one who knows about this case. *The only one.* And other than Dec, you're the only one that has access to my network."

I hear a sharp intake of breath, but Ella's voice comes out as a shaky whisper. "I would never. You may have reassigned me, and I will admit I was angry at first, but I *knew* it was out of love. It wasn't personal. So why would I do that to you?"

Fuck.

I don't know what to believe anymore.

I don't respond. I don't know how.

"Nova? I won't waste my breath defending myself. You can believe what you want. All I care about right now is you. I'm shaking. I feel powerless to help you, and despite what you think, I still *want* to help. Please. How can I help you?" Her voice is on the edge of breaking, but it's not her that breaks.

It's me.

I sob into the phone for probably five minutes, and Ella does nothing but listen.

When my rasping sobs become quiet whimpers, she asks more forcefully, "How can I help?"

I'm not sure why I believe her, but I do. I always have. So, with a shaking voice, I say, "Get Eagan and bring him to my apartment. One hour."

"Done."

"Please tell me the paperwork was finalized?" I beg Parker as he sits in Owen's office chair, looking like he spent the last thirty minutes crying.

He probably did.

"Everything is signed, but still needs the final approval from the board," he says at last.

"Will they give it, considering what's happened?"

Parker shrugs and hangs his head. "This wasn't how it was supposed to go. I'm no CEO. I have no idea what I'm doing. Those papers were only a precaution."

"Parker, look at me."

He obeys, raising his bloodshot, baby blue eyes to mine.

"You won't have to, because I'm going to get him out," I say.

"How?"

Parker looks so broken, which is precisely how I feel, but I also know who I am and what I'm capable of.

"I'm an undercover CIA agent who was sent here to put your brother behind bars for murder. But when I learned more, I realized your brother isn't the villain in this, and when I decided to help him instead, I was set up."

Parker's eyes widen at my blunt confession. "Holy shit."

"Listen, you don't have to trust me, but I'm going to get your brother out of this, and I need your help. I need to know if the company will pass to you. If the charities are protected. That's what he wanted."

Parker studies me for longer than feels comfortable, and I wonder if he's going to kick me out on my ass after my confession.

After my betrayal.

"Did he know?" Parker asks.

I shake my head, and the tears come unbidden once again. "I should have told him. I wanted to. I made far too many excuses not to. The biggest being that I wanted to find the evidence to save him first."

"You love him?"

I don't know how that's relevant, but somehow the answer to that question feels like it might determine my entire fate. Without Parker's help and access to Owen's personal files and house, I may not get what I need.

I don't hesitate. "Yes."

Taking my first deep breath since Owen was aprehended, relief washes over me at the admittance.

Parker nods as if it isn't a surprise. "You know, even if you get him out of this, he may never forgive you."

I try to hold back the sob in my throat. I've been crying far too much recently. "I know."

"And you're still willing to risk your career for this?"

Once again, there's no hesitation. "Yes."

Parker stands. "Then let's do this. What do you need from me?"

A small sob escapes my lips again, but I'm smiling. "Do whatever you can to make sure the board approves the transfer. I don't care what you have to do to make it happen. After, I need you to help me gather any and all physical documents related to the three most recent acquisitions. Anything that I can't find on the computer."

Parker nods. "I'll do it. But Nova?"

I nod, waiting for him to speak.

"Did my brother really kill them?"

I knew I'd have to answer that question eventually, but I am not prepared for it. I don't want to be the one to tell him, but I also don't want him getting all his information from the media and rumors.

"The evidence strongly suggests he did, but I'm no lawyer."

Parker inhales sharply. "And you still think you can get him out of it? You still *want* to?"

"Yes, I do. The men he killed had raped and murdered a lot of people, along with funding even more crime. Owen saved a lot of people by getting rid of those men, if he did kill them." I pause and study Parker, who looks panicked.

"He's not the bad guy in this, Parker. I think once you know more, you'll believe that too."

Parker runs a hand through his hair, looking away from me. "I hate him. I hate him for not telling me."

"I know, but he was trying to protect you."

"The bastard is always trying to do that."

Smiling at the annoyance in his tone, I know Parker feels nothing but love for his brother, despite the situation.

"I need to go," I say at last. "I'm leaving a few private security guards with you. If anyone finds out what we're doing, they might want to stop it. Tell no one."

Parker nods. When I turn to leave, his voice stops me. "Thank you, Nova."

"Don't thank me yet."

Chapter 29

I'm stopped by Noell before I can step out of the building, and I want nothing more than to run past her judging eyes, but I halt when she calls out my name.

"Can we talk?" she asks, her mouth drawn in a firm, no bullshit kind of way.

I nod, and she inclines her head toward her office door.

I'd never been to Noell's office, but it's exactly how I imagined it'd be—minimalistic, organized to the point of obsession, and not a spot of dust to be seen anywhere. I swivel my head to face her and find her as she always is: meticulously dressed, not a hair out of place. Her eyes scan me as if she's sizing me up. It may be the first time she's ever actually looked at me.

I've never understood her clear dislike of me, but I keep my mouth shut.

"Have a seat, Miss Riley," she says, motioning toward the chair in front of her desk.

I do as she says, even though I'm itching to get back to work.

She takes her time walking around the desk and sitting in her chair, and I find myself bouncing my leg to stop myself from bolting.

"I assume you know what happened to Mr. Mills?" I ask, trying to get the ball rolling.

Noell nods and narrows her eyes. "It's why I needed to talk to you. I want to help."

I cock my head to the side, studying her. She's clearly loyal to Owen, but she's also been his father's puppet, so I'm not sure I believe her.

She must notice that in my face. "I know you don't trust me, and I know I haven't been all that trustful of you—and rightfully so." I huff but let her finish. "However, I do think you're very intelligent, Miss Riley, and I do think that you care for Mr. Mills. Parker told me everything."

She's been in cahoots with Parker? This is a new development.

Noell sighs, slumping her shoulders. It's the most out of sorts I've ever seen her. "Is there any evidence I can help with?"

I straighten up, leaning forward. The thought hits me instantly. "Actually, there is something you might be able to help with."

"Anything."

"Can you look over all of the financials of the three companies that were acquired? Look for anything out of the ordinary. Money coming and going that seems odd or out of place."

Noell nods. "I can do that. It might take me a while to comb through everything, but I can do it."

If she can find any monetary evidence of wrongdoing, it might help our case. I'm not hopeful, though. These people knew what they were doing.

"Don't do it here. There's someone who's been hacking the company's system. I don't want them to get wind of what we're up to. Use a personal computer and meet me at my apartment."

Noell smiles, or almost does. "I'll be there."

I stand, and Noell walks me to the door of her office. I stop halfway out the exit and turn to face her.

"Thank you, Noell."

She gives me a curt nod, and I leave without another word.

I may not fully trust her, but I am not too proud to admit that she could really help us. We're going to need all the assistance we can get.

Ella and Eagan are at my apartment when I get there. Both sit rigid at the kitchen counter, studying me. I shut the door and quietly walk to the couch and fall onto it.

Ella furrows her brow.

I pinch the bridge of my nose, knowing they're waiting for me to say something.

"Where do we even start?" I finally say, my voice wavering from exhaustion and defeat.

Ella gives Eagan an encouraging nod.

"I think we start with figuring out who sent the evidence," Eagan replies, biting his lip.

I sit forward, resting my elbows on my knees. "How?"

Eagan leans over and pulls out a laptop from a grey computer bag sitting next to his feet. He opens it and turns it on, though his eyes never leave mine. "I think I can trace the documents, but I'll need access to your account."

Nodding, I stand, blindly following his lead, as if my mind has switched off to prevent overheating.

I sign in to my account on his computer. Ella watches me intently, but she still doesn't say anything, and I don't speak to her. I'm not sure what to say. I accused her of sending the evidence, but why would she be helping me now if she did?

Stepping back, I let Eagan sort through my files. By the look on his face, it's obvious almost right away that something's wrong.

"What is it?" Ella's voice is laced with worry.

Eagan turns to me, frowning. "Did you put the evidence of illegal wrongdoing of the companies Owen acquired in here?"

"Yes. I put them all in the same file."

Eagan turns back to the computer screen, rubbing his hand along the stubble on his chin. "It's not here."

"What?" Ella shouts.

My palms begin to sweat. I press them together, my heart rate kicking up a notch.

"There's no other place they could be?" he asks me.

My brain scans through what I may have done with those files, but it comes up blank. They should be there.

I shake my head.

"What does that mean?" Ella asks both of us.

Eagan's gaze falls on Ella. "It means whoever sent the evidence against Owen also deleted the evidence against the companies."

"But why?" Ella cries.

"Can we get it back?" I interrupt, and Eagan focuses on me again.

"I backed up all the evidence I sent you, so that isn't the problem. The problem is: whoever got into your account clearly doesn't want this evidence out there. Do you know anyone who might have reason to delete this folder?"

I shake my head again.

"Dec desperately wants that case dropped against you," Ella whispers as if she's afraid to speak. "And he's the only other person with access besides me."

I shake my head a third time. "He wouldn't do that. He knows my past. He knows how badly I want to take out the assholes in those crime circles."

"Perhaps he's doing it so you have a career long enough to actually take them out?" Ella suggests, though she doesn't sound convinced.

Standing, I pace back and forth. It doesn't make sense for Declan to do that, and yet, he's always been super protective of me, and if he found the evidence—other than the whistleblower—he might have been pissed I didn't tell him.

But he didn't seem pissed when he took Owen. He seemed devastated.

"This isn't adding up," I say, stopping my incessant movement. "Dec wants my case dismissed, but he also knows why I joined the CIA in the first place. He wouldn't delete the evidence. He'd arrest Owen, but he'd leave the other evidence for later."

Ella eyes me wearily. "Are you sure?"

No, I'm not, and suddenly I'm going over every interaction I've had with Declan over the last few weeks.

"Peyton said there's a rat. Someone who has been feeding information to whoever is after Owen. Could it be the same person who deleted the evidence against the companies? Or are these two separate incidents?" I ask them, trying to sort through the tangled web of what I know.

"Let's map it out. Put what we know into each scenario. One where they are connected, and one where they are separate," Ella suggests.

"If the rat is somehow connected to the evidence leak *and* the proof of the companies disappearing, then it can't be Dec," I offer.

"And if they aren't related?" Ella asks.

I inhale deeply. "Then Dec is our number one suspect."

"I'll try to trace who sent the evidence to Dec's computer and where they sent it from," Eagan offers.

"And I'll pry information out of Peyton, one way or another," I say.

Ella gives me a concerned look. "What if the rat, or whoever is after Owen, is now after you? With that evidence, they will know you're involved."

"This isn't the first time my mark has turned to targeting me. Remember that assignment in Russia a few years ago?"

Ella shakes her head.

"Well, I not only put the target behind bars but took out the *entire operation.*"

Ella huffs. "You like to conveniently leave out the parts where you almost die."

"But I didn't." I wink at her.

She tries to laugh, but it sounds desperate. "Nova, don't leave me out of this, please. Tell me how I can help, because I'm going to, whether you give me something to do or not."

I don't want her involved because if this all goes south, she risks jail time, too. But I understand why she wants to assist, and I've never been more grateful for a friend like her.

"Talk to Dec for me. Take him out for a drink." If there's one thing Ella is good at, it's listening, and Declan will probably need someone to talk to after what happened with Owen. In fact, I'm counting on it.

Ella nods and beams at me. "Done."

With our next tasks set up, I head for the door again. "Time to pay Peyton Radd a visit and find our rat."

Chapter 30

"I can't find him," Noah tells me at the cafe in the lobby of Regenerative Industries.

I can't help the frown and lick of frustration creeping up my spine.

Noah's face falls. "We know when Peyton checked out of the hotel. We're following every lead we have."

Running a hand through my hair, I drop into one of the empty chairs at the cafe. No one is around. After the news of Owen's arrest, it's been eerily quiet.

When I still don't say anything, Noah pulls out the chair across from me and sits. "We *will* find him, Nova. In the meantime, is there any other way to get the information you need?"

I suck in a deep breath, willing my racing mind to slow down. "There's one."

Noah's eyes narrow, and even his usually cheery mouth turns downward. "You mean Owen?"

I nod without looking at him. "I never got the whole story from him. We skated around the truth. I suspect he knows more than he ever told me. More than he told anyone."

Noah's frown doesn't disappear as he leans forward, reaching for my hand. "You up for that conversation?"

Meeting his eyes, I let him cover my hand with his own. "No. But what choice do I have?"

Noah pats my hand and pulls away. "You're going to tell him everything, too?"

It isn't really a question. He knows the answer, and so do I, but I nod anyway. "I have to."

"You ready?"

I snort. "No."

Noah pauses and studies my face for a few moments. "He's a good guy, Nova. I wouldn't underestimate him. He knows you, too. It won't change anything between you."

My eyes widen, and I shake my head. He can't be serious.

"It changes everything, Noah," I whisper.

You can't love someone if you don't truly know them. You can't build a relationship on lies. And when the truth finally comes out, which it always does, everything crumbles. I knew this from the beginning, and yet...I couldn't help myself.

Noah's eyes crinkle in the corners. His concern for me is written all over his face. "Was it worth it?"

His question throws me, and I tilt my head. I don't speak right away, though I've known the answer for a long time.

"Yes."

My heart is racing while I check in at the correctional facility where Owen is being held. With shaking hands, I'm barely able to sign my name on the extensive forms they make me fill out.

I've been going over and over what I want to say to him. What I want to start with. But I'm still terrified. Not of what I have to say, but because of what I know will be waiting for me. The betrayal, the lies, and—most terrifying of all—a broken man.

The guard walks me through the security gates and down a long hallway filled with prisoners, some of whom I put behind those bars. Most sneer and shout as my red heels click along the tiled floor. I ignore them, keeping my gaze forward and my hands in fists. Clammy sweat builds on my palms but don't wipe it away.

The guard opens a private meeting room door. Because of my CIA status, the private meeting was easy to procure.

"You'll have fifteen minutes," the guard says, his tone flat and devoid of any emotion.

"I was told I'd have as long as I needed?"

The guard shrugs. "Those were the orders I was given."

"From whom?" I push my anger down, but I fail to keep my voice even.

The guard raises a brow. "Fuck if I know."

I squeeze my eyes shut and pinch the bridge of my nose. "Thank you," I say between clenched teeth.

The guard doesn't hesitate as he slips out of the room and locks me in.

Usually, I have unlimited time to question prisoners. My CIA status gives me that clearance. Someone messed with it, and there's only one person who has the ability to do that.

Declan.

I pace back and forth, the wheels in my head turning. I'm trying to figure out why Declan would do that when I hear the familiar click of the door across from me opening, and I stop, my body going completely rigid.

There's the shuffle of two sets of feet across the smooth tile, but I can't look. Not yet.

"I'll retrieve you in fifteen minutes," the new guard mumbles as he pulls out a chair for Owen. The chair scrapes across the tile floor, echoing throughout the small interrogation room.

Owen doesn't make a sound. No sound of surprise, no greeting, no angry outburst. Nothing but utter silence.

When the click of the door closing behind Owen sounds, I suck in a deep breath and turn.

My heart stops in my chest when I see him. He isn't even looking at me. His head is bowed, his gaze on his hands, bound in his lap. He looks ten times smaller than I remember.

"Owen," I whisper, and I cannot keep the waver from my voice.

He finally raises his head. Slowly, as if it's taking all of his effort to do so.

Tears gather in my eyes, though I don't let them fall. They make my vision blurry, but I still see him. He looks as though he's already lost weight. There are deep circles under his eyes, and they look bloodshot, as if he hasn't slept in days.

I tentatively walk over to the table and pull out the chair in front of him. He tracks my movement but still doesn't say anything.

Sitting slowly, I want so badly to reach out and touch him, but I fold my hands in my lap instead.

"Owen," I repeat.

He drops his gaze to the table, refusing to speak.

"Please, Owen. I need to talk to you."

"So talk," he says, his voice gruff. He still refuses to meet my gaze.

I squeeze my eyes shut, willing the tears to stay where they are. "I'm so very sorry. I'm sorry I didn't tell you. I'm sorry it was me who landed you here. I know you won't believe me, but after I learned about everything, I tried to *save you*."

His eyes snap to mine and now anger simmers in them. "Tell me, Nova, how'd you get the evidence they're using against me?"

My heart hammers in my chest. He knows. He knows how I got the evidence. I was the only person he'd ever let into his house. This wasn't about me not telling him about my job. This was about the walls he let me tear down. The trust he gave me. And I broke it so thoroughly.

I hold his gaze, as hard as it is for me to do. His eyes bore into mine, and those tears I'm trying to hold back finally slip. "Your house." My voice cracks.

He huffs and looks away from me, the disappointment replacing the anger, and it feels so much worse.

"Owen, please," I beg, instinctively reaching toward him and coming up with nothing but a cold table between us. "This isn't over. I want to help get you out of here. I want..." I sputter a bit as more tears flow down my face. "Shit, I *need* to help you get out of here. I know it will never make up for what I've done. I know that what happened is irreparable. You don't ever have to forgive me. You can hate me for eternity. But I need to do this. I need to finish this. I need to get you out of here, and I need to get those assholes behind bars."

Owen slowly turns, but my words only seem to spark more of his anger. "So this is about you?" His question comes out as a low growl.

Shit. I deserved that.

I let my head drop, wiping away the tears on my cheeks with the back of my hand. "No. This is about saving your company and your charities. About saving your brother. About saving *you*. You may not believe that, and that's fine. But I'll ask you one more time. Will you help me?"

A silence stretches between us. I find the courage to raise my eyes to Owen. He's studying me intently. The anger is still there, but there's something else that has my heart thumping wildly in my chest—determination.

"What do you need?" he says at last.

"Any chance you have backups of your emails and files pertaining to the acquisitions? Someone wiped what I found." I cringe at admitting I hacked his computer.

If that fact is a surprise to him, he doesn't show it. "Who wiped it?"

"We don't know. That's what I'm trying to figure out. How all this fits together."

Owen cocks his head to the side and runs a hand over the stubble along his cheek. I track the movement unintentionally.

The corner of Owen's mouth kicks up slightly, or perhaps it was my imagination.

"You have a pen and paper?" he asks.

I nod, pulling them out of my purse and sliding them over to him.

"I made hard copies of all the correspondence with all the companies I acquired. They're at my house. I didn't trust them to stay on my computer. There might be something in there." He writes down everything I need.

My eyes widen. Something resembling hope stirs in my chest.

He pushes the paper to me, and I study it for a moment. "Have you told your lawyer about this folder?" I ask.

He shakes his head. "It only implicates me further, I'm afraid. But there's a chance there's something I missed the first time."

My heart sinks, and the hope deflates as fast as it rose. "So you truly believe there's nothing that can get you out of here?"

"No, Nova. I don't. I'm guilty. We both know that. I can't run from this. I knew I'd have to face it eventually. I just..." He trails off, running a hand through his hair and diverting his eyes. The chain between his cuffs sounds ominous. "I didn't expect...." I can tell he doesn't want to say his next words. "You."

My hands shake, holding the piece of paper with the information that I'd hoped might help him. He doesn't have to say it, but the implication is there in the words and the way his green eyes now pierce my very soul. He meant he didn't expect to fall for me.

"Nova?" he says hesitantly, his eyes never leaving mine. "I knew."

My eyes widen, but I'm not sure I'm surprised.

"I knew who you were. No person would have known how to deal with a gunman in the woods or be so calm about it. But I ignored it, because...because..."

He flinches and changes the subject. "You aren't in danger, are you?"

It's not his almost-admission or the question that throws me. He's angry with me, that's clear, but the fear he has about my safety almost brings me to my knees.

I respond as I always do when people ask me that question. "I'm always in danger. It's part of my job."

"That's not what I asked."

I know what he's really asking. He wants to know if he's the one responsible for my life being threatened.

I shake my head. "Owen, you are not responsible for my safety. Believe me, if you knew some of the assignments I've had, this one would look like a cake walk. I can't promise you I'll make it out of this alive. I can't ever promise that, but I have a really good team. A team that is risking their lives and careers to help me. To help *you*."

Owen leans back in his chair and rubs his tired, beautiful green eyes. "Why?" I almost don't hear the question as his voice is so quiet.

Suddenly, I'm angry for reasons I can't understand. I slam my fist on the table, making Owen jump, and I stand, leaning over the table. "You're seriously asking me why? Do you not see?"

Owen looks shell-shocked but squeaks out, "See what?"

I pull back and straighten my spine. "Do you have any idea how much the people in your life care about you? About your mission? About what you're doing for this fucked up world we live in? For fucks' sake, even Noell is helping, and she *hates* me. But she *loves* you! You are an idiot, do you know that?"

Owen appears stunned into silence.

"You seem all self-sacrificing, thinking that you aren't leaving anyone behind by ending up here. That everyone will be better off without you. But you're wrong!"

I start pacing back and forth across the floor, my heels clicking frantically.

"You are fucking loved, and somehow you have no clue." I shake my head, the anger still red-hot in my veins. "We're all risking something for someone. Isn't that what love is? Putting your heart on the line for someone? And all these people are risking a hell of a lot for you. So you better give me everything you know, or else I'll be back here, and this time I'll be behind bars right with you, and I will give you hell for the rest of your days!"

I stop my pacing and glare at him. Owen's eyes widen, and his mouth opens and shuts.

We hold each other's gaze for a few moments until the door behind Owen opens, and the guard comes traipsing in.

"Times up," he says, grabbing Owen's arm and pulling him to stand.

He's ushered to the door. Tears fill my eyes again, knowing that this may be the last time I ever see him, and I'm too much of a coward to say what I really want to.

Owen stops right before the door, and the guard lets him. He turns, tears clouding his own eyes. "Check the folder, Nova. And for what it's worth, I may hate you for what you've done, but I don't think I'll ever stop loving *you*."

With that, the door slams behind him. I'm left with nothing but utter silence and a heart that hurts in ways I never knew it could.

"I love you, too," I whisper into the quiet, but it doesn't answer me back.

Chapter 31

There's a frenzy of people at my apartment when I return. Ella and Eagan are parked at the island counter, heads smashed together as they search through files on Eagan's computer. Parker and Noell sit on the couch, rifling through papers that are spread haphazardly all over the coffee table.

I almost stumble when I see Evan and Jax rushing around the kitchen, chatting and cooking for everyone, along with generously filling wine glasses. Even they had come to help me?

Jax notices me first and gently places a plate of appetizers on the counter before approaching me carefully. Everyone else stops what they're doing and watches us.

"I take it everyone knows where I was?" I ask, though I know the answer.

They all nod as Jax stops in front of me, placing a hand on each of my shoulders. His eyes pinch together.

"I won't ask if you're ok. I know you're not," he says.

I suck in a shaky breath and let my forehead fall to his chest. He pulls me into a hug.

"How much do you know?" I ask into the softness of his tight T-shirt.

"We told them everything," Ella says, coming over to stand next to us. "They showed up and saw us all here and wouldn't stop asking questions. They worked most of it out on their own anyway."

"Are you mad?" Jax asks softly, pushing me away so he can look at me.

I shake my head. "I'm relieved, actually."

Jax gives me a cautious smile. "We've got you, Barbie."

I roll my eyes at the nickname, but my heart swells. If anyone can help Owen, it's these people. Those I trust with my life. The thought of Declan not being here, though, has my mouth pulling down into a frown.

Jax grabs my chin and pulls my attention back to him. Worry lines form around his beautiful eyes.

I step back and wave my hand at him. "I'll be fine."

God, how I wish that were true, but mercifully, Jax lets it drop.

I'm eager to get back to work, and perhaps it's because I want to ignore all the complicated feelings. That's what I've always done—pushed them away until they consume me.

"Anything?" I ask Eagan, moving toward the kitchen island to where he's hunched over his computer.

He peers at me over the top of it. "I have the backup I made from the evidence that was wiped, but there's nothing here anymore. Everything you saved on the companies and their illegal operations is gone. Whoever wiped the evidence also got rid of a lot more." He shakes his head, defeated. "I'm sorry, Nova. I'll keep looking."

"No luck on tracing who might have deleted it or sent it to Dec?" I ask the question, but from the look on his face, I already know the answer.

Ella answers for him. "No. It's all broken threads."

I turn to Parker and Noell next, the hope dwindling. The tension returns to my entire body, my nails digging into the skin of my palms.

"Anything?" This time it's nothing but a whisper.

Parker shakes his head, but it's Noell who speaks. "I found some interesting transfers of money. Inconspicuous payments spread out over years that are worth pennies in comparison to the overall financials of these companies. Most people would think nothing of it. Perhaps it's an employee paying for their morning coffee on the company's tab, but I found the same thing happening in all three companies. Same transactions, same amounts of money, all transferred on the same day over the last ten years."

My eyes widen, and I step closer to Noell. "What does it mean?"

She runs a hand through her perfectly curled hair, looking more frazzled than I've ever seen her. "I don't know yet. But it's odd enough to make me think it's connected to something bigger."

"Can you trace the money?"

"I can help her trace it," Eagan offers, hopping off his chair and reaching for the financial papers Noell highlighted and scribbled with notes.

"Do it," I say, finally giving my attention to Parker. The one person I was most afraid to face.

He must notice my tears, because his brow pinches. "How is he?"

I take a deep breath, letting my shoulders sink. "About as you'd expect. Defeated. Furious with me."

Parker stands and stops right in front of me, close enough that I have to angle my head up to peer into his sad blue eyes. "And you?"

There's only one word that comes to mind, that I can say—the truth. "Broken."

There's a deafening silence that follows, as if no one knows what to say. As if they didn't expect me to say it out loud. As if they didn't expect me to actually admit it, even if they saw it in me.

No one gets a chance to say anything because Noah barges into the apartment, his eyes wildly searching the room until they land on me.

"We found him. Peyton Radd is at Regenerative Industries right now."

Peyton sits across from me, feet propped on Owen's desk, a half-smirk planted on his face.

"Tell me what you know," I snap at him, unable to hide my irritation, knowing full well he probably could have prevented this whole situation.

"You haven't held up your end of the bargain," he responds with a lazy shrug.

"I don't have the authority to do so. That person is currently in jail."

Peyton lowers his feet to the ground and leans forward until his elbows are propped on the desk with his head held in his hands. "Come now, Miss Riley. You and I both know your boss wouldn't have left you empty-handed."

How the fuck does he know so much?

Still annoyed, I reach into Owen's top drawer and pull out an employment contract I found minutes before Peyton walked through the door. I slam the contract on the desk in front of him, just out of reach.

"Now talk," I say.

Peyton winks. "Have you found your rat, Miss Riley?" My face must give me away because he continues, shaking his head. "I pegged you for being smarter than that. Perhaps someone has been a distraction? Not that I can blame you—"

I slam my fist on the table, effectively cutting him off. "Get to the point," I hiss.

He holds his hands up in mock surrender. "Okay. Okay. I suppose it's story time." His snakelike smile returns as he leans back against the chair, putting his hands behind his head.

The way he looks at me sends chills down my spine. Every alarm bell in my head is screaming to kick the fucker out, but I know I need the information he has. He also knows I can't do this without him, and that's what makes the anger boil in my gut.

"Everyone assumes I'm always the bad guy, Miss Riley."

I snort but let him continue.

"But, you see, I'm a businessman like everyone else around here."

I want to point out that most businessmen don't go around assassinating people, but then again, that would be awfully hypocritical of me, so I keep my mouth shut.

"I take business where I can get it. I rarely pick sides. After all, this world only cares about money."

I can't argue with him there.

"Recently, I found myself in an interesting predicament. Oh, how you've woven a tangled web, Miss Riley."

"What is that supposed to mean?" I snap before I can stop myself.

Peyton shakes his head and waves his finger at my interruption as if I'm a petulant child. "I found myself in the company of a very interesting employer that just happens to have been involved in your precarious last assignment, but what's even more interesting is that you found yourself in the same situation with your current case."

My mouth falls open as Peyton squints, thinking for a moment. "Wait, I suppose it's no longer your current case, seeing as your target is in jail. And once again, the people you should be after are not only off the hook but richer than they were before."

I clench my fists under the desk. The heat of my anger creeps up my neck. "Who, Peyton? I need a name."

"Vivario." He smirks at me, watches me, his face slowly morphing into a smug smile as the truth dawns on me.

"Vivario. Vivarium. Reptiles. Snakes. The black snake crime syndicate," I whisper.

Peyton claps mockingly. "Very well done, Miss Riley. Now was that so hard?"

I want to punch the man in the face so badly that my hands shake with restraint.

Peyton stops clapping and leans forward. "This is where the fun part comes in." He pauses for dramatic effect, and I nearly knock him unconscious. "I was hired by the black snake crime syndicate to assassinate Owen Mills."

I suspected it, but the question I wanted to know most was: "Why?"

Peyton shrugs. "Why else? Money. He cut off the funds from those three companies when he acquired them by destroying the men who were bank rolling the entire crime operation. You can imagine how unhappy they were when they found out."

Peyton's smile turns sinister. He leans closer to me as if he has a secret. "And imagine their reaction when they found out you almost ruined their mission in Italy and then wound up protecting the one man that may have taken down the biggest crime syndicate in the world by murdering a bunch of rich creeps."

"What were they trying to do in Italy?" I ask, though my mind is beginning to link everything together, and I'm pretty sure I already know the answer.

"Get the CIA off their trail. They did an admirable job, if I do say so myself. Not only did you fail your mission in Italy, but now it's under investigation, halting all efforts to take them down."

"But how did they know?"

Peyton clicks his tongue. "Come now, Miss Riley. I know you're smarter than that."

I squeeze my eyes closed and take a deep breath, my composure on the brink of snapping. "The rat."

"Very good, Miss Riley."

"My rat is someone at the CIA." I suspected it. No one else outside the CIA, aside from Eagan, could have gotten access to my files. But that doesn't narrow it down much.

Peyton claps enthusiastically. "Very good! See, I knew you were smarter than you look."

"If I ever find myself alone in your presence again, Mr. Radd, you'd better watch yourself. I will not hold back on punching that smug smirk right off your face. Permanently."

Peyton winks. "I knew I liked you."

I ignore him. "Who's the rat, Peyton? No bullshit this time."

Peyton stands. "I'm afraid I don't know the answer to that question, Miss Riley. I've given you everything I know. That's something you'll have to figure out on your own."

I slam my fist against the desk, rattling everything on it. Peyton flinches but doesn't seem surprised by my outburst.

"And why, *Mr. Radd*, are you suddenly revealing all of this to me? Why are you switching sides in this little game of yours?" I can't help the derision that drips from my lips.

Peyton smiles so wide. A show to mask his own anger. "You see, I'm a betting man, Miss Riley. I like to place my bets where I know I'll come out on top."

"Yes, you've said that."

Peyton narrows his gaze but continues, "And I'm betting on you and Owen Mills this time."

"That seems like a terrible bet. If you haven't noticed, Mr. Mills is currently sitting in jail for the murder of three people, and my trial is only two weeks away."

Peyton chuckles. "You see, Miss Riley, I do very thorough research on all my targets and all my employees. I know your entire past. I know Mr. Mills' entire past. I know everything there is to know about the workings of the black snake crime syndicate."

"And you still bet on us?"

"Yes."

"Why?"

There's an odd glint in his eye as he smiles at me. "Because no one fights harder than a broken woman, Miss Riley. And you are most definitely broken."

I stare after him, my mouth gaping, as he heads for the door. But before my brain can sew together a single thought, he stops and looks back at me. "And perhaps you won't believe me, Miss Riley, but I'm also a bit of a romantic. I'd like to see love win just once, even with all cards stacked against it."

With that, he's gone.

Chapter 32

"It has to be Dec," Ella says, pacing around my apartment as everyone listens to the news I received from Peyton.

"But how? Why? It can't be him. We've been friends for a decade," I tell her.

She stops and faces me. "I know, Nova, but it's the only obvious choice. He has access to your accounts and the best hackers in the business, and he was recently appointed director, giving him even more clearance and control in the CIA and more sway with the board of directors. It just fits."

"It fits except that he would never do that to me," I snap, falling onto the large, leather chair next to the couch and burying my face in my hands.

Ella's voice is quiet this time. "Do you think maybe your relationship with Dec might be clouding your judgment here?"

I know she didn't say it to make me angry, but I can't help the rage. My hands instinctively ball into fists, and I slam them against the armrests on the chair. "I don't know!" My voice falls to a whisper an instant later. "I don't know anything anymore."

Ella places a supportive hand on my shoulder. "I'm meeting him for dinner tonight. We *will* figure this out."

I nod, miserable, when Noell suddenly shouts and Eagans face lights up.

"We found it!" she screams.

I'm out of the chair before anyone can blink. Eagan swivels his computer around to show everyone.

"What am I looking at?" I ask.

"The money transfers," Noell says, pointing to the screen.

I squint, trying to make sense of the numbers and words I'm seeing.

There's a tense moment of silence. My eyes widen. "Italy," I whisper.

"This is the proof we need! We can take them down, Nova. And it will likely help your case, too," Noell says, beaming, and I'm not sure I've ever seen her smile.

"But what about Owen?" I ask, happy that we're getting what we need to end the crime syndicate once and for all, but I'm still worried we won't be able to save the man I've come to love.

Everyone stares at me blankly except Parker. His face falls, and it looks as though he might cry.

I pull back from the computer screen. "Compile all the evidence against the crime syndicate. Peyton all but confirmed their headquarters is the Vivario in Sicily. I do not doubt that if we raid the place, we'll find the people in charge. In the meantime, I'm going to Owen's house. He said he kept all correspondence with the CEOs of the companies he acquired. I'm hoping there is something in there that can help us."

"Did he say there was?" Parker's hopeful voice makes my heart sink.

I shake my head. "He said it only implicates him further, but I'm checking anyway."

"Oh," is all Parker says as he slumps against the couch cushions.

On my way out, Parker blurts, "Do you want company?"

I don't turn right away. I want to say yes, but I also don't know if my heart can take it. I don't know if I'll be able to hold myself together in the one place that is completely and utterly Owen.

When I face Parker, he's looking at me expectantly, with misplaced hope dancing in his eyes.

"I could use the company," I squeak out.

Parker smiles, the identical dimple to Owen's making an appearance. My heart clenches at the sight of it. He jumps up off the couch, grabs his half-drank coffee cup and his black leather jacket, and follows me out the door.

Noah's waiting to escort us. He leaves behind a few of his security guards to protect the apartment.

None of us says anything on the thirty-minute drive to the small, stone cottage. Noah stations himself outside the house, checking the perimeter. Parker grabs the hidden key under the flower pot by the front door, and I roll my eyes at the idiocy of hiding it there.

When we both step inside, it's silent. The only sound comes from the faint hum of the refrigerator in the kitchen.

Parker walks toward the sink. A few dirty dishes sit there as if someone's still living here. Nothing, it seems, has been touched since Owen's arrest. It still smells like coffee, with a hint of pine. A hint of Owen.

I choke down the emotion threatening to burst and turn right, toward the living room. The books haven't been touched. Owen's notes are still spread across the coffee table. I blindly follow the directions Owen wrote on the piece of paper he gave me at the jail. The folder we're looking for is tucked under the couch cushion closest to the window.

Sure enough, when I pull the cushion up, there's a sizable manilla folder overflowing with papers.

I smell a new batch of coffee and register the quiet clanking of dishes. I read copies of email after email. The reasons why Owen did what he did solidify with each one I read. Those men were monsters, and Owen knew it.

I'm so absorbed in reading that I don't recognize Parker standing right in front of me until he shoves a steaming cup of coffee right under my nose.

I finally look away from what I'm doing and mumble a quick thanks as he plops down next to me. He takes a large sip of his own coffee before asking, "Find anything?"

I shake my head. "Aside from the fact that all of these emails make me want to murder these men all over again?"

Parker raises a brow. "That bad?"

"That bad."

"But nothing that might help him?"

"Not yet."

We sit in companionable silence for a while as Parker reads the emails I've finished, the crease in his brow deepening with each one.

I'm three-quarters of the way through, and am about to give up, when a single word catches my eye on the next paper.

Kill.

I quickly read the email, my heart rate kicking up and my back tensing.

Parker senses my change in demeanor. "Did you find something?"

I don't answer right away. I race to finish what I'm reading, but the tension in my body increases with every sentence.

"Shit. I think I may have something," I finally say, grabbing the next one, hoping for even more.

"What is it?" Parker asks.

I stop, even though I want to keep going, to see if this is actually real or not.

"There's a small chance we can lessen his sentence or even get him out of this," I say at last. "'Small' is the keyword here. Owen thought the emails would implicate him further, but I think, due to a few choice words used, we may be able to claim self-defense."

Parker's mouth drops open. "Really?"

I nod. "These men weren't careful in how they spoke to him via email. There are pretty clear death threats in here. And if I can get Peyton to testify that he was hired to kill him, we might have a chance."

"How the hell are you going to get Peyton to testify? Won't that land him in jail?"

"Not if I can work out a deal with him. To drop the cases against him in exchange for helping take down the black snake crime syndicate *and* testify on behalf of Owen."

"Well, shit," Parker says, running his hands through his curly blond hair.

My heart beats as though it might burst out of my chest. I don't want to get my hopes up. I don't want to have to rely so much on Peyton. But I also can't believe there's even a chance Owen might walk away from all this.

My hopes are instantly dashed when I hear Noah yell from outside, followed by a series of rapid gunshots.

Snatching the papers, I stuff them into the folder and drop to the ground, pulling Parker with me.

"Get behind the couch and stay there," I demand, pushing him toward it.

"What about you?" he asks, his voice high-pitched.

Pulling a gun from the back of my pants, I shove the folder in his arms.

"I'll be fine. Trained agent, remember?" I say with a slight upturn of my lips, hoping to ease his fear even though my panic is creeping dangerously close to the surface. I don't know how many men are out there, and there's only Noah and me.

I hand Parker my phone. "Call Ella. She'll know how to get us help."

I crouch and slink toward the front door and the sound of shouting and gunshots. *Noah, you fucking better be alive.*

Peeking my head above the window ledge next to the front door, I notice three shadows among the trees on the opposite side of the driveway. When

I scan the area they're shooting at, I finally relax, if only a little. Noah crouches behind the car, reloading his gun.

He's alive.

A plan takes root in my head, and instead of trying to reach Noah, I decide to use him as a distraction. I slink along the floor, careful to not be spotted through the windows. When I reach the dim hallway, I stand and make my way to Owen's bedroom. It's dark, with the curtains drawn across the French doors leading to the outside. His bed is only half-made, and the desire to crawl in it and breathe him in is strong.

Shaking my head at the stupidity of my body's response to being in this place, I make my way to the closed curtains.

Peering through the small crack between them, I search for other shooters. When I find none, I peel back the fabric and inch the doors open. Careful to stay hidden, I slink along the side of the house, sticking to the shadows.

I still hear gunshots and the voices of the men in the trees shouting directions to each other. Inwardly, I smile at their frustration in not being able to get a good enough angle to take Noah out.

Noah's booming voice echoes across the field of flowers in front of me, taunting them.

I shake my head, mumbling, "Cocky bastard."

When I reach the corner of the house that faces the driveway, I plaster my back to the cold stone behind me and ready myself. I know I need to be quick. I won't get more than one or two shots before their guns are turned on me.

Time seems to slow when I step around the corner, my pistol pointed at the man closest to me. He doesn't see it coming, and the bullet pierces him in the back, exiting through his chest. His cry thunders through the air as he falls, but I don't spend another moment on him. I release a second bullet aimed at the person twenty feet from him.

I aim for his chest. The man's head swivels at the sound of his comrade's shout. The bullet misses, piercing his shoulder instead. Dropping the gun, he shouts for the remaining shooter to take me out.

Instantly stepping behind the side of the house, I calculate that I have approximately two hundred feet where I'm completely exposed. I have to be faster than the other gunman, or I'm dead.

I take off running, aiming for the door to Owen's bedroom that I left open.

Noah shouts in frustration.

They took the bait.

I will my legs to move faster as I close the distance. I only have seconds before I'm exposed.

As the gunshot sounds, I grab the doorframe, pulling myself into Owen's bedroom and instantly drop to the ground. A bullet grazes the wood frame on the outside of the door, splintering it.

I kick the door closed with my foot, yanking the curtains closed so the shooter has no clear line of sight.

It works, but not well enough. A bullet passes through the glass, shattering it, and I duck as the pieces rain across the room. One catches me on the cheek. Blood drips down my face and neck.

Ignoring it, I will myself to move. I crawl through the bedroom door, kicking it shut behind me. Moving down the hall toward the kitchen and living room, I shout, "Parker!"

"I'm still here!" he answers back.

My relief is short-lived. I hear my assailant push open the broken French doors in the bedroom behind me.

"You need to get to Noah!" I yell as my brain scans the room for the best place to hide.

Another gunshot sounds outside, and I desperately hope it's not Noah at the other end of it.

Parker appears from behind the couch, clutching the folder like his life depends on it. His eyes are wide, and he's shaking.

"Get to the car, Parker. Tell Noah to take the papers somewhere secure. Now!"

Parker looks like he might not listen to me, but when the door to Owen's bedroom opens, he beelines for the exit, slipping slightly as he grabs the handle and pulls himself through.

I throw myself behind the kitchen island, hoping the shooter will come into my line of sight so I can take him down. That's the best-case scenario, though I know he's probably smarter than that.

It's an eternity waiting for the footsteps to draw closer. My heart hammers in my chest, the familiar sensation of adrenaline pumping through my veins. My body becomes completely still, my vision laser-focused. My arms hold the gun in front of me, not a tremble in them.

The footsteps stop short of the opening to the kitchen.

"It's over, Miss Riley. Your evidence is in our hands, and your friends are caught."

I roll my eyes at the clear lie. The obvious intention is to frighten me into submission.

Instead of answering, I move as silently as I can across the wood floor.

"I know exactly where you are, Miss Riley. There's no escaping this."

I back up against the wall. I know he's in the hallway directly on the other side. I'm banking on the fact that he'll think I'm still behind the island, trying to get the best angle to take him out.

I wait for him to make his move, knowing it's only a matter of seconds.

As I predicted, he steps slightly past the kitchen wall, looking directly where I just was. Another careful step, and I press the trigger. The bullet goes straight through his thigh, and he screams, falling with a loud thud against the wood floor. The gun he is holding bounces out of his hand.

He reaches for it, but I get there first, scooping it up and aiming both weapons directly at his head. His eyes go wide as he stares up at me.

I shake my head. "You want to know why I'm so good at my job?"

When he doesn't do anything but grab his bleeding leg and moan, I say, "Because men like you *always* underestimate women like me."

The front door whips open, crashing against the wall.

"Nova!" Noah's panicked voice shouts from the doorway.

I smile. He's safe. We're safe.

"In here!" I shout back.

When he rounds the corner and finds me standing over my target, his shoulders slump, and his lips turn up. "That's my girl."

Ella switches on the light in my bedroom, and I bolt upright, wiping the sleep from my eyes. Jax and Evan both groan simultaneously next to me. We've barely slept in the last forty-eight hours.

The look on Ella's face has me bolting out of bed. Tears streak down her face, her eyes bloodshot from crying. I fear the worst, but I wait for her to speak.

"It's not Dec, Nova."

The fear and pain I've held tightly wound up in my chest finally release, and identical tears streak down my face.

"How do you know?" I ask with a shaky voice.

Ella raises a brow. "Besides the fact that the second you were brought up, he burst into tears?"

"Shit. I've never seen Dec cry."

Ella lets out a shaky laugh and falls into the chair next to the bed. "Neither have I."

I remain standing, swaying back and forth, full of nervous energy.

"He told me everything, even though it broke about a million rules. Everything he has on Owen's case, on your case, on the black snake crime syndicate. He put most of it together himself with very little information."

I huff, stopping my swaying body. "I'm an idiot. I should have trusted my gut. He could have helped us."

Ella wisely doesn't comment, because even though she suspected he might be the rat, in the beginning she encouraged me to talk to him about everything.

"I didn't tell him the evidence we have because I was still afraid he might be our rat, but as the conversation went on, and the more he revealed..." Ella trails off, more tears spilling from her eyes. "He's risking his career for you, Nova. He told me he's going up against the board with the shitty evidence he has and will resign after. He is fighting for you."

"Fuck."

How could I have so badly underestimated him?

There's a long silence where no one even moves, though their eyes are trained on me.

I take a deep breath, meeting their expectant faces. "I'm going to Dec with all of it. I'll explain everything."

It's the answer they were all anticipating, but as I quickly exit the room, Ella's voice trails after me. "If the rat isn't Dec, then who is it?"

I stop in the doorway, turning enough to notice her face.

I'd already figured it out as she was speaking. Perhaps I'd always known, and I'm angry at being so foolish and as blind as Peyton implied. But my fragmented memories and dreams finally make sense. There's only one person with the tech skills. There's only one person who was in Italy with me when everything went to shit. And there's only one person who has a vested interest in my trial going well. Not because they care about me, but because they care about being outed as a double agent.

"It's Gray."

Chapter 33

"You broke protocol!" Declan shouts into the phone.

"Dec, I had to. You know why."

"I can't protect you anymore, Nova. You're on your own with this one." He sounds so defeated that tears spring to my eyes.

"I know. You don't have to, Dec. You never had to, though I appreciate that you always have."

Declan sighs. "Even if you take down this crime syndicate *and* provide evidence clearing Mr. Mills, I don't think I can get you your job back. Not with so many infractions."

"I don't want it." I hadn't even let myself think those words. The CIA is my whole life, but as I look around the room at the people who've risked their own lives and careers to help me, all of them zeroed in on my conversation with Dec, I realize the CIA might not be what I want anymore. This job isn't my whole life.

They are.

"You've worked so hard, Nova. How can you say that?"

"Because I've realized there's more to life than this. There's more than putting bad guys behind bars." I don't know why I'm suddenly whispering. "I want to *live,* Dec. I'm done. No more chasing revenge that will never fill the hole in my chest since my father's death."

I hear him sigh on the other end of the phone, his voice also coming out as a whisper. "And Owen?"

"What about him?" I rein in the anger that throws me off at the mention of his name.

"What if you can't get him out?"

It's a practical question, one I've avoided asking myself for fear of the answer.

"Then at least I tried. At least I can live without the regret."

There's a long silence. He knows I'm full of shit.

"He has the best lawyers in the city, thanks to his father," Noell says carefully.

My head snaps to Noell, who sheepishly smiles at me. That's a story I'm going to have to pry out of her when this is done.

Declan continues, "And your evidence is good, especially with your whistleblower, but if you can't get Peyton to testify and show up to court *on time*, then I think the best you can hope for is twenty years."

I growl, unable to help my reaction. That fucker better testify.

Noah chuckles from the doorway, leaning against it in the easy way he always does, arms folded across his chest. It's almost as if he's looking forward to the hell I will rain down on the man myself.

"I'll get him to testify," I say through gritted teeth.

Declan laughs this time, probably since he knows full well the facial expression I'm wearing. How did I ever doubt him?

"But what about you? Are you coming to the trial? Are you testifying for him?" he asks.

I've dreaded this question, but there's no way I'm sitting this one out, not if it helps Owen. "If the lawyers think it will help, I'll testify. Regardless, I'll be there."

I notice everyone's shoulders drop a little at my words.

Another long silence has me already anticipating Declan's next question. "And Gray? Do you have any evidence?"

Declan sounds like he wants to track the man down and strangle him to death. I don't blame him. I want to do the same.

"Not yet. Eagan's working on hacking his computer now."

The use of Eagan's name has Declan asking another question. "That reminds me, Eagan."

Eagan's head snaps up from the computer, and he pales.

"Once you gather all that evidence, I'd like to have a chat with you in my office."

Eagan's eyes widen, and Ella holds back a laugh, smothering it with her hand.

"Stop being an ass, Dec," I hiss.

Declan laughs. "I'd like to offer you a job before I resign."

Eagan visibly sighs, and Ella beams at him, patting his knee in moral support.

"I'll be there, sir," Eagan says.

Declan huffs. "Please don't call me sir."

"It makes him feel old," I say sarcastically in Eagan's direction.

Declan snorts, then clears his throat. "Get the evidence, and then we'll take him out. We'll take them all out."

"Thank you, Dec," I say, though it's not enough. It will *never* be enough after all he's done for me.

"You never have to thank me, Nova. There is nothing I wouldn't do to help you. You are the sister I never had."

There are nods of confirmation all across the room, their faces bright as if they share similar feelings toward me, especially Jax.

"Shut up before you make me cry again," I snap at the phone.

I hear his laugh, and I wish I could reach through the phone and throw my arms around him.

"Let's go take down those motherfuckers," he says, and I smile at everyone surrounding me. At the family I never knew I'd have.

I find myself staring at the one man I had hoped to never see again. His snakelike smirk is plastered on his face, as if he already knows what I'm going to ask him.

"We all know you're a smug bastard, Peyton, and that you're really only here to gloat, but for once, could you please not give me hell for it? I've had a rough couple of days," I seethe.

Peyton laughs, looking around at my entourage who insisted they be here for this. Noah is definitely here to watch me punch Peyton. Parker wants to help convince him to testify for his brother, and Noell is here because—I'm now almost positive—there's something going on between her and Parker, though she'd never admit it.

Eagan is ready to record everything being said for evidence purposes. Ella is here for me and Eagan, and Jax and Evan are excited to witness what I've really been doing in my career.

Though when my gaze finds Jax, who smirks back at Noah, I change my mind—he's here to watch me punch Peyton, too.

Who am I to deny them?

I play the part, though, biding my time.

"Proceed, Miss Riley," Peyton drawls, crossing his arms over his chest and resting his dirty shoes on Owen's desk again like he owns the place.

I try not to throw his damn feet off the desk. Not yet, at least. I need to get verbal confirmation that he'll testify.

"I need you to testify for Mr. Mills."

Peyton laughs. "Not a chance."

I stand leaning across the desk. "I think what I have to offer in return might be something you're interested in."

His lips curl into a sneer. "I'm listening."

Stepping out from behind the desk, I plop on the edge of it, close to Peyton. "You have ten warrants for your arrest. Did you know that? Turns out, it's hard for this company to hire you with all of those warrants. Impossible, even."

Peyton's sneer turns to a frown as he sits up, planting his feet back on the floor. I track the movement.

"I'm listening," he repeats.

"It's simple. You testify for Mr. Mills—and yes, you will legally sign that you intend to do so, as well as provide verbal confirmation, which is being recorded as we speak—and the CIA will drop every warrant. You will be free to work here."

Peyton sits up straighter. "All ten?"

I nod.

Peyton raises a brow, his lips twitching. I know I have him even before he speaks. "You have a deal, Miss Riley."

Peyton stands, holding out a hand for me to shake. I smile sweetly, reaching for his hand.

And then I punch him square in the jaw.

Unsurprised gasps circle around the room. Noah takes a few steps closer, his eyes trained on Peyton, but he's laughing so hard that I don't think he'd be able to protect me if he needed to.

Peyton rubs his jaw. His fingers swipe away blood on his lower lip. "Touché, Miss Riley. I deserved that."

This time I reach out my hand. "Truce?"

Peyton eyes my hand skeptically but smirks. This time, though, the grin doesn't twist my insides. He grabs my hand and gives it a firm shake. "Truce."

I nod, pulling away. "Welcome to the company, Mr. Radd. I'm sure Mr. Mills will love his new assistant."

Chapter 34

I hesitate at the doors to my CIA office. I haven't set foot in here in months, and for good reason.

Ella grabs my hand and gives it a squeeze in silent support.

I reach for the door and open it. Everything is the same as it was before I left. Not a paper has been touched, but it feels different somehow—foreign.

"Dec will be here any minute. Do you need anything?" Ella asks, falling into her assistant role like she'd never been kicked out of it.

"No, thank you." I'm still standing in the doorway like an idiot, afraid to enter my office.

Ella pats me on the shoulder before turning and heading to find Declan.

"Dec tells me you have the evidence, and Mr. Mills is behind bars?" Gray's voice pulls me out of my trance, and my instincts are instantly on high alert. I want to kill the man for what he's done. For all the people in that square who died. For the entire mess I find myself in. But I can't say a damn word. Not until Eagan has what we need.

I play the part I've always played so well. The submissive, people-pleasing woman. I turn and smile sweetly. "We do. Enough to get the trial dropped. At least, that's what Dec says."

He sighs as though he didn't believe Declan until I confirmed it. "Good. That's good."

I didn't notice his tells before, but I do now. I thought it was fear of losing his job at the CIA, but now I see it for what it really is. He's afraid of a blown cover. He's scared of his own damn shadow. Because perhaps he knows I'm not exactly who I pretend to be, either.

I'm something so much worse.

I cock my head to the side, still smiling. "Afraid of something, Gray?"

He narrows his gaze, and something changes in his face. He knows I know, or at least he suspects that I do.

My smile widens as I wait for his answer.

"Not at all, Miss Riley. Just worried for your career."

I wave my hand at him. "Don't be. I put in for my resignation. I have nothing left to lose." I emphasize the last part.

His eyes widen, and there is genuine fear there. He stumbles over his words. "I thought this job was everything to you?"

"Perhaps you don't know me as well as you think you do, Mr. Gray."

"Oh, Gray, did she tell you I am also stepping down after the trial of Mr. Mills?" Declan comes up beside us.

If possible, Gray's eyes widen even further. If he didn't know he's fucked before, he certainly does now. Our resignation means we're coming for blood.

Gray takes a few steps away from us, stumbling a little.

I look down at my nails. "You know, that little warehouse you said was abandoned and empty? Well, turns out"—I pause and look him dead in the eye—"you're a big fucking liar."

All color drains from Gray's face as Declan waves a hand at the seemingly-empty hallway. CIA agents swarm Gray, and among his shouts of innocence, Declan leans in close and whispers to me, "Eagan sent the evidence we need to put him behind bars, along with the drugs from the warehouse."

I lean my head against Declan's shoulder as the agents tug Gray down the hall and out of sight.

"What now?" I ask.

Declan's draws me further against his side. "We get your boyfriend back."

Peyton reluctantly complies with all of the lawyer's demands, and much to my delight, I learn his birth name is Edwin Irving.

Noah has no qualms using it against him, and I'm here for it. I haven't laughed this much in ages.

Though Peyton acts miserable at his new predicament, I can tell he's happy with how it all turned out. I catch his smiles when he turns his back on everyone, and a light in his eyes that wasn't there before.

This is exactly what he wanted, and we played right into his hands. I can't find the energy to be mad about it. Not if it gets Owen out of jail.

"Ten A.M., Peyton. If you are late, I will personally hunt you down and make your life a living hell," I warn.

Peyton frowns, knowing full well that I will come through on that threat. I will do anything to make sure the trial goes *exactly* how we've planned it. Owen's lawyers are thrilled with all the evidence we collected.

"How is he?" I ask one of them, Laurie, an older woman with silver hair and a kind smile.

"As well as you can expect him to be, given the circumstances. I think he's more optimistic since we presented the evidence and the case we're going for, but he doesn't want to get his hopes up."

"I think she's asking if he's asked about her," Peyton interrupts.

I shoot him a glare that could kill, even if what he's saying is true. He laughs and holds up his hands in surrender, turning to grab yet another cup of coffee from Owen's bar. No one's slept in days.

Laurie chuckles at Peyton's words, and my face heats, but her smile quickly fades as she answers, "No, dear. He hasn't asked about you."

Parker's been latched onto every word the lawyers have said, but he quickly switches his attention to my reaction, his face falling.

I nod. I didn't expect anything more, but damn if it doesn't hurt.

"Does he know she's involved in getting the evidence?" Parker asks, lips pulling into a thin line.

Laurie nods. "He's been told everything."

I change the subject, unsure I can take any more of this. "We will be there, on time." I glare at Peyton for emphasis. "And we'll be holding our breath."

Laurie gets up and smiles at me, patting me on the arm. Her colleague quietly gathers their papers and stuffs them in their duffel bag.

"For what it's worth, Miss Riley," Laurie continues, "he'd be a damn fool not to see what you've sacrificed for this evidence."

I nod, willing the emotion to stay buried deep, deep down. "Thank you."

No one says anything as the two lawyers leave. It's as if her words sit heavy in the room, and everyone is too afraid to set me off.

"I'm not a damn ticking time bomb for fucks' sake," I snap. "You all look as though someone died."

Noah scratches at his beard while Parker's face flushes. Noell squeezes his hand, and no one misses the movement.

"I'll kill him," Parker mumbles.

I raise a brow.

"I'll kill him if he doesn't forgive you for this. I'll never forgive him. That will show him!"

I laugh, loud and hard, clutching at my stomach. His words are so juvenile and so much like a younger brother that my chortle soon turns into a sob.

To have that kind of love.

Parker doesn't hesitate to come wrap me in a hug. He smells a bit like Owen, and it only makes me cry harder.

"I'm so tired, Parker. So fucking tired." I sob into his chest.

He strokes my hair gently. "I know you are. It's almost over."

Tomorrow. It ends tomorrow.

Chapter 35

I'm surprised to find every seat in the courtroom completely full. Every single employee at Regenerative Industries and every person Owen has ever helped with his money—and his big heart—is here. Maybe I'm not so surprised, but it throws me a bit. After all, this man murdered three people, and yet everyone still came to support him.

If I ever get close enough to Owen ever again, I'm going to throttle him for not fighting harder for himself.

Parker's gaze drops to my clenched fists, and he laughs.

I'm not mad at all the people taking up every single seat, but I'm mad at Owen for ever doubting himself and the love that these people have for him.

"He'll see it," Parker whispers in my ear, giving me a big enough smile to flash that dimple of his.

"He better," I mumble as a familiar face steps in front of us.

"Charlotte!" I shout, instinctively pulling her into a rough hug.

She chuckles into my hair, embracing me back.

"You're here!" I squeal a little too enthusiastically. I didn't think the head of the school, or any of the other people involved in Owen's charities, would show up.

She smiles widely. "Of course I'm here." She looks at Owen's brother and back to me. "Parker told us everything, and there's never been a moment when any of us doubted Mr. Mills and what he was trying to do. It doesn't matter the outcome of this trial. We will be here to support him."

I smile back at her, squeezing her one more time before she finds a seat amongst all the volunteers and workers from the charities set up by Regenerative Industries.

Even more people flood into the courtroom. Someone nudges my shoulder, and I turn to find Declan smiling. "Seems I need to meet this man properly."

I snort. "Did you ever doubt my choices?"

"Well, yes." There's humor behind his words.

I scoff, shoving his arm.

"What can I say? On paper, the man is a murderer. How could I condone that relationship?"

"He has a fair point," Parker chimes in next to me.

Noell snorts but refrains from comment.

"You shouldn't judge a book by its cover, Dec," I say. "Haven't you learned that by now, simply from being around me for the last ten years?"

Noah laughs behind us, and I shoot him a quick wink before returning my attention to Declan.

"Fair point," he replies.

I turn to Noah. "Is Peyton here?" My heart rate kicks up in preparation for that little shit bailing on us.

"I escorted Edwin here myself," Noah says with a triumphant grin.

Parker shakes his head, and I can't help the small giggle that escapes. It's mostly relief. And a little bit for the use of Edwin's name.

The judge enters the courtroom before I can say anything else, and a silence descends over everyone. The judge looks around at all the people filling every spare inch of the place and gives a questioning look to the security guards. They shrug as if this has never happened before.

The judge seems confused but drops it and, with a wave of her hand, ushers in the prosecutors and defendants.

I brace myself for Owen's entrance, and Declan reaches for my hand and gives it a supportive squeeze.

Owen looks like he always did. Dressed in a suit, showered, with a stray strand of dark hair falling across his brow. My heart practically stalls at the sight of him, but the tears gather when he finally looks around the room at everyone who showed up.

For him.

I notice the subtle change in his expression. The sudden realization that maybe he's not the monster he thinks he is.

A single tear falls down my face.

Peyton performs his role perfectly, and I silently swear to thank him for that sometime soon. Everything else goes by the book, and the prosecution looks shell-shocked with the evidence presented. All-in-all, it goes exactly how we'd hoped, but the jury is unreadable, and when we're dismissed for a lunch break, my nerves take over.

Declan sticks by my side like glue, even when his phone is clearly blowing up with messages from work.

"You don't want to get those?" I ask him, stuffing another bite of a cafeteria sandwich in my mouth, desperately trying not to think about how Owen is doing.

Declan shakes his head. "I only have a week left of this anyway."

I scrunch my nose, my hand halting my next bite. "You're resigning right after my trial?"

"What's the point of staying any longer? You won't be there, and I'll likely be fired."

I sigh. Even if I wanted to, I couldn't convince Declan to do anything. He's made up his mind, and when he does, it's as though nothing could change it.

"I know that look," he says as I stuff the last of my sandwich in my mouth.

I raise a brow and smirk.

"You don't agree with my decision," he says, slightly amused.

"Of course I don't, dumbass."

Declan's eyebrows furrow at the insult, but he doesn't stop me from continuing.

"You did *nothing* wrong. You followed protocol. It was me who didn't. And though we know the mission in Italy got thirty-five people killed, at least we know why now, and that it had nothing to do with you or me. We were doomed from the start. And everything with Owen... You didn't even know what was going on because I chose not to tell you. If you think for one moment you aren't fit for the director position, I will quite literally throw you through that wall over there." I point past his head for emphasis.

He doesn't fall for my antics and keeps his gaze on me. "What if I'm resigning because I want to?"

I glare at him. "If that's true, which I know it's not, then I'd support your decision."

He huffs. "You think you know me so well, don't you?"

"I'm pretty sure I know you better than you know yourself."

He raises a brow in challenge.

"First, you like your coffee sweet as hell with extra whipped cream, even though you order it black in front of others."

Declan pales, and I sit up straighter in my chair, ready to take the fucker out.

"I also know that though a million women throw themselves at you, you politely decline because you've been pining over Jax for the last five years."

He scoffs.

Oh, I have him now. But I'm not done because Jax and Evan are headed our way, and their timing couldn't be more perfect.

I hide my smirk, knowing Declan hasn't spotted them yet. "And if you just told him, he and Evan both aren't against adding more people to their little group."

Declan's mouth falls into his lap, and Jax steps beside him.

I lean back in the chair, crossing my arms, a triumphant grin on my face.

Jax's gaze catches on my smile before he looks between the two of us, Declan's eyes widening the longer Jax lingers.

Declan shakes his head at me, as if asking me to shut the fuck up.

I laugh but don't miss the hand Jax casually places on the back of Declan's chair.

"Don't listen to her, Dec. Whatever it is she's saying," Jax comments.

"You have no idea what I just said," I argue. "I actually think you'd fully support it."

"If it has anything to do with sex, I'm in," Evan says, coming up to the other side of Declan's chair and resting his hand on it with the same casualness.

I stifle a laugh, slapping my hand over my mouth, and Declan suddenly looks horrified.

I wink at Evan. "It might."

Evan finally looks down at Declan, and I notice the instant it clicks, though Jax seemed to figure it out the second he picked up on Declan's wide eyes and my grin.

I shrug, standing up and grabbing my food tray. "I'm going to find Ella." I'm still unable to hide my smile.

"I'm going to kill you," Declan says through clenched teeth.

This time, I laugh without restraint as I walk away, back to the courtroom. Back to Owen.

Chapter 36

Owen's trial drags on for a week, and the ruling happens to fall the day before my own trial starts.

I'm nothing but nervous energy, my legs bouncing frantically while I sit on a crowded bench in the courtroom. Owen's trial couldn't have gone better than it did, but that doesn't mean he's off the hook. The best-case scenario is a reduced sentence or house arrest.

I'd take either one.

The courtroom silences as the prosecution enters. A minute later, Owen walks in with his lawyers, looking as though he didn't get any sleep last night.

My heart clenches at the sight of him. All I want is to wrap myself around him so we both can finally sleep again. But I know that even if he gets to go home, I won't be going with him.

Declan must sense my tension because he puts a supportive hand on my knee, easing it to stillness.

I blow out a breath when Owen finally sits.

The judge comes in next, followed shortly by the jury.

There's a tense silence as the judge asks the jury for their verdict. I don't think a single person takes a breath.

The judge scans the verdict, not a single muscle changing in her expression.

When she looks around at the jam-packed courtroom, she finally allows a small smile to grace her lips.

"The jury finds Owen Mills innocent on all counts, citing self-defense."

The courtroom instantly erupts into shouts and cheers. The prosecution looks as shocked as I feel.

Innocent on all counts? Not possible.

Everyone is out of their seats in a second, trying to get to Owen. I stay seated in stunned silence, the crowds' bodies blocking my view of him. Declan sits with me, squeezing my knee even harder.

I know I'm in shock as my hands begin to tremble fiercely.

Declan grabs them and rubs them between his own. "Nova?"

I meet his eyes, and there are unshed tears there. "What are you going to do?" he whispers among the loud commotion all around us.

My voice wavers when I answer him. "I wasn't expecting him to go home."

Declan gives me a comforting smile and holds up a hand to stop whoever is approaching us. "He's going home because of *you*."

I nod, not really registering anything.

"Are you going to try to talk to him?"

"He'll never forgive me," I whisper.

"You'll never know unless you try. You've done harder things than this, Nova. Isn't it worth a shot?"

I might sob, so I deflect. "I'll try if I don't trade places with him and land my ass in jail tomorrow."

Declan doesn't fall for my antics, rolling his eyes. "You won't end up in jail, dumbass." He throws my insult back at me. "You took down the largest crime syndicate in the world and provided evidence that landed your target in jail—and then provided evidence clearing him."

"But I broke about a million laws and rules to do so," I grumble like a child.

Declan shakes his head, finally pulling away from me and standing. "Allow yourself a win, Nova. You deserve it."

I nod, but it doesn't feel like a win if Owen never wants to see me again.

I don't ever work up the nerve to speak to Owen in the courtroom before security starts kicking everyone out. I'm too afraid and too wrapped up in conversations and congratulations from everyone at Regenerative Industries. The few times I catch sight of Owen, I don't think he even notices I'm there as he chats with everyone around him. He still looks tired, but the tension has fallen away from his shoulders. A small win.

I walk out of the courtroom with Declan, Jax, Evan, Ella, and Eagan surrounding me. No one speaks, which I'm thankful for because my emotions can't handle any questions.

I've gotten Owen free. The relief finally hits me along with severe exhaustion, and I almost stumble down the concrete steps.

Declan grabs me under the elbow and holds onto me until we get to the car, where he gently settles me into the backseat without a word.

Jax and Evan flank me on either side as Declan slides into the front and says a quick goodbye to Ella and Eagan. They pile into the car next to us. Ella gives me a quick wave, along with a concerned glance, before heading back to my apartment.

My brain decides the best thing to do with the emotional overwhelm is to fall asleep with my head on Jax's shoulder.

Jax carries me up to my bedroom, cradled in his arms, and deposits me gently on my bed. Neither he, Evan, or Declan say a thing as they pile on the bed, surrounding me with their warmth.

I almost cry at their silent support but pass out before a single tear falls.

"Up!" Declan's voice booms, throwing open the curtains, letting the light filter through the window and spill across the bed.

I throw my arm over my face, groaning at being woken up from the best sleep I've had since Owen got arrested.

"Time to get your ass cleared and be done with all these trials."

Declan encourages me to get up by pulling my arm away from my face and flinging new clothes at me.

I look down to find that my friends removed my shoes, but they didn't touch the clothes on my body, leaving me to sleep in the uncomfortable pantsuit I chose to wear to Owen's trial.

I smell coffee and bacon and groan again, but this time out of pure pleasure.

Declan laughs. "Jax and Evan made breakfast."

I snap my head to him, wagging my eyebrows.

He shakes his head like I'm a child, and I giggle like one.

"I don't know whether to hug you or punch you for interfering with me and them," Declan says.

"The correct answer is to thank me."

He snorts, pointing at the clothes I'm supposed to change into. "You have five minutes, or we'll be late, and then the board will definitely throw your ass in jail."

I huff, but it sounds more like a whine.

Declan chuckles and shakes his head again. "Five minutes."

He's out the door before I can protest.

I take a deep breath, straightening myself out. I can do this. I can get through this one last thing.

I flip through the notifications on my phone before heading out to the kitchen, where the three men are flirting with each other. It's filled with messages from Ella, Parker, and Noah, all checking in with me and asking if I've heard from Owen.

The answer is a resounding no.

I try not to pout while I make my way to the kitchen, but of course they all notice, frowns falling on all three faces.

"Haven't heard from him?" Jax asks as Evan rounds the counter and plops a plate of food in my face.

I shake my head, not hesitating to dig in. I can't even remember the last time I ate a full meal without feeling queasy.

"Have you tried contacting him?" Declan asks.

I nod. "I texted him to tell him congratulations on the outcome of the trial."

"And nothing?" Evan asks, surprised.

"Nothing," I say, my heart in a vice.

No one speaks. What can they say? I know Owen is mad. I just hoped he'd at least say *something*.

I interrupt the awkward silence. "I'm meeting with Parker about my current position with Regenerative Industries and requesting a transfer, obviously. I can't be Owen's assistant anymore, and plus, I already gave the position to Peyton." I wink, trying to hide my devastation.

None of them falls for it. They all frown at me.

I throw up my hands. "Can I just get through today, and you can all hound me about this tomorrow?"

They nod and rush to help me get out the door.

I'm grateful for them, but there still seems to be a gaping hole in my chest, and I don't know how the hell to get it to go away.

The board peppers me with a million questions, and I answer them with nothing but the absolute truth. I present my case in a way that lets them know I didn't follow protocol, but I use the evidence to help them understand why I made the decisions I did.

Declan testifies in my favor, which isn't common for directors to do. They are supposed to remain unbiased. Declan made it clear from the start that he had no intention of remaining neutral, and if he loses his job, then it is a sign that he shouldn't work for the organization anymore. I agreed to his request to help me, even though I wanted to protect him from this.

We're both exhausted as the questions continue past lunch, and the board doesn't make any move to release us for a break.

"You went against protocol five times. You lied to your director. You omitted important information. You were involved in thirty-five civilian deaths..." The director continues listing off all the things I've done wrong, and I flinch at each one.

When he puts it that way, I deserve to be locked up.

"But," he says, pulling off his glasses and looking me in the eye, "You took down a crime circle we've been hunting for twenty years, and the number of lives that will be saved as a result... Well, it's not measurable, but it's invaluable."

I hold my breath, waiting for the decision I suspect they've already made.

"It has come to our attention that you no longer desire to work for the CIA?" he asks.

I nod because I don't think I would be able to speak without a tremble in my voice.

"In light of that information, we would like to let you know that your job with the CIA is not at risk. You have the position if you want it. And we will not be pressing any criminal charges against you. Nor will Italy be pursuing any criminal charges. Internationally, you are free to go."

My mouth drops open, and Declan is smiling so widely that it seems like his face might split in two. I don't say anything, flabbergasted.

The board member who read my sentence shuffles his papers before standing and smiling at me. "Don't be so surprised, Miss Riley. You're an excellent agent, and you did what you needed to. What many haven't been able to do for two decades. If you broke a few rules, well..." He shrugs and then gives me one more grin before he disappears from the conference room.

Declan and I watch as the rest of the board members leave, all nodding at me and offering smiles. When the door clicks shut on the last person, Declan finally turns to me.

"Holy shit," he says.

I'm still not able to say a word. None of this feels real. Not this hearing. Not Owen's trial. Not the fact that I took down the largest crime syndicate in the world.

Nothing makes sense anymore. I should feel relieved, but instead, I feel numb.

Somehow, this all means nothing without Owen.

And I'm so very tired.

Chapter 37

I meet Parker at Regenerative Industries after my trial, my heart rate pounding out of control at the thought of running into Owen.

My eyes are wandering the room when Parker says, "He's out at the farms with Charlotte."

I meet his gaze across the table from me in the office cafe. Surprisingly, or maybe not so surprisingly, the place is packed again. Everyone seems settled back in, and it's business as usual.

"Oh," I say, unable to form any more words than that.

Parker frowns. "He still hasn't said anything to you?"

Parker looks surprised at the shake of my head, which has me wondering if Owen's said anything about me.

"I thought he'd have reached out by now." Parker can't hide the sadness behind his words.

I reach out and give his hand a gentle pat, plastering a smile on my face. "I'll survive. So, where am I being transferred, boss?"

Parker shakes his head at the term. "Owen is still your boss, Nova. I'm only trying to keep the peace around here." I scowl at his response, which makes him laugh. "I know how much you love working with the charities, so I got you a position working with Charlotte over at the community farm school."

I almost squeal with delight.

Parker laughs again. "I thought you'd like that. It's mostly administrative stuff, though. Not much fun, but you can work from wherever you want. No need to be on site or in this office. You'll have to attend mandatory meetings, but that's it."

It's the best I could hope for, actually. "Thank you for doing this for me, Parker. I can't tell you how much I appreciate this."

Parker's silence has me searching his face, which is suddenly far too serious. "Nova, you should never, *ever* thank me. What you've done..." Parker chokes on his words a bit, totally throwing me off. "You have my eternal gratitude, and there are no mountains I wouldn't move for you. I hope you know that. For fucks' sake, this whole company would no longer exist if it weren't for you. You do know that, right?"

Well, when he puts it that way. "I guess I didn't really think about the broader implications of getting Owen out of jail. I was only focused on him."

Parker nods. "You don't ever have to cross paths with him if you don't want to, but if you want my opinion—"

"I don't," I snap.

Parker chuckles but continues, "You should try again."

I don't give him any response because I don't know what to say to him, so I stand, holding out my hand. "I'll see you Monday for the charity meeting. And don't forget to have Peyton set up the plants I left in Owen's office."

"You aren't coming to my birthday party?" Parker asks, clasping my hand and not letting me go.

"I don't think that's the best idea," I reply sadly.

Parker shakes his head, dropping my hand. "I understand."

I spend the weekend punching things. Literally.

Everyone I know and love is at Parker's birthday party, and I'm too chickenshit to face Owen, so instead, I punch holes all over my apartment until my knuckles are bleeding so badly that I'm dripping blood everywhere.

I really need to get myself a punching bag or start going to a new gym.

Declan paid off the apartment with CIA funds so I could stay here, but my salary probably can't afford to redo all of the walls, so I finally stop, my anger mostly spent.

I'm attempting to wrap my knuckles when there's a knock at the door.

I stop, dropping the wrapping material and grabbing my phone.

No messages.

Who would be here on a Saturday night at this hour?

I cautiously approach the door, halting my instinct to grab a knife. The doorman would never let anyone up that I didn't know.

I crack the door to find livid green eyes glaring at me.

I step back so fast that I almost trip over my own bare feet.

Owen barrels into the apartment, not breaking eye contact as he practically yells, "You replaced yourself with Peyton fucking Radd!"

Oh shit.

I can't help the laugh that bubbles up, and I smack my hand over my mouth to stop myself.

Owen's eyes flare when he sees the blood, and I drop my hand, putting both of them behind me.

That's when he finally looks around and notices the mess I made of the walls.

When his eyes meet mine again, they've softened, and there's a hint of amusement in them.

"I don't have a punching bag or a gym membership currently," I spit out as a way of explanation.

"And why, Miss Riley, were you beating up your apartment?"

His low voice and close proximity have my body trembling. It's completely inappropriate, but I cannot help it. How do I answer him? How do I tell him everything I'm feeling right now and before he walked through that door?

"I was angry," I say, hoping that's enough of an answer for him.

"You're angry? You're the one who hired my assassin to be my personal assistant in your place."

Somehow, I hold back the chuckle, but the smile I cannot help. "I had to, or he wouldn't have testified."

Owen shakes his head, and I think he's going to finally step away from me, but he doesn't. "I told him I'd give him a job. I *did not* tell him he could have *your* job."

"It's the only job he was qualified for that was in the pay range he demanded." I pause, realizing something. "He doesn't start until Monday. How'd you find out?"

Owen's eyes sharpen. "For some reason, Parker thought it would be a good idea to invite him to his party, and sure enough, Peyton couldn't stop talking my ear off about his new position."

I stifle yet another laugh.

Owen narrows his gaze and takes another small step toward me. "I see you find this very amusing, Miss Riley, but I do not. I snapped when he started talking about *you*."

My eyes widen, and I can't help the "oh shit" that escapes my mouth.

"That's right, Miss Riley. I wasn't too keen on how he was speaking about you."

I jump in to defend Peyton for some odd reason and start rambling like an idiot. "He apologized for touching me. He told me it was only to get under your skin to get you to listen to him, which I think was genius and worked very well."

I look up to find Owen glaring at me, and so I just keep going like the dumbass I am. "And he promised he'd never do it again, and he did everything I asked him to do, and he helped us get you out of jail, and he helped me get off with no jail time in my own trial, and the crime syndicate is no more, and he played a *huge* role in that, and I just couldn't say no when he asked for my job."

I squeeze my eyes shut and scrunch my face up, ready for his harsh retaliation.

When I'm met with silence, I crack one eye open to find him watching me with a slight grin.

I punch his shoulder before I can stop myself. "You asshole! You knew all of this and made me stand there and ramble like a complete fucking idiot."

All Owen says is "Edwin" before he actually laughs.

I huff and turn to walk away, but he grabs my bleeding hand and holds it gently, giving me an out if I want one.

His face softens, the smile disappearing as he stares down at the carnage of my knuckles.

I open my mouth to say something, but snap it shut again, slowly pulling my hand away.

"You knew from the beginning what I'd done?" he asks, still staring at my now-absent hand.

It isn't really a question, but I nod. My voice shakes as I explain. "I knew what you were suspected of doing. When I got to know you, though, I wanted to believe it was all a misunderstanding. I didn't want to believe it was true."

My hands itch to touch him, and I curl them into fists to stop myself. His eyes track my movement.

"Why?" his voice cracks as he says it.

"Fuck Owen, if you haven't figured out why by now... Did you not see the people who showed up for your trial? Who showed up for *you*? Who decided they didn't give a fuck what you'd done because you've created a better world for every one of them?"

I don't know how, but suddenly Owen is closer. Close enough that his familiar scent washes over me, and I suddenly can't breathe.

"What you did for me..." Owen stumbles over his words. "What you did... How can I ever thank you?"

"Thank me?" I shake my head. "You shouldn't be thanking me. I lied to you. I was the person responsible for putting you behind bars in the first place. I let you believe I was a different person."

I can't find it in me to meet his eyes, so I stare at his broad chest. My nails are now digging into my palms so hard that droplets of blood form.

"Are you a different person?" he asks.

My head shoots up, and I narrow my gaze, not understanding his question.

"The way you were with me was that you, or was it an act?"

I squeeze my eyes shut, trying and failing so miserably at hiding my emotion. When I open them, a single tear slides free, tumbling down my cheek. "At first, it was an act. You were just another target. But damnit if I wasn't absolutely livid at how fast you were able to tear down every wall and boundary I'd put around myself the moment my father was murdered. I *wanted* it to be an act. I was so desperate to keep my distance and yet I...couldn't."

I finally look into his beautiful green eyes to find them glassy, but he doesn't say anything, so I continue with my rambling. "You weaseled your way so easily into my life. It felt as if you belonged there. Like you'd always been there. And fuck did I want to murder those naked women in your office. I'd never felt so..." I trail off.

"I think the word you're looking for is jealous."

Damnit. The way he is smiling at me, with the easy arrogance I am used to...

I roll my eyes, and he chuckles but lets me finish. "If you're asking if you've been with the real me, then the answer is yes. In fact, I don't think I've ever been more myself with anyone."

Owen narrows his gaze as if studying me.

When he opens his mouth, my stomach tightens so hard that I think I'll puke. "I love you!" I blurt far louder than I intended.

His eyes widen, and he takes a step back. My fragile heart is so afraid of rejection that I still can't stop the tumble of words coming out of my mouth. "I should have told you that at the jail. Hell, I should have told you before that moment. I was a coward. And scared—"

Owen cuts me off by grabbing my chin and forcing me to look at him. He leans in, impossibly close to my lips, and whispers, "How is it that you can put the most notorious criminals behind bars and survive multiple shootouts without backup, but you're afraid to tell me you love me?"

My voice wavers a bit. "Because you scare the shit out of me, Owen Mills. Because I'm afraid to lose you again."

"You never lost me, Nova. I was yours from the moment I laid eyes on you."

His words send a shiver down my spine, but I remain frozen in his grip, staring into depthless green eyes. Eyes I never thought I'd be able to see again.

Owen rests his forehead against mine, and his breath skates along my lips. "And you saved me, Nova. Not just from this trial but from myself. You made me feel like I was worth loving for the first time since my mother died. Most importantly, you gave me a reason to keep fighting for what I believe in."

I can't stop the second tear escaping down my cheek. This time, Owen releases my chin and wipes it away with his thumb.

"The plants, too. You filled my office with plants even when you thought I'd never speak to you again."

This time, I smile through my tears. "I promised you plants for your office, Mr. Mills."

"Our office."

I cock my head to the side. "You mean your and Edwin's office."

Owen laughs, and it's a balm for my weary soul, erasing all the tension that I've been holding for far too long.

"You're mine, Miss Riley. You always have been, and you always will be. If you'll have me."

Fuck if those words don't flow straight through me. I reach up to pull him toward me and he smiles, the dimple making an appearance the second before our lips crash together.

And it feels like coming home.

Epilogue
One Year Later

"You're passing the company to me?" Parker shouts at Owen, his eyes wild and ping ponging between me and Owen as if the decision was also mine.

I put my hands up in surrender, backing away from the barely-contained rage simmering in Parker's eyes.

Noell stands in the corner of Owen's office, and Edwin was dismissed before the meeting. The information is confidential. For now. And ever since Edwin became a free man with his name cleared, it's as if he can no longer keep any secrets.

Owen puts a placating hand on Parker's shoulder, but Parker shrugs it off.

"You're ready," Owen says.

"What if I don't want it?" Parker shoots back, but it isn't sincere. We all know he's had his sights set on running things over the last year, and to everyone's surprise, he more than exceeded expectations. Much to Noell's disappointment.

Owen rolls his eyes at his brother. "You're ready, and you'll be better at this job than I was."

"Because I'm more handsome?"

After the words are out of his mouth, Parker backs away from Owen so far that he nearly knocks Noell over.

Noell snarls and sidesteps him.

I can't see Parker's face, but I'm pretty sure he winks at her, which only causes her scowl to grow.

Parker turns his attention back to his brother. A dangerous smirk that speaks of violence graces Owen's face.

Parker sighs, relenting. "I'll take the position, but you could have given me more of a warning."

Noell grunts her agreement, causing Owen to glance in her direction, but Parker pulls his attention back by saying, "I assume this has to do with Nova."

I scoff, but Owen answers. "We've been through enough."

No one argues, and though the last year has been wonderful, putting the company back together was more work than either of us anticipated. We found ourselves working day and night to keep everything afloat. As a result, our happy ending didn't turn out quite like we'd planned.

"What do you need me to do?" Parker asks, his voice softer now.

"We'll make a formal statement next month. We need to inform the board and secure their votes."

Noell snorts.

Parker turns to her. "You don't think I can win over the board?" His voice is full of challenge.

The two of them couldn't be more different, and the last year proved that they don't exactly see eye-to-eye in business either. But no one can deny that Parker is hard-working and wants to succeed.

"We'll see" is all she says, but her response has Parker beaming at her like he's won something.

Owen ignores whatever is going on between them and steps to my side, squeezing my hand. "Also, I'm cashing in on my company stock and giving the money away."

This doesn't surprise anyone, but Noell rolls her eyes.

"We'll keep enough to hold us through retirement, but no more," he adds.

This also doesn't surprise anyone.

Parker's smile grows, and he rubs his hands together conspiratorially.

Owen eyes him. "No private jets."

Parker pouts, and I almost laugh.

"It will be your company, nimwit. Your brother can't stop you from buying a private jet," Noell chimes in from her corner, her arms still locked across her chest.

"See, she gets it," Parker says, pointing his thumb over his shoulder at her.

"Not hard to *get* you when there isn't much *to* you," Noell replies, which has both me and Owen trying desperately to hold back a laugh.

Parker frowns, but there's a flash of challenge in his eye.

Noell's mouth twitches.

"Are there any more questions? Or can I get out of here now?" Owen asks everyone.

Noell and Parker shake their heads, and Noell marches out of the office before anyone dismisses her. Parker follows her with his gaze until she's out of sight.

"Well, let's hope there aren't any other CEOs that need to be"—Parker stops and runs a finger across his neck—"while I'm in charge."

"You aren't the murdering type," Owen says, grabbing his jacket from the back of his office chair and rejoining me by the door.

"I could if I needed to be," Parker replies.

Owen and I both laugh, each clapping him on the back as we exit the office.

"What? I could be!" he shouts after us as Owen grabs my hand and winds his fingers through mine.

"Where to?" he asks, his green eyes sparkling as he looks at me.

"Home."

Six Months Later

"I could get used to this," Owen says, leaning into me.

We're sitting on the front of a large catamaran as it slices through the Adriatic Sea. I've been to the Greek Islands, but not like this. Not where I could fully relax and not have to worry about throwing anyone behind bars or putting my life in danger. This time, I can actually enjoy it. Enjoy the little things. Enjoy Owen.

"I'm never leaving," I reply, melting into his side.

He's silent for a moment, his eyes on me.

"How'd we get here?" he asks in a whisper.

I glance up to find disbelief etched across his features. Sitting up, I swing my legs over his lap so we're face-to-face.

"I don't know, but we're damn lucky." I brush my lips against his.

"Will Parker fuck everything up?"

"Likely."

We both laugh, and Owen runs a hand through my windswept hair.

After Owen's trial, rumors of what happened spread like wildfire. The media began to spin it as a *Robin Hood* tale, and the public devoured it. Ultimately, stocks for Regenerative Industries skyrocketed, and the company was able to save itself from bankruptcy, all while continuing to fund Owen's projects and paying all employees fairly.

But the stress of what happened to us, along with the exhaustion of running such a large company, took its toll. We decided, together, that it would be best to give Regenerative Industries to Parker and spend time away from the public spotlight.

I let Owen process everything, all the while reminding him that I'm here. That *we're* here. Together.

"I'm proud of you," I say sleepily against his neck, my legs still wrapped around him.

Instead of acknowledging my statement, he turns it back on me. "You saved my life, Miss Riley."

"It's Mrs. Mills now, or have you forgotten?"

Owen hums against my ear. "I haven't forgotten. It just doesn't have the same ring to it."

I chuckle. "No, I suppose it doesn't."

The sudden sound of a speedboat inching closer has me on my feet and on alert, my adrenaline spiking. Owen is right behind me, his hand tense on my low back.

As the boat gets closer, aiming to secure itself to ours, I reach for the bottle of champagne out of instinct, prepared to use it as a weapon. Owen notices but doesn't comment, instead stepping slightly in front of me as if to protect me.

The driver comes into view.

"What the fuck, Edwin!" Owen shouts.

Edwin, in linen pants and a linen shirt and wearing a straw hat and sunglasses, is driving a very expensive boat as if he's done it a thousand times before.

He probably has, knowing him.

Owen waves to our captain to lower the sails while Edwin expertly ties his boat to ours. We greet him in the back, where he pulls off his sunglasses and grins at us conspiratorially.

I cross my arms over my chest, waiting for him to drop a bomb on us. This level of theatrics must mean something big has happened.

Edwin clears his throat and opens his mouth, likely to ask for a drink since his eyes scan the bar filled with many bottles of expensive alcohol.

Owen growls, and Edwin turns his attention to him, hands out in supplication. "I guess the drink can wait." He pauses for effect, and I can't help but roll my eyes as Owen visibly gets more frustrated.

"Your brother's missing."

The End

Acknowledgments

The story of how this book came to be is actually quite amusing. This idea of a billionaire Robin Hood vigilante came to me randomly while I was reading the Kings of Sin series. I had a desire to write a billionaire romance, but not your typical one. So, Blurred was born through this crazy idea that I could turn a billionaire romance on its head. The mystery part of the story came about while I was already writing. I intended it to be a suspense, but somehow Nova's story ended up blending with Owen's story, and I loved how it turned out, even though it wasn't planned that way. In the end, it was a story I hadn't even planned on publishing, and then my alpha readers demanded that I publish it. So, they are the true reason this book is in your hands today.

To my alpha and beta readers: you gave me the courage to publish this book, you cheered me on, you brainstormed with me, and you made it very clear that these two knuckleheads deserved to have their story told and shared with the world. I couldn't, and wouldn't, be an author without you all! Some of you have been around since book one! And are still here for my third book, and I couldn't be more grateful.

To my spicy swap writing group: your encouragement, your feedback on my blurb, your feedback on the spicy scene, and all the times you've heard me rant about this industry. Thank you. Truly. Without you, I would have given up already.

To my book incubator writing group: Thank you for your support, encouragement, and accountability (and also for your shocked faces when I announced I'm publishing my third book in 11 months). You've been with me from the start, and I couldn't have done this without you. A million thanks.

To my editor, Tori: What would I have done without you? You made my writing so much better! Thank you for pointing out my bad habits and helping me fix them! This book is so much more readable because of you!

Lastly, to my family: I know I get a bit crazy sometimes when I'm writing because I'm so immersed in the story that I struggle to separate myself. Thank you for putting up with me! And thanks for putting up with my absolute obsession with writing. Especially my husband. How could I do this without you? You are my everything, and my inspiration for all these crazy, amazing MMCs. Thank you for making me laugh and believing in my stories.

About the Author

Brilynn O'Neal lives in California with her husband, three children, two dogs, two cats, ten chickens, and lots of honeybees. When she's not writing spicy, emotional stories, she's outside soaking up nature and saving bees.

Follow her on Instagram, Tiktok, Threads, and Pinterest @forestsand-fantasy